*L*ove
Among the Survivors

Doreen-Louise Willis

Grace and Bruce Martin from Doreen-Louise Willis

© 2001 by Doreen-Louise Willis. All rights reserved.

No part of this publication may be reproduced, stored in a retrieval system, or transmitted, in any form or by any means, electronic, mechanical, photocopying, recording, or otherwise, without the written prior permission of the author.

Cover Illustration by Shirley Reynolds

National Library of Canada Cataloguing in Publication Data

```
Willis, Dorreen-Louise
     Love among the survivors


ISBN 1-55212-959-4


     I. Title.

PS8595.I5686L68 2001         C813'.6        C2001-903057-6
PR9199.4.W54L68 2001
```

TRAFFORD

This book was published *on-demand* in cooperation with **Trafford Publishing.**
On-demand publishing is a unique process and service of making a book available for retail sale to the public taking advantage of on-demand manufacturing and Internet marketing.
On-demand publishing includes promotions, retail sales, manufacturing, order fulfilment, accounting and collecting royalties on behalf of the author.

Suite 6E, 2333 Government St., Victoria, B.C. V8T 4P4, CANADA
Phone   250-383-2864   Toll-free   1-888-232-4444 (Canada & US)
Fax   250-383-6804   E-mail   sales@trafford.com
Web site   www.trafford.com   TRAFFORD PUBLISHING IS A DIVISION OF TRAFFORD HOLDINGS LTD.
Trafford Catalogue #01-0361   www.trafford.com/robots/01-0361.html

10   9   8   7   6   5   4   3   2

Writing is called the lonely profession, so I am deeply grateful to my friends for their help and encouragement, to my Writer's Group in Victoria, and especially to my best friend Lorraine Burnett who helped and encouraged me, then got in there and did the typing.

Thank you.

Chapter One

Anne came home from town and immediately washed out her brand new hairstyle. It was not a great day for her, just back from a week in Reno and re-adjusting. This morning after a good night's sleep in her own bed and a general refurbishing of skin, hair and clothes, she started out well.

She went downtown to pay the few bills that had accumulated and then, feeling frivolous, went into a new dress shop. As she moved through racks of same-colour, same-style dresses, a sales clerk appeared. She flicked her glance over Anne.

"There isn't much in the larger sizes," and added, "I could try to find something," in a don't – ask tone.

Anne was crushed. "Don't bother, I'm just looking," thus permitting the sales clerk to chalk up another point for herself in her daily battle against the world of trade and commerce.

Anne retreated to the bank to exchange her American currency back to its colourful Canadian counterpart. As she waited a solicitous young troublemaker pointed to a chair. "If you want to sit while you're waiting, I'll keep your place for you."

Finally, in a teashop near the bank, a waitress brought her the senior's menu without even asking and then confided that they featured herbal teas.

"I'm 63, she muttered to herself. "I'm only 63. I'm not even a senior yet." She looked around surreptitiously and vowed to stop talking to herself.

"Sixty-three is not exactly decay," she thought defiantly. She mournfully pondered her new Reno (the old ladies' capital of the world) hairstyle and knew it was a mistake. As she sipped her Red Zinger, she decided it would be the first thing to go. She knew her face was haggard, the result of a long bus trip after a week of shows and slot machines. She shuffled home in her sensible shoes and her old lady's hairstyle and slumped on a bench in the garden. She gradually calmed down as she watched the light drain from the enclosed garden, studying it with the expertise of a retired florist.

The Complex was beautiful. Thick green lawns surrounded units of ten apartments. Scalloped edge flower beds were packed with flowers in the style of an English country garden. Discreet ornamental iron fences prevented skateboards, bicycles, motorcycles and delivery trucks from driving along the curving walks. There were ornamental iron benches that offered rest, and Anne was resting. Her friend Robbie joined her. "You look like you'd rather be in Reno."

"No, I just feel as if I've aged twenty years this morning."

"Not with those legs. You look like a kid to me, too young for this place. Anne, how did you end up here anyway?"

"It was a palace to me. Martin left a lot of debt when he died."

"Don't say anything if you don't want to, but I thought you were a florist with your own exclusive Vancouver emporium."

"It's a long story. It's not that I mind talking about it to you, but it's so long and dreary. I inherited Dad's flower shop, then I sold it and bought a fabulous one right across from the main hospital."

"So far, so good."

Anne nodded. "It was great. I was well off, well trained by my father and in firm control. Then I met Martin de Kyp at a florist's convention. I thought he was nice and one thing led to another so that when he asked me to marry him I did. Then I learned that he was in bad health, so he looked after the books in my business. He had worked in a shop for less than a year then found he couldn't work anymore. When he died, I learned the shop and even Dad's house were financed to the limit." Talking over the disastrous past put today's annoyances in a better perspective. She laughed.

"Another time I'll tell you about his trip to Mexico for a wonderful six month cure that cost the earth (in advance) and he stayed three weeks. He died two weeks later."

"In all our bridge games over the years you never told us your big tale of woe."

"Oh, well, I'd rather forget about it. Besides, it's not nearly as exciting as the tales you tell. Let's have some tea or something."

Living in seniors housing didn't help her present mood much but when she was 55 she was ecstatic to find that she was able to move in. It meant no more money worries; everything else she was sure she could cope with. If her neighbours were elderly, they were hospitable and quieter than her previous ones. And those elderly neighbours became her friends, Robbie, Mary and Lottie and they played awful bridge together.

Robbie Fairley was seventy-four, a widow with two children that she says she never sees. She isn't very tall and she is stooped now. She has dark hair heavily streaked with grey. She is strong and capable and has been Anne's special friend almost ever since Anne arrived.

Mary Burke was then eighty, a widow with pale red hair that needs quite a lot of expert attention. She is naturally slim, is a very good cook and talks knowledgeably about slimming diets while serving fabulous cakes and squares. Her younger daughter Ellen is special but Mary moved to the complex to join Lottie. She says her elder daughter became impossibly bossy when her father died.

Lottie Simpson was eighty-four. She had endured a sensational divorce and she sometimes enthralls the bridge club when she feels like talking about it. She dyes her hair black once in a while then wears scarves for months as it slowly and excruciatingly grows out. She seems to have children but they haven't been around for years. Lottie thinks they are laying low until the divorce talk cools. They blame her for not keeping quiet.

Anne had been almost overcome with the dark mood of that gloomy day but when she considered Lottie she counted her blessings. Lottie says that she was part of a love quadrangle of two couples who had been friends forever until she realized that her husband had been sleeping with the other two, also forever.

When he threatened Lottie with his fist, she left the house and went to the police station, a lawyer, an accountant and the Y.W.C.A. The rest, as they say, is history…a history that the bridge club has been raptly hearing for years. Anne chuckled and went indoors, thinking of her bridge night to come and its possibilities.

At bridge on Tuesday, she looked around at her friends with satisfaction.

"What did you do to your hair, Anne?"

"I washed it."

"That expensive set would have lasted for a while yet."

"That's why I washed it. Two no trump."

Play was desultory as they ruminated about their trip and the changes in the complex while they were away.

"Have you seen the new couple, Ivy and Harry?"

"Yes, and wow!"

Anne had missed the coffee morning and had gone downtown instead. "Harry?"

"Harry is gorgeous. His wife, Ivy, is nice but she is in a wheelchair and has oxygen with her all the time."

"Wait until you see Harry, Anne. He's the sexiest man!"

Lottie spoke up. "He came to my place to use the phone and the smoke alarm went off."

When they stopped laughing, Robbie asked which one of them was standing near it at the time.

Anne met the newcomers on Wednesday at the morning coffee break. Harry and his wife introduced themselves to Anne and after Harry placed Ivy's wheelchair he sat between her and Anne. His grey eyes were noticeable because his look was so intent. He was tall and the physical energy that was obvious in his every move obviously kept him trim and everyone else stimulated. When he turned the full voltage of his piercing eyes and a very wide smile on Anne she felt like Lottie's smoke alarm. It had been quite a while since Anne had met such an exciting man, certainly never in The Complex.

After a calming moment, she spoke to his wife. Ivy's hands were skeletal, her skin was pale as wax and she breathed with difficulty but still her eyes were friendly and she smiled.

Anne asked if anyone had shown her around.

"Later I could show you a few ins and outs."

Harry looked pleased and asked if he could do a few things while Anne was with Ivy.

The two women toured the garden and Ivy admired it all. In the library, Ivy found a book she wanted to read. They passed the poolroom.

"If Harry plays pool, there's usually someone looking for a game."

"Harry doesn't have much time for recreation. He's always been so involved in his construction company that he never learned to play. Even now, he seems to find a lot to do although he retired from the company five years ago."

They saw the nurse's room and the manager's office. The communal hall for large groups, community meals, monthly birthday parties and large coffee parties was empty and dark at the moment. Anne only kept Ivy out for a half hour then took her back to their apartment and helped her into bed.

"Thanks for spending so much time with me, Anne. Harry hasn't had so much time off for months. We have two daughters, but Marjorie, the older one, is living in Calgary with her husband and two children. She phones every night. Annette, the younger one, lives just over the water but she doesn't come over. She prefers to have her Dad go over there. She's quite spoiled, I think, but Harry doesn't see it. Men aren't very bright sometimes." She smiled faintly and closed her eyes as Anne left quietly.

Harry and Ivy slipped into the daily life of The Complex. They were obviously used to socializing and they were pleasant company. Ivy went steadily downhill which was expected by everyone, including Ivy. Anne formed the habit of spending a half hour with her every day just before lunch.

"Annette was on the phone again last night. She's divorced and has a ridiculous house over there. She works part time as a cosmetics consultant. We help her when she's really in trouble but I think it's best for her to struggle a little. Harry dotes on her and no doubt gives her more money than I know about. Men are such fools. They don't know when to say no. All it takes with Annette is a bit of wheedling. Oh, well never mind that. Do you have a family?"

"No, we never had children. Martin's health failed just after we married. I don't brood about it but it would be nice to have grandchildren."

"Don't quit yet...marry a grandfather," said wise Ivy.

It was a beautiful summer, sunny and calm with enough breeze to make the heat pleasant. It rained on and off but always at night, keeping the trees and grass green and verdant. The flowers thrived but as the weeks went by Anne felt that, unlike the flowers, she wasn't thriving. She was so nervous and restless that she found it impossible to settle to anything. Even though she reminded herself that she had everything she needed, nothing was wrong, still she was unhappy. She was so irritable that it took effort to smile and be pleasant. Her time spent with Ivy, and often Harry, was easy but otherwise she was so tense and stressed she longed for escape. She supposed she needed a change like a return trip to Reno. She would talk to the bridge club. Over the years they had supported each other through a variety of crises. Lately, Anne had confided in them about Martin's betrayal.

"I can't help wondering if he only married for a lifeline when he couldn't look after himself anymore."

Lottie thought about it. "I wouldn't think that, Anne. It's probably true that he saw you as the answer to a prayer but you don't realize what you have. You give an impression of strength and calm and Martin probably needed that. I think he fell in love with you and took a final grab at happiness."

Mary agreed. "You're good looking...more than you know. It would be wrong to lose confidence in your marriage, Anne. You were happy then, and you had over ten good years. I think he got desperate at the end. People do."

"And you're a great comfort sometimes." Anne told her friends. They always had been, but that was before. This time, when she suggested a trip they showed a different kind of understanding, not at all comforting.

"Reno. Now there's an idea. We haven't been there for weeks."

"Can't. No money." Robbie was inclined to be a spender. "I just bought a recliner." She looked sideways at Anne. "You don't need a break anyway. You just had one. Anne, I've got to say it. We're friends, aren't we? Your trouble is that you have fallen for Harry and you won't face facts."

They went back to playing their own kind of bridge and discussing Harry's many attractions so that Anne had time to gather her wits.

That night, Anne was sleepless and furious because she realized that Robbie was right. Not only was she in love with a married man, but his wife was her friend, her sick friend. And he was elderly, anyway. She was resentful of being adolescent, in spite of her advanced age and experience. She was so conscious of him. She was back to blushing and stammering. She had gone through her whole life on an even keel emotionally and she hardly expected to be confronted by such a ridiculous situation at her age. She was a wreck. Eventually she went to sleep.

Chapter Two

When everything was going well with the residents of the Complex, security and contentment were demonstrated by bickering, complaining and symptom recitals. Thus, peaceful enjoyment of coffee on Monday morning was very loud when Sid introduced a new word of gentle allure into the din.

Millie's usual "Isn't it cold!" was heard.

"Seventy degrees."

"Yes, but that horrible wind. Wind gets into my joints. I hate wind. In Ontario we never get wind like this."

"Yeah, right." A man's voice from another table. "They just had a tornado a week ago."

Millie was a chubby lady wearing two heavy sweaters over her fleece track suit. She subsided and tasted her coffee. "Ugh. Who make it this time? It's much too strong."

"Eva, and if she hears you complaining about it again she won't make it and you'll have to do it." Silence as this horrible fate was contemplated. Sid spoke up.

"Anyone heard of Arden?"

"I think it's something to do with cosmetics."

"No, it's a place. A ghost town. My son is up there helping with a fish study. I'm going to keep them company for a while before his wife goes nuts from the isolation. They're the only ones there." He smiled wryly. "Probably I'll drive her nuts after I've been there for a while."

"Imagine a place that hasn't been taken over by greedy developers. I don't think so."

"There must be something wrong with it."

"It's probably horrible; that poor young wife."

Sid pondered. "Well it's only accessible by boat."

Someone groaned. "And there's no work anywhere in the area now that logging is so quiet."

"Was it a logging town then?"

"Yes, although they built it near an old whaling station."

"Whaling's quiet all right." Everyone laughed and began to talk about other things. A very tall, very thin woman with very thick glasses observed,

"I don't wear cosmetics anymore. I can't see to tart myself up properly and I don't want to look like a clown." A baffled look came over her face when she heard a snort from the men's end of the table, followed by a snicker.

Kindly Anne said hastily, "Rosalie, you'd never look like a clown but I know what you mean. I've almost quit wearing makeup myself, except for powder and a bit of lipstick." She hoped that made up for her recent grumpiness; she felt better anyway.

Sid left for his holiday and the mornings were diminished by his absence. His quiet sense of humour and nonjudgmental attitude were missed. Harry especially missed his ally against the bored, complaining atmosphere of idle people who had once been active. He listened to a ninety year old man from another building who joined them occasionally.

"Mini storage for people…that's what we have here," he raved. "Stay out of the work force and fork out money for the grandchildren. If you volunteer you're taking a job away from some young guy. If you give an opinion you're outdated. If you do say something they call relevant, the young ones are incredulous, as if the poodle dog said something clever. Where do they think we've been all these years? We've been where they are now. Looking for work that's scarce, raising kids on nothing in a scary economy, trying to keep a place to live. We could help a lot if they'd listen. We could keep on battling a bunch of overpaid specialists who have a chokehold on the economy."

There was truth in what he said but it had all been said many times before. With Sid it was different. Sid didn't have the resentment in his voice; he was constructive and full of ideas.

The quiet summer days went by slowly. It was always quiet at The Complex in the summer when many of the tenants were away. If families came to visit, they usually went sightseeing and nobody saw them.

Ivy and Anne became friends. Anne spent time with her and they talked every day. Ivy was just a few years older than Harry and if her body was failing, her mind was as sharp as ever. She watched Anne become jumpy and irritable and could hardly miss the cause of her misery. She resolved to put her thoughts in order and speak to her friend.

"When I die…."

"Please don't hit me with that so suddenly, Ivy."

Ivy chuckled. "We've all had time to get used to it. I have my faith, Anne, and I don't mind now although I sometimes worry about how. But never mind that, I was going to say, when I die, Harry will need someone to look after him. We've been married for so long and I've shielded him a lot because he really is an innocent in some ways. And you. Please don't get upset if I say I hope you won't go all girlish and think of me as a barrier between you and Harry."

Anne looked down at her hands clenched in her lap and said nothing. After a minute, Ivy continued,

"I know you love him and I'm glad. If it's worth anything, I give you my blessing for the future." She chuckled as only Ivy could. She could find humour in anything.

"If we were Mormons, old-fashioned Mormons, we could share him now, but we aren't and we can't. I really don't mind sharing him with you, Anne. We are all compatible if you know what I mean. You look after him too, dear."

She waited for a second and knew that Anne couldn't answer. "If you don't mind I'd like to go to sleep now."

That was Ivy, forthright, brave and so very frail.

The hot days arrived and Millie stopped wearing her toque in the garden. Peter used to call her Millie-Is-Always-Chilly but now that Peter had died there was no-one to call her pet names. She was just Millie and people tended to avoid her.

Back to School advertising started telephones ringing in grandparents' homes. Budding student grandchildren found reasons to telephone. Everyone else planned fall teas and bazaars. Garage sales began to lose their appeal for the women although the men still quartered The City looking for bargains. Even winter didn't stop the men in their restless quest for deals and something to do.

By September Ivy was almost helpless. She still came down occasionally for a visit with everyone but she and Anne spent most of their time together in Ivy's bedroom. She talked about Harry constantly.

"He is a building contractor who supposedly retired five years ago, but you know Harry. He still sticks his nose in every chance he gets and the company, meaning his old partner, never did get around to buying him out. They have a haywire arrangement where Harry is a paid consultant and his money just lies around in the company, going up and down with the economy. I think I was the reason that Harry retired and they planned it that way because it's been down for a long time and he would have lost on the deal. He and Mike are good businessmen. We're all right, very well off in fact. Neither of us spends much except to travel. I love to travel."

Twenty minutes later Harry came home, Anne was becoming accustomed to his sudden appearances and hardly trembled at all. This time she was sitting down so all was serene and she hoped no-one noticed her agitation. She made tea, happy to have something to do with her hands, and arranged cups and cookies on a plate. A knock on the door.

"Hello, Sid. Good to see you."

They heard all about Sid's summer in the country. His wife had died when Randy was a baby so he had raised his son and they were close. He liked Monica. The two young people had been glad to have him there.

"Arden is quite a place, Harry. There are twenty-five houses there, built in the Sixties."

"Well Sid, are any of them habitable?"

"Sure. They need roof repairs pretty quick and there is plenty to do on them but they're better than I expected. It was a logging town as we thought but the company never did get off the ground and after their first five-year lease was up, they left. It wasn't as productive as it should have been in the free-wheeling Sixties."

"You picked up quite a few facts."

"More than you know. I saw one house there that I decided to go for. There was an old real estate sign on the dock, so I called them. They gave me the company representative's address and I wrote to ask about buying the house. I offered them five hundred dollars."

As Sid talked he grew more and more animated and the rest listened carefully.

"You couldn't live there in the wintertime, could you?"

"Originally I thought it would be a fine summer place and it would. I think I'd like to stay at least one winter. It's a lovely location. It isn't right on the coast, fortunately, because even the east coast of the Island is pretty hard in the winter, but Arden is in a big cove that is sheltered from northerlies and most of the easterlies."

"But how did you get there?"

"Randy picked me up in the Fisheries boat. It's about an hour by boat from The Port, maybe less. You would have to charter a boat normally."

"Would Randy be there over the winter?"

"Nope, his contract is finished on October fifteenth."

"You can't stay there alone," said Harry.

"Maybe not. Anyway, the interesting part is that I just got a letter from the company lawyers."

"Not five hundred dollars, I'm sure." Anne was as engrossed as everyone else. "You could never find a house in B.C. for that nowadays."

"No, fifty thousand dollars." Sid was grinning, hardly able to contain his excitement. Harry rocked back in his chair, amused at Sid's pipedream. Anne and Ivy waited. Ivy was limp but alert.

"Do you want to go to bed for a while, Ivy?" asked Anne.

"No," she gasped, "I want to hear Sid's story."

"I got a letter saying I can buy the entire property for fifty thousand dollars. The title to one hundred and fifty acres, all of the houses free title, the jetty and amenities already installed." He explained further. "The company folded and one man in Australia is holding what's left of the assets. He's the one I heard from."

Harry kicked away his footstool, sat up and said,

"The whole thing? Sid, have you any idea what you're going to do with it?"

"Nope, just one house, but you know me, I'll think of something. I just have to figure out where to get fifty thousand dollars…I know the bank won't go for it. I'm broke and retired. I haven't got it…yet. That's what I'm in town for."

Now it was perfectly quiet. The implications of this remote place, waiting for life to come back was intriguing.

"Is it in a forest?" asked Anne.

"It was cleared and now it's a lovely grassy slope, falling down very gradually to the seashore. There is a low granite outcropping four of five feet high right across the waterfront so there's no erosion at all. The field at the back slopes upward then it's level enough to cultivate. Beyond that is forest and an old farm.

"Is there water?"

"That's the big thing. Yes, and the houses are plumbed. The big community well needs a lot of work but there's water all right."

Anne made another pot of tea but, thinking of Arden, not of seniors who should cut back on their tea and coffee intake. They were not primarily seniors but friends having a very interesting conversation.

"Give it to him, Harry."

They all gaped at Ivy as though she had just hit a high C.

"Give it to him. That's not much money for all that adventure. We could take it out of my travel fund that I haven't been using lately." She paused for breath and turned to Sid. "We can make out an agreement for you and me with the understanding that if one of us dies, it will be paid off. Can we do it that way, Harry?"

He walked over to the small gallant lady and took her hands, "Of course we can, Ivy." Tears welled in his eyes as he went into the kitchen.

Ivy winked at Anne. "That will keep some of my money from greedy little Annette," she whispered wickedly.

Sid was transported to a world of his own. He would own all of those houses and all of that land and a jetty and he didn't have a penny to develop it with. Details. He was out of The Complex.

Chapter Three

Ivy's final act on earth was the signing of the agreement for Sid's property. She triumphantly smiled as she drew her wavering signature and went peacefully to sleep. Two days later she drifted away during her afternoon rest with Harry sleeping beside her. Those who cared for her were grateful that she was found composed and peaceful with a faint smile on her lips. She had only lived at The Complex for a few months but she was well liked and her loss was felt. Harry was bereft without her and Anne, along with the bridge club, did what they could to help him along.

His two daughters arrived for the funeral. Anne offered her apartment to Marjorie and her family and moved in with Robbie for the duration. Annette, the younger daughter, arrived on the day of the funeral and planned to leave right after the service. She came to The City on the ferry and seemed to see no reason to stay and support her father. She was in her father's suite when Anne arrived. They were introduced.

Annette was full of questions. "Do you live in The Complex? Are you married? Were you a friend of Mummy's?"

Harry was grinning as his younger daughter asked all the questions except the ones she wanted to ask. Why was Anne here? What was she doing in Harry's apartment? Who was she? Ivy's funeral was today and already Annette was possessively taking charge of her father. When Marjorie, her husband and two children arrived the atmosphere cleared. Anne immediately liked her and thought she was like Ivy.

After the funeral they returned to Harry's apartment then went down to share the lunch the other tenants had prepared in the common room. Marjorie talked about the ferry trip that became exciting when their son disappeared.

"Here we were on this huge ship with all those car decks and Chad was gone … just gone. We checked all the obvious places, bathroom, pop machine, video games. No Chad." She looked at Chad in mock anger. "The only other place I could think of was overboard. And all of the cars in all on those car decks were worrisome, as well."

"Ah, Mom, you know I would never talk to strangers."

"Well, we looked out the front window and there was a passenger feeding seagulls. Of course Chad was right in there. He wasn't more than twenty feet away but who would have thought to look out of a fifteen foot window!"

The chuckles were cut short by Annette. "I hope you gave him a darn good spanking!"

Marjorie shook her head and hugged an abashed Chad.

"It was good of you to come to the funeral, Anne. And, of course to give up your suite. I hope we'll see more of you while we're here."

"I won't have time to visit." Annette said. "Daddy told me I could sort out Mummy's jewellery as soon as Marjorie arrived and I have to get the ferry home right afterward."

This program was as good as any so Anne, John, Chad and Catherine went to Anne's apartment while the other three disappeared for a while. Anne made coffee for everyone and produced juice for the two children.

When the others arrived, Annette was talking. "But I want to take them today. I have a party next week and I want to dazzle everyone with the diamond earrings."

"First the Will, Annette. Now I know your preferences in case Ivy didn't specify the individual pieces and I'll have them cleaned and appraised and insured for you. I'll let you know when to expect them when I see the lawyer on Monday. You can stay until Monday, Marjorie?" She nodded.

"Don't you let Marjorie take any of it either and don't go giving any away to the people around here." Her glance slid off Anne. "It isn't as if she lived here for very long."

It was a relief that Annette was as good as her word and left for the ferry with Harry driving her to the dock. Marjorie offered to go with them but Annette vetoed that. Daddy's girl, indeed. Anne took Marjorie and her family sightseeing after they finished lunch and, as planned, drove into a park on the highway. Harry soon arrived bearing fried chicken and drinks. The impromptu picnic was the right way to finish the day.

"I wish I had my trunks," said Chad.

"Chad the Intrepid." Harry walked down to the water with him so he could feel the frigid water. When Chad didn't flinch, they planned a day at the beach before the young family went home.

Beside Chad, who was five years old, eight year old Catherine was inclined to disappear into the background. She was a quiet little girl and seemed to be as enthralled by her brother as everyone else was. Her clothes stayed in place, her hair was always neat and voice was soft. Anne felt drawn to the child, almost protective. When she said how quiet Catherine was, Marjorie laughed.

"Don't worry about Catherine. Half of what Chad gets into is at her instigation but she's an observer. When anything is going on she looks more than she talks. Of course she's on her best behaviour now. She knows why we're here and she really loved her grandmother." Marjorie choked. "We all did."

Anne's eyes filled with tears. "I haven't known Ivy very long but we spent time together every day and I know how much you have lost. I feel as if I have lost a real friend."

Marjorie's arm went around Anne's shoulder and they were quiet. Anne liked Marjorie. How could Annette be so different!

The following day, Anne (laden with sunscreen, tee shirts, sun hats and sunglasses) took Chad and Catherine to the beach. She had had no contact with children and her offer to take Catherine and Chad was outstanding. Her heroism was unrecognized however. She wanted to give Harry, Marjorie and John time to deal with Ivy's estate but she was nervous. Would they do as they were asked? What if…? Still she offered. The children were thrilled, the parents were grateful and Harry thought it would be helpful since he planned to ask for help with Ivy's personal possessions.

They liked the beach. Anne sat under a shady tree and dispensed all the sunburn foils she had been provided with. She had a book but she was afraid to take her eyes off the two prairie children in case they drowned. They ran and screamed and jumped into the icy salt water while she admired the brown legs and sturdy little bodies of Harry's grandchildren. For a while she was part of a family again and she loved it, but she took her duties seriously and never took her eyes off them. Actually they didn't go into the water all that much, but they did build an impressive sandcastle. Sometimes a quite ordinary day becomes memorable and people are framed in gold and that is what happened then. She never forgot the beach, the sun, the children and the dream.

"There's Grandpa," called Chad. Harry walked toward them, elated and subdued. She could read his dear face clearly. He had been through such sadness and now he had finished a difficult job.

"Is anyone hungry?" The day became ordinary. Marjorie and John were not far behind and they all ate hamburgers and chips on the beach. (My poor low fat diet, thought Anne.) They stayed until sundown to enjoy the pink and blue sea and sky. In the stillness, the crying, chattering birds were loud as they gathered for the night. There was even an eagle soaring among the seagulls.

The next day the family had to leave. At Catherine's insistence Anne went to the airport with them and tears filled her eyes when all the loveliness went out of the Departure door. Harry steered her out to the car with his arm around her, suddenly realized what he did and felt in his pocket for the car keys. By mutual consent they got out of the car at The Complex and went their separate ways, tired and sad.

In the ensuing weeks they were together a lot. They seemed to casually run into each other, for coffee, for walks, for entertainment around The Complex. They met on Sundays for brunch and a drive.

One Sunday, Harry's phone rang just before he left to take Anne out.

"Daddy, it's Annette. I haven't heard from you for days and I wondered what you're doing." They talked about small things and Annette asked about Anne. "Do you ever see her?"

"We generally spend Sundays together."

"Mummy hasn't been gone for very long and already you are running around with another woman."

"Now, Annette, it's not like that."

"Never mind, you're probably going through a late male menopause and you'll soon be over her. Bye, Daddy, see you soon."

It was August. Hot, dry days, blue skies and sunshine. Harry and Anne were sitting in his car in a hilltop parking lot overlooking The City. Harry had something on his mind.

"You know, I'm getting back to normal. Ivy was ill for such a long time, almost four years. I think I was prepared for her to go years ago. She made sure of that. Did Ivy talk to you much?" Anne nodded. He continued, "She talked to me about you. She said, Harry I know how you feel about Anne." Anne stiffened, and Harry's voice was husky. "I know you, and you're going to feel so guilty after I'm gone that you'll let her get away. You are a faithful man, but when I'm dead, I'm gone Harry and where I'm going, I won't be concerned about Harry. If I want anything, it will be that you won't be lonely. Is this kind of what she said to you?"

"Yes, she was very concerned about you. She said you were always faithful but she didn't want you to go to extremes." It sounded so much like Ivy that they both smiled.

"I feel so restricted around The Complex that I can't spend time with you. How would you feel about going on a cruise with me?" He added shyly, "Ivy has been ill for years but I'll tell you this, Anne. I can still make you happy in bed."

It is one thing to have dreams but the sudden step into reality took some getting used to. Until Harry arrived, she thought she was content with her life, and she liked to think she was established for the remainder of her life. Her home, her friends, her pastimes were all very pleasant and ordered. Harry offered travel and change and excitement and this was not necessarily welcome.

"I don't know, Harry. Could we talk about this later? In a few months perhaps, so I have time to get used to you?"

"I think I'm in love with you Anne. Am I out of order?"

"No, you've been on my mind for a long time. It isn't that. It's all the changes. No matter what we say, this is going to change things between us and I'm not sure I want changes. I don't travel with every man I meet. Mind you," she added judiciously, "Nobody else has ever asked me."

"You could be right. Maybe it's too soon for me to try making a new life. I guess we'll just have to get our kicks out of trying to confuse the gossips around the place." He started the car in an atmosphere of dissatisfaction. Nothing had been settled and they were just as undecided as before.

He stopped the car suddenly, took Anne in his arms and kissed her thoroughly and for quite a long time. They were both breathless when he started the car, smiling broadly, and drove home.

In spite of logical discussion, kissing became a habit in no time. Harry soon determined every turn in the pathways that wasn't overlooked. There were frequent reasons to visit her apartment which offered even greater scope. Anne co-operated in this. They spent increasingly long hours together. Always, for the sake of confusing the gossips they left The Complex and went out to brunch and for a drive on Sunday. The gossips were not confused because they had experience in the game and Harry and Anne had none.

"I'm new at being a swinging single, Anne. Is there any place you would like to go? There must be dances and clubs panting for our patronage. Are there still movies?"

"Anywhere," said Anne. "It doesn't matter. Why is it that I am grey haired and you still have brown hair with only a few grey hairs at you temples?"

"Genes, for one thing. Also," he patted the top of his head with her hand, "You have all of your hair on top."

He kissed the hand he held. "Your hair is not grey, it is molten moonlight, it is shimmering moonbeams. I like the way you wear it all soft and loose instead of curled and permanented (permanted?). I think we should get married."

"Mm hm…what? Oh, Harry, for Pete's sake. Married. Well. You're not serious." She had just been thinking that her hairdressing appointment would have to be changed to no perm so it wasn't easy to switch to this tremendous subject. "Time," she babbled. "I have the nicest apartment I've ever had. I have plans for the rest of my life."

"Take all the time you like but this isn't all that sudden. Even Ivy knew I was in love with you, Anne. She told me not to let you get away."

Later, when she was alone she tried to consider his proposal seriously. It had taken years to get her life in order. She finally had an adequate income, an apartment she liked, friends. She even had a good bridge club. Now, with this proposal she would have to change everything again, for this would not be Harry's idea of life at all. He liked to travel, play golf and he liked novelty. Anything could happen when he was around. Obviously, Harry was wealthy. The thought of that higher standard of living was attractive but it would be demanding and she just wanted to coast from now on… or did until Harry came along.

She would be a fool to say no if she loved him but did she love him? Oh, she was crazy about him and lit up inside when he was around but what about the long haul? Would they go the way of so many older marriages? What if one of them got sick? What if she did and Harry was faced with another invalid wife? What if he ended up in a wheelchair?

What if the sky fell? Good night. Still she lay, sleepless and wide eyed until she realized that she did not want to imagine life without Harry.

Harry went home whistling. When he got settled he phoned Annette. "I can't wait to tell you. I just asked Anne to marry me." He and Annette had always been close and he was eager to share this moment with her.

"Did Anne say yes?"

"Not yet but she will. She loves me as much as I love her."

"You love Mummy. You can't love Anne although she sure tries hard enough."

Harry was blithe. "Anne will come around."

"Daddy," Annette said loudly. "You can't marry Anne. Mummy has only been gone for a few months and you are reacting to grief by denial, by falling for the first scheming woman that comes along. In a year you won't even recognize her name."

They talked briefly about Annette's job and the new kitchen cabinets that Harry would install in her house.

"But I can't come on the weekend because Anne and I always spend Sunday together."

"It has to be the weekend. I work."

"Part time. Maybe Anne could come too. It would give you two the opportunity to get to know each other."

He spent the rest of the time describing their future life. They would all take a cruise together. Annette could come and visit every weekend that she was able and they would come over so that he could meet all of her friends. They could go camping when the weather permitted. He recited Anne's virtues for a long time. When he got off the phone he thought with satisfaction that he had brought Annette to his way of thinking.

Annette had given up on her besotted father and decided to take another tack, when she said, "We'll talk about it later. Bye, Daddy."

When she got off the phone, Annette began making plans. There was no way that Anne was going to be part of the family…or for that matter, marry him. Anyway, it was obscene. He was almost seventy, How could he talk about love? If he isn't careful, people will think he's senile. Maybe he is. Maybe he has Alzheimer's.

For a few days Anne and Harry lit up The Complex. Anne was still unsure but Harry took a future yes for granted. When they went for coffee with the group they shone. While they were sure that nobody suspected their relationship, residents of The Complex had already taken sides for or against them. One faction thought they made a very nice couple and each of them would be a wonderful spouse. They were both popular and it was felt that Harry had been so good to Ivy for so long and now he was through a bad time. Both of them deserved a little happiness.

The other side relished the thought that late marriages never work. Poor Anne would then have to come back to The Complex, worse off than ever. He would probably take a stroke in no time. Her legs would give out and he would lose interest. It was noticeable that it was always Anne that would suffer.

One evening Anne received a call from Annette.

"Daddy wants to come over for the weekend to fix my cupboards but he says you won't like it."

"Of course he can go over. When did you think you could work it in?"

"Daddy and I will plan that."

Anne got the message but put the possessive tone down to jealousy. After all, this was Daddy's girl. "Sure, anytime is fine with me. We won't make any plans for the next few weekends that can't be changed."

"You shouldn't try to tie Daddy down with plans anyway. He's still grieving for Mummy. When he gets back to normal he won't want to be involved with anyone in an old folks home. He likes to be active."

Anne was upset with the turn of the conversation. "It was nice of you to let me know about the carpentry, Annette. Call me again when you feel like it."

"You'll never marry him. Marjorie and I have talked about it and we don't think it's right. He won't go against his family. Good bye, Anne."

The conversation changed the situation for Anne. She had only considered the marriage between herself and Harry but if Annette was so hostile and Marjorie didn't approve, it could spoil everything. Harry loved his children and his grandchildren and he certainly never would give up seeing them. She had seen other older couples who were always apart at Christmas and other family times but that wasn't what Anne wanted for them. Older marriages subject to adult hostile children don't have much chance of success. She worried and decided to talk to Harry about the new development. She still hadn't actually said she would marry him.

The next day was Tuesday and she ended up telling her bridge club about Annette's attitude.

Anne, Mary, Lottie and Robbie made a congenial foursome with their own laid back style of play. Purists would faint and aggressive players would burst a blood vessel but this group had found their own perfection. It was usually the high social point of the week although recent developments threatened to overwhelm the routine. Robbie ventured to remark,

"Have you got anything to tell your dearest friends, Anne?" The three dearest friends laid their cards on the table face down and leaned forward to hear.

"Well, nothing's settled but Harry did ask me to marry him."

"You don't look ecstatic about it, I must say."

"Nothing's ever perfect, I suppose. I am settled here, and happy."

"So you could live here. What else?"

"Harry's daughters. Especially Annette, the younger one. She is definitely against it."

"You can ignore her," Mary suggested. Anne shook her head. Mary continued, "Children can cause so much trouble. My oldest still tries to control everything I do. That's why I moved to the Coast. She insisted that I sell the house after Ralph died, then she sold the furniture, found an apartment and put me in it. I was in no condition to resist. I finally moved out to join Lottie. We've known each other since high school. My daughter still tries but long distance rates are on my side."

"Could you talk to Harry about Annette?" asked Robbie.

"I'll certainly do that but I don't want it to look as if I'm putting him in the middle when it isn't me that is doing it."

"How do you feel about gaining children and grandchildren all at once?"

"I think I like the idea, especially Marjorie and her children. They were great people until Harry began to talk of marriage."

"Have you talked to Marjorie?"

"No, but Annette said...."

"I wouldn't trust Annette's interpretation of Marjorie's thoughts."

"First of all, I have to discuss it with Harry when the time is right. Two no trump."

The bridge game continued. Actually they became so engrossed that they continued playing all afternoon. At six o'clock Mary served tea.

"Isn't this great. We don't have to listen to any complaints because dinner is late."

"Let's send out for a pizza."

"Retirement's a drag."

Anne's present way of life was very attractive in comparison with the turmoil of her feelings and those of Harry's family. She and her friends had come to rest. All four of them had been married, suffered widowhood (except Lottie and her astonishing divorce after forty-eight years of marriage). All had children except Anne. They had worked when they could, lived through a couple of wars and at least one Depression. They had learned how to live, how to expect trouble as a part of life and how to survive. Now they were safe, comfortable and happy. They were at nobody's beck and call, they ate when and what they pleased and endured no-one's grumpiness or criticism. What a good life. Pensions were small but so were expenses.

"Money isn't everything," they often remarked.

Chapter Four

That evening Harry drove out into the country to a small restaurant that served delicious food and had practically invisible waiting staff. The food arrived course by course and choices were minimal, re-inforced by all the necessary implements and condiments so that their conversation was quiet and uninterrupted. As they enjoyed salmon steaks Anne spoke.

"Annette phoned me."

"Good." Harry was pleased. "I know that both of the girls will welcome you into the family."

"It wasn't exactly a welcome."

Harry was relaxed and happy. "Don't worry, Anne. She'll come around. She's always vocal about what she wants but underneath she is a loving girl and she'll come around."

Anne could feel the point of the discussion slipping away. "She is against my marrying you, Dear. She objects to your not being free on weekends. She thinks we're too old. She doesn't want you to marry anyone."

"You girls are just going to have to sort things out between yourselves."

Anne had a sudden revelation of the future. Annette would not give up and Harry would not intervene. She wasn't charmed with the prospect of such an uneasy life. They talked inconsequentially through the rest of the meal. Anne ordered a large, rich dessert. Why not?

In the car, Harry drove to the waterfront so that they could walk on the wharf and enjoy the evening. The soft lap of the waves on shore was the only sound. The wind always dropped at sundown and at present there was an almost imperceptible breeze. The rising moon seemed misshapen as it slowly showed itself over the horizon. They watched in silence until Anne broke the spell.

"Harry, I can't marry you," she blurted tensely.

"Sure you can," he smiled as he enveloped her in his arms.

"No, Harry, I finally decided that I simply can't go ahead."

"What's all this, Anne? We love each other. We're both on our own. Why can't you? You're just having pre-marital nerves." He produced the cliché triumphantly as though he had just invented it. "Once you get through the wedding, everything will be fine."

"Please, Harry. I said I wanted to think it over and I have."

"But why? What's wrong. Tell me and we'll talk about it." They walked side by side, she with her two arms wrapped around her purse, and he looking at the boards under his feet. He glanced up and she shook her head.

"Don't do this to me, Anne. Please. I know we're right together."

Anne's eyes filled with tears. They returned to the car. With Harry's arms around her and the box of tissues in her lap, she cried her heart out but she didn't change her mind. Incoherently, she tried to say she couldn't leave a life of peace and certainty (and the bridge club, she said wildly) for a life of bickering and hostility in addition to the uncertainty of health, the future and aging bodies. It was just too much to consider.

He couldn't think of anything more to say. He didn't understand all of what she was saying but his poor Anne was beyond reasoning. He couldn't bear her unhappiness when he knew he was the cause. He took his arm away, dried her eyes for the last time and started the car for the despairing half hour trip home.

He took her to her door and neither of them even considered his coming in. He put his hand on her arm in farewell and it ended. All of the happiness, the glow, the anticipation of the future and thoughts of a family, ended.

The first few days went past as she kept herself busy in her apartment. She wrote letters to everyone she could think of and put herself on a weight loss program at home. She followed an exercise video with a perfectly shaped woman in a suit that looked like a pop can and who had never had a broken heart in her life.

She typed a resume and began to apply for work as a florist, first in The City, then the province, then Canada wide.

Later the fog began to dissipate, but, instead of moving into the sun she still walked under a black cloud. Now she realized what she had done. Harry had given her something to look forward to, always, ever since he and Ivy had come into her life. He has a brightness about him that affected everyone around him, but not her, not any more. Now, when it was too late she was able to think. Well, moping around the apartment wasn't the best way to get her life going again.

The bridge club was her consolation. They sympathized, talked it over then let it alone. She had avoided the morning coffee break because of Harry, but Robbie told her that he must be away. He didn't come in either so she had better start her day with coffee as she had done before, said Robbie.

Now she only had to deal with the gossips and Harry wasn't there to help confuse them. Lottie thought she might as well talk to them then they would go on to something else. The following morning she was back in her old place beside Robbie braced to face the firing squad.

"Are you going to give up your suite, Anne? I have a friend who wants to live here," someone lied shamelessly.

"No, I'm not going anywhere."

"Is Harry moving?"

"I don't know. Ask him."

As the bridge club predicted the group went on to talk about Bert, who had fallen in a shopping mall. He broke his arm and went to the hospital in an ambulance to have it set. They predicted his complaints about malls not being designed for old people. Too many lights and stairs. "He needs new glasses," someone said. "He's had those for nine years, he told me, and they were off a stand in the drugstore."

Heads turned as Millie came in. "Isn't it cold!"

"It's eighty-five degrees, Millie!"

"Isn't it hot!" she said, not missing a beat. She was wearing slacks and a twinset with a silk scarf around her neck.

The worst part was over and the pointed interest moved on. Anne went everywhere as before but with a new sadness. She listened to morning reports of events that interested the speakers; their fall on the stairs, the result of someone's tests. They talked about events to come and everyone was a little more comfortable because of the extended family feeling they enjoyed, especially when they could each go home when they wished.

Anne's home was cleaned to gleaming perfection—even her doorknobs were polished at the end of two months on her own. Her clothes were laundered and pressed and mended, every button in place and every wrinkle eradicated. Bridge on Tuesday prevented her from waxing her rock collection.

Eventually Harry was seen in The Complex and he ventured into the coffee room one morning. All the side glances in the world didn't faze Harry. He spoke to her and sat at the end of the table with the rest of the men. Rosalie appeared with her face lumpy with bites.

"What happened to you, Rosalie?" asked Bert. "What bit you?"

"No-see-ums. I was at my friend's place up-Island and we went for a walk in the woods. We both came home like this."

"Are you sure they were no-see-ums?"

"They said so but I can't be sure. I didn't see them."

Harry laughed, and after an unbelieving silence, so did everyone else. Rosalie said,

"I made a funny, didn't I?"

But life wasn't really back to the way it was before and it never would be, for Anne. The bridge club lent their support without talking about it. Everything had been said when Anne told them she had decided not to get married. They all understood her reservations and problems so they just continued their ritual non-bridge, afternoon or evening, and their plans for a trip to Reno.

As usual, every week they watched the lottery program with excitement. So far, no-one had a ticket with more than two numbers out of the required six, but there is always next week. Then came next week.

Anne, Robbie, Mary and Lottie always watched the television draw together. There were the usual lost tickets, time checks and shifting of chairs. The usual ruminations about what a person did when they won all that money and what the bridge club would do if one of them won.

Robbie was emphatic. "If I win, I'm going to take the bridge club to New Zealand. We have always talked about it but if I win, we'll go. Maybe tonight's the night."

Silence as the first number was called. Afterward, moans of despair as they checked their tickets over came a small voice saying, "Lottie."

When there was no response she said to the woman beside her, "Mary."

Everyone stopped talking and looked at Robbie. Her voice was shaking and her face was a most peculiar colour, suffused and blotchy.

"Are you all right, Robbie?"

"Lottie." Then silence. She pointed to her lottery ticket and someone's chair went over as they all leaped to her side. Her astounded friends read five, six, numbers and the bonus number exactly as they were called. It looked as if Robbie had won a million dollars. Lottie fainted, well, as good as. She got very giddy and had to lie down. Robbie was in a trance. The man next door was called in to check the numbers then sworn to silence. When a man confirmed it, they knew they were right. Robbie was a millionaire. She was, too. Well, actually, she shared a huge jackpot with several other winners, but for a widowed senior it was as good as a million. Her picture was in the paper and she was interviewed on television. She didn't mind the publicity; she had no wish to hide her new wealth.

Soon the four friends were in a storm of travel brochures. They were comparing airline schedules in Robbie's apartment. "What's the weather like in New Zealand in the fall?" asked Anne.

"I don't know what it's like anytime." Lottie said.

"Wait, I think that's in one of my brochures." Robbie re-filled the kettle.

"We'll have to know—what about clothes? Let's start another list."

The phone rang and Robbie answered it promptly. There were so many calls lately. The others listened with increasing attention to Robbie's end of the conversation.

"Hello?...Who?" A long pause. "Yes, all right...next week? You'll have to hurry because we're on our way to New Zealand...We? The ladies I play bridge with...Of course I'm coming back.... Tomorrow? I thought you said next week. Oh, that's nice of you, fitting in with my schedule. Yes, good-bye."

She replaced the receiver and turned to her waiting friends. "My son. My son, Gardiner. He's coming out from Toronto. Isn't that wonderful! Everything is wonderful since I won the money. He's calling tomorrow to tell me when he will arrive."

Imagine. This was new and discussion was brisk. They decided to suspend any real plans for now and not make reservations until Gardiner left.

The next morning, the now-routine discussion of Robbie's fantastic win (it could be me next time) included Gardiner's anticipated visit. That morning he had called to say that he was able to pick up a cancellation and would be arriving tonight.

"Ask if the guest suite is available."

"Yes, he'd probably prefer that to my backbreaking hide-a-bed."

Remarks about Gardiner's fifteen year hiatus between visits were, on the whole, sympathetic. After all, children are children for life if they're not too busy.

"Or if there's a big enough reason to put in an appearance." All in all, Robbie was well liked and it was thought that she could look after herself.

That day was also the day that Robbie heard from her daughter in Calgary. Gardiner had called her to tell her of her mother's win and she wanted to congratulate her.

"Before I had time to tell her about Gardiner's visit she said she is coming here this weekend. I didn't say any more, Anne. I thought it would be a nice surprise for her. Imagine, Gardiner and Shirley and I together after such a long time."

Gardiner arrived, all barbered and suited as a Toronto businessman would be. Nobody met him because he arrived in a rental car, and went directly to Robbie's apartment. After that, nobody could find out anything. Robbie didn't call anyone and they couldn't think of a good reason to call her. Robbie didn't come to coffee the next morning.

"They drove away at nine," volunteered Agnes. Her apartment window overlooks the visitors' parking lot instead of the garden.

"Isn't that nice. Gardiner took her out to breakfast. My, she must be happy to see him."

"She didn't look happy," said Agnes. "She looked flustered. You know how she keeps dropping things when you rush her. She dropped her keys twice and her purse three times on the way to the car." Agnes thought for a minute while everyone waited expectantly. "She dropped her sweater, too."

"How did Gardiner look?"

"Annoyed." Everyone laughed. They were all familiar with the hazards of getting Robbie into a car.

The next day produced another bombshell. Robbie phoned Anne late in the evening. "Anne, it's Robbie. I phoned to tell you that everything's changed. I'm going to Toronto in the morning."

"Is everything all right?"

"Oh, yes. Yes, just fine. It's just that he could only get a couple of days off because he's so busy at work and he wants me to go back with him for a visit to the old home town."

"You know, it might be fun to go back after all this time and you can get some real shopping done there."

"Anne, I'm so sorry. I feel so guilty."

"Guilty?"

"Well, we were going to New Zealand and now we'll have to put off our arrangements until I get back and I don't even know when that will be."

"Oh, Robbie, that was just fun. You go and have a good time and let us know when you're coming back and we'll meet you and you can tell us all that's been going on."

As they were saying good-bye, Anne suddenly remembered, "Robbie, what about Shirley? She's supposed to arrive tomorrow, isn't she?"

"It's all right. Gardiner took care of that and we're going to see her in Calgary on the way."

When the friends met the following morning, Agnes reported that Robbie and Gardiner were gone. They left very early and Robbie had three suitcases, big ones. Gardiner was wearing a very nice blue topcoat.

The bridge club still talked about the trip to New Zealand some day but it wasn't the same without Robbie and her excitement. After a harrowing silence, Lottie received a hasty letter from Robbie saying she was having a wonderful time. Gardiner and his lady friend were showing her the sights. Excellent restaurants that were new since she lived there, the parks, the residential areas in Toronto were all completely changed and beautiful.

They had fallen in love with a nice house that was huge, and still had an in-law suite as well, and Robbie had bought it (underlined). She was excited with all the sudden changes and now they had an appointment with a lawyer for the next day to sign the papers. Since Gardiner had given her furniture to the manager of The Complex, hers would all be new, including a recliner.

The bridge club discussed Robbie's situation. They couldn't play bridge with just three players and so far, they hadn't replaced her.

"I suppose Gardiner really is her son."

"Oh, yes, he must be."

"Sometimes children are more ruthless than strangers."

It was a worrying time. They consoled themselves with the fact that Robbie was no fool and at seventy-four, seemed well able to look after herself.

"Her daughter, Shirley, knows about it."

"We think. Gardiner told her, he said."

"If we don't hear from her again soon, we'll call Gardiner's number." With that they had to be content. It was the suddenness of the move that worried them for their friend's sake.

Anne had to laugh at their dramatic fears when Robbie phoned a couple of weeks later. The phone rang just as she was leaving to meet the bridge club.

"Hello, Anne. It's Robbie. Are you busy Thursday afternoon?"

"No more than usual. What's up?"

"I need someone to meet me at the airport." She sounded all right, casual and calm.

"Yes, of course I'll meet you. Now, with that out of the way, what's going on? Are you all right? Does Gardiner know you're leaving?" There was a lot to talk about and Robbie explained most of it. Anne finally interrupted.

"You're going to have to win another lottery to pay for this phone call. Let's save the rest until you get here. Oh, I'm so glad you're coming home. Where do you want to stay?"

"That's another thing. Will you ask the manager if there is a suite available? If there is, I'll take it."

Robbie came home on Thursday as planned. She was back in her old suite with the furniture intact. She hadn't been gone long, just over two weeks. When Anne, Robbie, Lottie and Mary settled down in Anne's living room, Robbie finally told the story…she had made Gardiner very cross.

"I was thinking over the house purchase and how it really fulfilled a dream for Gardiner, but what about Shirley? I always believed in giving them equal treats…."

"Treats!"

"Well, yes. Gardiner thinks of the house as his. I gave them treats that were equal in value all through their lives. When Gardiner and I went to the lawyer about the house transfer I asked to speak to the lawyer alone for a minute. I asked him to transfer the equivalent amount of cash to Shirley and I gave her address in Calgary."

Her friends were impressed. "We thought…."

"We were afraid…."

"What if…."

"I know what Gardiner thought, and Shirley for that matter, but when you've lived this long you learn about people, eh? And about money. All that experience in the Depression taught me all I want to know about money and what it can do to people. It was fun while it lasted, and now I'm practically broke."

Back to the old routine and this was Mary's night for the bridge club. "Is it all right if we don't play bridge this time? I have a surprise for everyone." She showed them to chairs arranged around the television set and placed popcorn at each place, then turned on the V.C.R. WELCOME TO NEW ZEALAND flashed on the screen.

One of the reasons they got on so well was that they shared the same mad sense of humour. They laughed, how they laughed, and Robbie was the first one to see the joke. Then they settled down to watch the film that Mary had borrowed from the travel agent in the shopping center. Later they decided they really must book for a trip to Reno.

"Robbie, did you ever pay off your recliner."

"Of course I did," she said, with dignity.

"Then let's book tomorrow."

"The recliner, I might add, wasn't in the suite when you got back. I didn't say anything," said Lottie, "but I think it went to someone needy."

"I guess it's gone forever," Robbie pondered.

"Never mind," said Lottie wickedly, "You can probably buy some of Harry's furniture," and they all started to cry.

It had been a really bad time for the bridge club.

Chapter Five

The Reno trip was still in abeyance. The bridge club members were limp after the recent tensions and wanted rest, not stimulation. Harry was seldom seen around The Complex for which Anne was grateful. She knew her feeling for him wouldn't change and that she had made a mistake. She waited for an opportunity to talk to him. He came to coffee one morning soon after she began to make plans.

"What was the name of your company, Harry?" some man asked.

"Mikhar."

"Oh, my car. I called it Miker when I saw it in the paper."

"We were young when we started up and we called it by our own names. Mike and Harry."

"It's a darn shame you retired ten years ago. It has just been sold for eight and a half million."

Harry's eyes sought Anne's. "Yeah, it's a shame."

Anne couldn't finish her coffee. She left with the other, smiling and contained, although her new mood of optimism was gone. She knew that Harry had not sold out of the company because Ivy told her so. How could she even think of telling him she had changed her mind when all that money from the sale changed everything, including the tie between them. Harry would never try to force her to change her mind and she could never approach him now. She never wanted to see him again.

Annette appeared the following morning, surprisingly, in the middle of the week. Well, maybe not surprisingly if she had read the financial news and quit her job. Anne was relieved that it was no longer her problem and she didn't even have to look at Annette's triumphant smirk. Harry went away on the weekend and Anne thought he was finally going to fix Annette's cupboards. She found herself looking for him but he didn't arrive on Monday or even that week. After a month of waiting, she gave up. He was gone forever. He had only moved to The Complex in the first place to be close to the hospital for Ivy's daily treatments. Still, he should have said good-bye when he left and even a month later when the phone rang she felt a lift to her spirits, but it wasn't Harry.

"Hi, Anne, it's Annette. Have you seen Daddy lately?"

"No, I haven't. It's hardly likely I would, don't you think?"

"I mean around that grubby old seniors' place."

"No." It wasn't grubby and this time Anne wasn't going to let Annette poison her life. She waited.

"I went to Daddy's a month ago and I haven't heard from him since. Do you think he died of a heart attack somewhere or lost his mind because of Mummy's death?"

"No, Annette, I don't think either one is likely. He's probably just found the time to take a holiday."

"He wouldn't, not without me. I told him I was ready any time he wanted to take a cruise or anything."

"If I hear anything that will help, I'll let you know."

Afterward Anne pondered. Annette had come to see him and he had left town. He wasn't avoiding Anne necessarily; maybe he was getting away from Annette. He hadn't given up his suite as far as she knew even though he could do that without coming back. Where would he go? Arden…of course. He had joined Sid when everything in The City overwhelmed him. Here she was worrying while Sid and Harry were likely having the time of their lives, fishing, swapping stories and re-building old houses. Arden was a sort of dream place to escape to…quiet, calm and far from life's turmoil. Of course he's there. She could stop worrying and go to bridge.

She told them about Annette's call and they discussed her effrontery but that was Annette. Mary looked thoughtful.

"If there's all that money involved, maybe you should have taken your chances on managing Annette."

Robbie loyally retorted, "Money isn't that important, Mary. If she had walked into a trap of misery and dissension, love wouldn't have lasted long."

"Yes, and she'd be back here, loaded."

"I'm back and I was loaded and I still say that money isn't everything." She paused. "Well, actually, money did bring Gardiner and Shirley back and gave me a memorable time back east."

Mary patted Anne's hand. "I know you're not mercenary, Anne, I'm just considering the possibilities."

"I know. Naturally I've thought about it, but the real problem came from knowing that Harry wouldn't support me when I needed him. That wouldn't change and I couldn't handle it."

After that day, Anne didn't want to go back to bridge any more. It wasn't that her friends were against her but they knew her situation so well that she couldn't get away from her problems in their company. She needed a new interest to replace cleaning her clean suite. Every time the phone rang she glared at it, sure that it was Annette or some other major pest. The phone rang, she closed her eyes for a minute and answered.

"Anne, it's me. Harry. You've got to come to Arden for a holiday."

"Harry! Arden! I can't possibly...."

"You have to come. Bring the bridge club. There's plenty of room. The thing is I have to come back to get some papers signed and I'll be staying overnight on the nineteenth. If you decide to come, I'll bring a station wagon. Make up your mind. You don't get a fantastic offer like this very often. Check with your friends and I'll call you at the same time tomorrow."

Seven o'clock she noted, so he'll be calling tomorrow at seven even while she was telling herself she wanted nothing to do with it.

"It would be helpful if you could get sleeping bags."

"We all have them, Harry, from our fishing trip last year. I can't say one way or another but I'll talk to everyone."

"I'd appreciate it if you would talk to everyone but Annette. Good night, MY DARLING." The line went dead.

He hung up before she could answer but she could hear him laughing, and a great weight lifted from her heart. She put a bottle of white wine in the fridge to cool and phoned Robbie, Mary and Lottie. None of them were busy.

"Who has anything to do in the evening?"

They all met at Anne's place looking worried.

"For once I have good news, well, interesting news. We were wanting a holiday and we can have one if we want one that is inexpensive, slightly mysterious and the opposite of elegant…and we'll probably have to work." Anne's happiness shone from her face and her whole manner was changed.

They chorused, "Arden." They looked at each other then her. "Yes."

"Good-bye, Reno," somebody added.

As Anne poured the chilled wine she told them what she knew. Harry would take them back with him after his appointment in The City. They discussed what they would need.

"For how long? A week?"

"We'll miss bridge night so we'll have to take cards."

"Right, first things first. Cards."

"We'll have to think about food. Is there refrigeration?"

"I seem to remember talk of a light plant, but we'd better not depend on it."

"Right. Cans and dried stuff like spaghetti, rolled oats, flour. Sardines and canned salmon."

"No way. I'm going to fish." Robbie loved fishing and had instigated last year's fishing trip.

"Right. Powdered milk and eggs. Fresh vegetables."

"I think I'll crank up my bread machine." Lottie was heard above the chorus of voices. "I can make enough to last us the whole time."

They decided to take work clothes, sweaters and sturdy shoes and one pant suit for civilized appearances. Their heavy leisure suits and long underwear would be comforting on the Coast at night when the lovely civilized heating system at The Complex was far away.

"I'll take my camera."

"Binoculars for birds." By this time they were all writing busily and drinking wine thirstily.

"Wine. Lots of wine in case of snakebite."

"Are there snakes, do you think?"

"Who cares. Lots of wine in case."

"Should we take swimsuits?"

"Only if they go on over long underwear. The water's cold around this Island."

"I think we should take them. There may be a lake…how big is this place anyway? Maybe there's an old leftover pool."

Wine and excitement were taking their toll.

"Sid really likes sweets. Let's have a cookie bake and take a stockpile over to him. I'll bet nobody cooks for him like we used to."

"I hope not." This was a new thought. "You know, we really don't know what we're getting into and we can't ask if Sid has a live-in."

"Who lives there?" Robbie wondered.

The others recited, "Sid and Harry, Sid's son and daughter-in law. And?"

"This is really living. It's an adventure. We can at least be sure that Sid and Harry will look after us and mastermind accommodation, transportation and safety. The rest is up to us."

"Salt." Said Mary suddenly. "My husband used to have a fit because every time we went out on a picnic I forgot the salt. I'm going to take five pounds of the stuff."

"Are we going to tell the other tenants where we're going?"

This led to more discussion. Anne repeated Harry's provocative statement that he didn't want Annette to know.

The wine was beginning to take hold and Robbie peered around owlishly. "I will not tell Annette," she said judiciously. "I think…I'm not going to tell anyone. If Harry wants to spill the beans he can, but if we tell everyone, they'll all want to come with us, especially if they remember that Sid said there are twenty-five empty houses."

"Shhh." Anne served crackers and cheese before they went back to their separate apartments, tiptoeing exaggeratedly.

When Harry phoned the following evening the news was all good. They were going back with him and were bringing everything they needed. Harry said there were beds since Sid and he found an auction of hotel fittings and they bought all the beds. He was excited and so was Anne.

"Let's not talk about anything serious until we can sit down with all the time in the world. But there's nothing to worry about, Anne, I won't say or do anything to upset you. Ever. I promise. You can tell the bridge club to bring their canes to fend me off.…

"Oh, Harry, you nut." She laughed. Everything was funny and lighthearted again.

"See you this weekend."

They had two days to make their preparations and they did their best. They didn't know what they were getting into but they knew there was a station wagon and there were four of them and Harry so they kept the packing at a minimum. They were having a grand time, knowing all the while that The Port had all the stores they could wish for and they didn't really need to haul everything from The City.

At last Harry arrived in a very big, not very new station wagon. They sat in Harry's apartment discussing the holiday departure time and decided that ten in the evening was a good time to load for a quiet getaway. Nobody was around at ten in the evening but at five in the morning there were people walking all over the place. They loaded everything at ten o'clock with no audience. It went well enough with the four pillows just making it, crammed into odd corners.

They left The City at seven in the morning and had breakfast on the road. The trip to The Port took hours as they dawdled through shopping centers and coffee shops. At The Port they met Sid and he treated them to fish and chips before they followed the men to the dock. The charter boat, a converted trawler, was waiting to take them to Arden.

Anne thought that Harry had timed their arrival for the best time of day. When they tied up to the jetty the town of Arden was bathed in benign late afternoon light and the sea and the winds were calm. Arden. There were three rows of houses. The lowest, closest to the waterfront were small, almost cabins. There were eleven of them, placed in a curving row above the high granite ledge that extended across the whole sea front. Pebbles formed the slight beach.

The second row of houses, ten of them, seemed to be two-bedroom classics of the sixties and were also in a curve facing the beach. They were about a hundred feet behind the front row and sited so that they had an unimpeded view of the water. The top row consisted of four larger two storey houses, two on each side of a double track that led up into the cleared fields above.

The six of them stood gazing upward at this strange anachronism of thirty years ago. The houses were shabby but in surprisingly good condition with only a sagging porch here and a strip of missing roofing paper there to bear witness to their abandonment.

Sid, characteristically, had moved into one of the bachelor houses in the lowest row, while signs of determined repair on one of the two storey houses at the top testified to Harry's choice, also characteristically. Their porches were straight and their rooves were tight. You could see the results of their industry.

Each occupied house had a neat pile of firewood stacked in the yard and a day's supply on each porch. Then Anne noticed that three houses in the middle row showed signs of activity. The end one to the left had smoke coming from the chimney. Two on the far right had a stack of wood each and their porches were swept as well as being straight. The men had put a lot of effort into their comfort.

"I thought while it's light we would walk up and look at the houses to see what you want. There are two beds in each bedroom so you can all share one house or you can go two to a house. They're ready to live in."

The houses were fine. They needed paint and new sinks, and the wood stoves were rusty but otherwise the years had been kind. Obviously the previous tenants had expected to return. The houses had been left in good condition. It was amazing that boat-owning vandals missed them when wreaking their particular kind of spite.

The women decided they would share one house. There was enough room and it would be more fun.

"What about the house at the other end, Sid? Is that where your son lives?"

"That's right, that's where Randy and Monica live. You'll like her and she sure will be glad of some company. Randy's at work now but he'll bring the stuff up when he comes home if that's all right. I don't carry any more that I have to."

"Yeah, Sid, but you don't seem to mind climbing all over the rooves of all these houses."

"That's right. We all have our limitations but roofing isn't one of mine. Randy carries the rolls of roofing up for me. I want all of them watertight by winter."

"That's a big job, Sid. Can you do it?" asked Robbie. "I hate to point it out but you're no younger than I am."

"Sure, Robbie, I know. We have a crew coming over to do the four top ones and the middle ones that need it. We do the bachelor houses for fun. You're closer to the ground on them."

They noticed that Sid was talking more than usual and they suspected that he liked the additional company as well as his daughter-in-law did.

Harry looked rested and relaxed and very happy. He had been through a very stressful year. Ivy's illness and death, the sale of his company and all the extra work that entailed, then a love affair with Anne that must have taxed him to the limit. How wonderful to have Arden to escape to. Anne looked at him fondly. How nice it was going to be. No peering eyes and a whole week together to restore their relationship and plan the future, if there was to be a future.

Coffee was ready at Sid's house. He produced a tin of ubiquitous Danish Butter Cookies. "There are no home-made cookies in this bachelor set-up. Otherwise, anything else you want, if you see it, you can have it. You didn't happen to bring any cookies?" He asked hopefully and beamed when the women nodded.

Later they walked up to the second road and met Monica. She was shy with the sudden influx of so many people but Sid was right, she was glad to have company.

"I'm so pleased to meet you. I love this place but it is somewhat lacking in female companionship. Come up tonight when Randy is home and we'll show you the night life." Everyone looked at her, surprised. "We're it."

They proceeded to their holiday house as the men described the amenities. "We've put in an outhouse temporarily. There is a system here for sewage but we're still working on it, so in the meantime you have your little house out back. We have different plans for the future."

"Up above the town there is a abandoned farm that must have been productive at one time. There are still fruit trees and even old berry canes. I don't know when they cleared out of the house. There's a house and a well and out-buildings such as a barn and chicken house and other sheds."

"Is that part of your property, Sid?"

"Sure is, and I have plans for it."

"You're not going to farm next!"

"No, but if we have people living here in Arden. I'm going to lease it to some nice young farm family and we can enjoy the produce. They can sell here and in The Port. Isolation did in most of these lush old farms. Fortunately," he added shyly, "we have enough capital (thanks to Harry) that we can hire all the transportation we need, which was more than the old farms could afford."

Seeing Sid in his element made it difficult to imagine him living in a small apartment in The City. It said a lot for his nature that he had always been good tempered in those circumstances.

"A dog, Sid! You should get a dog. If I lived here," claimed Lottie, "I'd have a great big dog."

"A cat or two lends a certain ambience to a house, too. It seems calm and settled." Lottie was the practical one, born and raised in the country in Ontario. "When you do get animals, get strays with no place to go, poor things, and they should be neutered unless you want them to multiply."

Sid watched the others as their enthusiasm began to grow and he knew that pets were apt to arrive quickly. "I'm not going to do anything until I get the title deeds to the place."

"Haven't you got them?" asked Robbie, diverted from the enticing animal shelter idea.

"Is anything wrong?"

"We couldn't bear it if you didn't get this place."

"I don't think there's a problem. I've paid the money and got a receipt. It's just that Australia is so far away and that's where the previous owners ended up."

Harry turned to Anne. "How long are you planning to stay?"

"We thought a week, if it's all right with you and if it's convenient for you to take us back then."

"We picked that time because the Fall Fair is coming at The Complex and we want to get busy on that. The committee will decorate and generally look after the organizing, but they need help and all the handiwork needs to be sorted and priced. I do jams and jellies." This was Mary's big project of the year.

"What about you, Sid? Are you still wanting to stay over the winter in Arden?"

"Sure, it's going to be interesting. The bad weather doesn't last all that long."

"Are Randy and Monica going to stay?"

It seemed that the young couple planned to go back to The Port when the fisheries contract ran out. Sid wanted to stay and he didn't mind being alone. Everyone looked at Harry.

"What are you going to do next, Harry?"

"I can't make any definite plans yet but I wouldn't mind the winter here with Sid."

They were going to install radio telephone which was a relief to their friends. Harry had chartered a boat in The Port to service Arden with a schedule still to be decided. Sid was stockpiling food, kerosene for the lamps and the old power plant and he was cutting and stacking firewood in his spare time. He almost made it sound attractive to have a few weeks of peace.

"When the weather is good you can come and visit me," Sid added hopefully....

"Christmas." Lottie was caught up in the magic of Arden. "It's always the worst time of the year to travel in Canada but we can choose a time to just nip over between storms."

"I'll put Christmas lights on the jetty for you all if you'll bring a turkey."

"Wait a minute. Our families. Mine always have plans. I always have Christmas with my daughter, Ellen," said Mary.

"Oh, let's just say we're going on a cruise. They'd believe that." Robbie laughed wickedly. "My kids may have plans for me this year but I have a feeling it would include my going to them. If I'm not available they can go skiing or something."

Anne noticed that Harry wasn't saying much but he was happy. His big smile was back. They ate the penne, asparagus and chicken casserole that Robbie had brought, and fresh salmon that Sid had caught that morning, then finished off with Lottie's cake and cantaloupe.

Later they walked to the other occupied house. Randy and Monica were ready for them. Randy was very like his father, wide shouldered and sturdy but he was much taller than Sid. They were a pleasant couple and it was true that Monica was happy to have company. The week would be busy if they did everything they planned that evening. The next day was for berry picking and they would help Monica make blackberry jam and jelly, and fill as many jars as they could find with soft fruit. There was no freezer.

"Blackberry wine is lovely. We always used the last of the berries and the very first huge ones in wine at home and I continued the tradition," said Robbie.

"Did you happen to bring any recipes?"

"No, but I can start you off and send the books when I go home so you'll have instructions in time for the next steps. I can write out what you will have to do before we go back."

"I don't have any equipment at all."

"All you need is a big, clean plastic pail, wooden spoons and glass bottles. Cheesecloth is useful if you have any."

"What about a crock?"

"They're all right but I find them cold and you can't use one that has had pickles in it or your wine won't work. You can use anything else as long as it's non-metal and very clean. It's best to boil everything. Now they like to complicate matters with additives but I think of wine making as a cottage craft and the old method suits me. I like the wine better, in fact. The additives give people heartburn that my wine never does."

"There are old apple trees up on the farm, very overgrown but I've seen a few apples," offered Sid.

"It seems early but if we find some useful ones we can bottle some applesauce."

"And make a couple of pies, I hope," sighed Randy.

"This is going to be a busy week."

"We'd better go to our place and stoke the fire."

"It's all right, I did it," said Sid, "but we should turn in if we want to make an early start tomorrow."

Harry spoke up. "Can't I take Anne out tomorrow?" He smiled at her. "I thought we could pack a lunch and go exploring and talk things over."

They all agreed that Anne could start learning to pick berries another time, and milled around getting flashlights and coats for the great trek home. The women's cabin was warm but they added more wood and closed the dampers, to ward off the waterfront chill for the night. The trusty light plant would run for another half hour, until eleven o'clock so they had time to get settled before the lights went out.

Silence fell as their sleeping bags grew warm and soon the only sounds were the crackling fire, the sussurating waves and the onshore wind moving the nearby trees.

Chapter Six

The following morning was the beginning of a hot, sunny day. The women wore heavy shoes and work clothes for berry picking and walked up the road between the houses and over the hill. Tall grass was everywhere, glistening and whispering in the sun. The sea was very blue, slightly lipped with whitecaps. The sky was cloudless.

"Are there any bears around here, Harry?"

"I've never seen one but it would be wise to expect them. There's bound to be, especially in the berry patches. Keep an eye out and don't argue is my plan. If I talk loudly they try to avoid me. If I see cubs, I go home by the shortest route and I don't get between mother and cubs. Mother love in the bear world is formidable. We haven't heard anything about bears, but come to think of it, we haven't heard about anything else either."

They walked across the old farm, bypassing serene old buildings, grey and weathered in the sun. There was an old orchard with a few apples and plums. Pear trees could be seen with only single occasional pears withered on the branches. Berry canes, raspberries, gooseberry and currant bushes, were struggling to survive.

A double track went through the farmyard continuing from the jetty at Arden. The track continuing across the field led the bridge club and Monica into the trees at the far side, while Anne and Harry veered to the left on a game trail into the woods. They found a knoll that overlooked the land below, the beach and the sea. That first morning, Harry and Anne sat on a rock on the summit and watched the berrypickers far below.

"No bears that I can see," observed Harry. He put his arm around Anne and she leaned against him comfortably.

"I have to talk about the situation with Annette first, Anne. I made a mistake with her."

As he talked, his mind went back to the last time he had seen Annette when she had come to see him at The Complex. It was after the sale of Mikhar had been reported in the newspapers. They discussed money and he told her of his plan to give her and Marjorie a portion now instead of an inheritance in the future. He felt that they could use it now and he wanted to be free of the burden of financial complications and expectations within the family. When Annette asked how much money he made from the sale he told her quite truthfully that it would be somewhere over four million dollars. He laughed when she talked as if she would receive two million dollars.

"Not likely," he said. "I thought you would be thrilled with half a million."

She pouted but he could see her eyes change as she realized what she could do with it. "At least you won't have to give that Anne any of it."

"No. I'm sorry to say no."

"Well, I made sure of that." She laughed. He looked at her, stunned. "She didn't have to think she could marry my Daddy just because he was rich and vulnerable. I got rid of her for you."

"I loved Anne."

"You loved Mummy."

"I loved Ivy and I loved Anne." He was shocked. He remembered telling Anne that the girls would have to sort it out for themselves and he winced. Annette was headstrong but she was also sweet and loving, at least with him. He recalled Ivy telling him that he let her get away with too much. Now he could see that Ivy herself had been treated with contempt by Annette and he was the cause. In the politics of family life, he had let Annette play the role of Daddy's girl at the expense of Ivy, and probably Marjorie. "I don't think I can discuss this right now, Annette. I have to think, I've made so many mistakes that I don't know where to start. I'm going out for a couple of hours. You can phone your friends as usual and I'll be back in time to drive you to the ferry. In a few days I'll get in touch with you, I promise."

When he came home she was gone. He wrote to her once but business matters were handled by his lawyers, including the transfer of her funds. He told Anne about that day and the long recital ended.

"Annette broke us up, didn't she?" Anne protested by shaking her head, but Harry went on, "I didn't understand when you said she had phoned but I do now. As I have always said, we are right together. Please let this be a big rock on the road to romance and re-consider. Please marry me."

"Yes."

"What?"

"Yes." It wasn't often that she could surprise him so she loved to do so. It took him a while to realize that he could relax. She said yes.

"We are supposed to be watching for bears," she said breathlessly after a long, long kiss.

"I don't see any."

Later they had lunch, hard boiled eggs and buttered fresh bread and water. "You're a wonderful cook." He was besotted. Nevertheless, the ease and simplicity of transporting such a lunch had its appeal.

"Where were you born, Harry?" asked Anne dreamily.

"Weyburn, Saskatchewan but we moved to Regina when I was four years old."

"Do you have brothers and sisters?"

"I had two brothers quite a bit older than I was but they were both killed in the War."

"Were you brought up in Regina then?"

"Well, Dad went there to manage a lumber yard and that's where we stayed all during the Depression." He laughed, "That's where I learned the building trade. When I was quite a little kid we used to build chicken houses and sheds to try to sell lumber. One time, I must have been fourteen, Dad sold the lumber to build a barn and he threw me in, too."

"What? Harry!"

"I mean it. By that time I was getting pretty useful and Dad was a creative salesman. Part of the deal was that I'd go and help with the framing. Actually, the owner paid me to help with the rest of it so it worked out all right. Dad never wasted anything. He used leftover pieces to build wheelbarrows and gates, benches, lawn swings, you name it. It got so that I made most of them. I even sold birdhouses door-to-door once when I was wanting money for something."

"So that's how you became a builder."

"Yes, and of course after the War there was a fantastic building boom. That was when Mike and I went into partnership and it was a profitable time to start out. You couldn't go wrong if you tried. Dad taught me all he knew about keeping books and Mike spent his early years as a carpenter then estimator so we had a pretty good background. There was no shortage of tradesmen, good men, with all the returned men looking for work.

I met Ivy in 1952 in Calgary. (I'm glad you knew Ivy before she died.) We had a big contract there so I stayed for a year, then we married and Calgary became my base. Ivy's father was wealthy and she invested all of her own money in the firm. She was like that, generous.

That's why, when the company was finally sold, I gave the girls the money. I wanted to see John and Marjorie started in something worthwhile while they're still young enough to have the stamina. Annette will probably blow hers but there's nothing I can do about that and she knows that's all she's going to get. She signed a kind of quit claim on my estate, a release."

"What does John do?"

"So far he hasn't been able to get much of anything. He's all right, he tries hard, but it's different now. You need money to start. Part time and contracts are the norm at present. I don't know a man can ensure his future except by going into business for himself. John had been working in computer programming but he hasn't found his field yet. I hope to get some time to talk with him when they come to the wedding." He tightened his arm around her shoulder and kissed her. "I want to get that worried look off his face. Mind you, they have that money now which should help. He's a good man and he and Marjorie have a good marriage. I hope that's all right with you," he added.

"Of course. The best thing that we (we, doesn't that sound lovely?) can do is give them security."

They spent the rest of the afternoon exploring some of the many game trails that wound enticingly along the hillsides. They found wildflowers and animal burrows of mysterious provenance. They ate a few berries as they walked reverently under the huge cedar trees that seemed to be the essence of all old forest, brooding and remote.

On the way back, they stopped at the farmhouse. It was old with a large low ceilinged living room, a big kitchen and one bedroom downstairs. Narrow steps ascended to the second floor hallway and two more bedrooms. In the style of the time, there was one bathroom, downstairs, and there were not many rooms in all, but they were large. The remains of red gingham curtains were still blowing in the kitchen windows, ragged and stiff with dust. A large fieldstone fireplace almost covered the end wall of the living room. A family could be comfortable here if they didn't mind the isolation.

"We'd better not go upstairs," said Harry. "Those stairs were not too sturdy in the first place and they look really shaky now."

They went outside. The barn was dusty in the heat of the sun but the dirt floor seemed ageless, quite even and smooth. A chicken house with sagging chicken wire and a few small utility buildings clustered around the barn.

"Is it possible that Sid won't get Title? Now that he's shown an interest can they change anything?"

"It should be all right. They quoted a price and Sid paid it. I'll feel better when he gets the actual deeds, though. I like to have the paperwork in my hands in any transaction before I make any firm plans."

"I don't think I could stand to have anything go wrong now that I've spent time in this wonderful place."

"Could you live here?"

"Oh, yes. I can see some problems, especially it's being remote."

"Would that bother you? We can always go on a trip once in a while."

"It won't bother me now, with you. We could use some kind of medical care. The City has amenities for seniors that we don't have here…hospital, doctors, dentists, chiropractors, chiropodists, electricity, refrigerators, running water, entertainment." Seeing Harry's sad expression she laughed. "The only real problem we'll have to solve is emergency medical care. The Port isn't that far away."

They talked about it again in the evening after dinner. Harry invited everyone up to his two-storey house, all warm and with enough chairs to go around. He announced very formally that they were getting married. Robbie, Lottie and Mary put their arms around Anne, and cheered, then they hugged Harry. Sid shook everyone's hand. Randy and Monica, after an astonished moment of wonder at the noise, joined in heartily. Harry disappeared into the kitchen and re-appeared with a big bottle of reasonably cold champagne.

"Harry, when did you buy that?" asked Anne accusingly.

"When I went to The City to get you."

"What if I hadn't changed my mind?"

"I didn't intend to let you leave until you did. After all, it's our charter boat and our station wagon. Sid would have stuck by me."

"Are you going to live here?" Again the big question.

"Summers certainly," they said.

Harry explained. "Sid and I have plans for improvements. We can manage power, one way or another. I have the boat service on a regular basis and maybe even a helicopter for emergencies. As Anne pointed out, our main problem will be emergency medical problems. If Sid will insist on working on his roof, we have to be prepared if he falls off and there are all the other problems that come with grey hair. We have radio telephone and we can probably do better than that. There's plenty of firewood. We thought we would buy all the building materials for repairs and new sinks and stoves and water pipes, things like that, and have a barge bring it all over at once. Randy will be finished his contract with fisheries in the late fall and he seems to have unlimited large, fit friends so we have all the labour we need."

"As far as organization goes, Sid owns the land and the buildings and I rent my place from him. I don't particularly want ownership, just access."

They listened carefully.

"Could I rent a house, Sid?" asked Robbie. "I could live in a bachelor house if you have plans for the others. Harry can have his two-storey house." They all joked about his mansion because nobody else lived on the top tier and Harry was up there in solitary splendour.

"It all depends on getting Title. We don't want to get in too deep until then."

Lottie and Mary said they loved Arden and wanted to rent a house if possible.

The week sped by with the guests picking berries, canning, making jam and jelly and starting wine. Monica soon had enough food preserved to feed an army. They put the wine in the kitchen of the empty house next door to Monica's to keep the bees and other assorted insects out of their own house.

"Be sure to keep the cheesecloth over it because flies carry the vinegar bacillus and your wine will turn to vinegar. That's good for pickling, though. One year all of my pickles were a beautiful deep red because a whole batch of raspberry wine went to vinegar. Of course, wine vinegar is a gourmet cooking ingredient now." Monica was listening carefully, especially in regard to wine vinegar.

Lottie made bread twice and showed Monica her method. Wood stoves were no problem. Almost every Canadian over sixty learned to cook on a wood stove and they all poked the fires and rattles stove lids with insouciance. Now that there was a possibility that they would spend time in Arden they cleaned cupboards and talked about wallpaper and paint.

It was a perfect holiday for the city guests. They walked up to the old farm every day and frequently took picnic lunches. The men were not committed to any schedules so they were present at the various impromptu events. They hiked up to the knoll and clambered down to the water where it was accessible. They collected shells and poked in tidal pools. They fished from the dock although they didn't catch much. Sid fashioned a crab trap with fishnet and an old wheel rim he found in the barn.

"Where did you learn to do that, Sid?" he was asked as they ate their first feed of crab.

"Prince Rupert. I was a fisherman."

"You were! You never told us that."

"My legs went which is an occupational hazard. It turned out all right for me but I couldn't go back to fishing because it slowed down when the fish stocks began to go. I sold my boat and moved to Victoria. Fishing's improving now but it's a hard way to make a living."

"That's why Randy works for Fisheries."

"He always loved fishing. It nearly broke his heart when I sold the boat but it seemed like the best thing to do at the time. If only he gets a permanent job with them. He can go fishing in his spare time, I tell him."

"We'd better get a pressure canner," observed Lottie, "so we can keep some. Imagine having all the crab you want."

Sid laughed at her. "Why preserve it when you can just go down to the jetty and get some fresh ones?"

Swimsuits were never in the water during that holiday but the women sunned themselves once or twice. They sat around a campfire in the evening, listening to the lapping of the waves and the wind gently moving the trees. Once they cooked corn and bacon and beans on the campfire, savouring the camp coffee.

"Don't drink the last mouthful or you'll get coffee grounds in your teeth."

"We've got to make time to look at the bachelor houses. Sid may let us live here someday."

The days seemed very short and the visitors never seemed to accomplish all they planned but the following morning they went down to inspect them.

Although the houses closest to the water were small, just twenty by thirty feet, they were weatherproof. There was a main room and a bedroom, with part of the bedroom space used for the bathroom. Sid thought the bachelors probably lived in a float camp and the couples lived in these but they were called bachelor houses now.

"I was afraid they didn't have plumbing and Harry would have to build outhouses."

"Can you do that, Harry?"

"Someone built some here." Mary pointed to the new little houses built for their visit.

"He's a building contractor, for Pete's sake."

Anne smiled, remembering Harry's story of his early career. "He really could. He told me he has built about a hundred outhouses in his time."

"But millionaire Mikhars don't build bathrooms as a rule," said irrepressible Lottie.

The pipe dreams went on as the week flew by. Nothing would be done until next spring if they did decide to move over. Anne would come to Arden in the spring. The water system would go forward in the spring. Always with the reservation that the Title deeds would have to be in Sid's hands first. The plan, the optimism, the walking and the simple food made everyone energetic and cheerful. Nobody had trouble sleeping. Mary and Lottie were both over eighty and yet, tanned and lithe, they thought it seemed possible for them, too. Sid and Harry and Randy were there to look after them, they thought. Actually, the two retired men were there to play carpenter and fish and indulge their fantasies but the bridge club agenda fitted in with theirs well enough. There had been a lack of decent food and this past week had been a revelation of what meals could be like.

Realistically, they waited until the deeds were secure in Sid's hands. They were old enough to realize that life was full of surprises and not always pleasant ones.

"Expect the best and prepare for the worst," isn't a bad philosophy.

On Saturday as they waited on the wharf for the charter boat, Mary said, "Don't forget the lights on the landing. We'll be here for Christmas with a turkey and all the trimmings."

They were picked up as arranged and the boat chugged across the now familiar water to The Port. They retrieved Harry's station wagon and drove home, stopping once for dinner. It wasn't really necessary to arrive after dark, but they did with what they called a fiendish delight in causing confusion to the gossips.

Chapter Seven

A shrieking siren split the air as they separated reluctantly to go to their own apartments. It would be strange to be alone after a week of sharing the bathroom and discussing the day's events before going to bed each night, but no-one would complain that it was too quiet. A series of sirens and horns sounded at the intersection as several vehicles rushed madly to a fire. Car horns and brakes sounded almost continuously. The pale light of The City almost overwhelmed the faint stars trying to be seen through the murk. Another ambulance passed, siren yelling and horns hooting as it went through the same busy intersection. Someone in the building turned on a television set, very loudly, then turned it off. The women used to sleep soundly in all the commotion but it would take time to get used to it again.

In Harry's building it was just as noisy. He was kept awake by the clatter of skateboards in the parking lot and the same sirens to and from the hospital. It was very hot and he could either open the windows and endure the increased racket or leave them closed to lessen the noise and breathe the stale air of the building. How he missed the stillness and moving air he was accustomed to, and he couldn't wait to go back to Arden. Finally, he slept fitfully.

He would have a long meeting on Monday but Sunday was for them. They decided to enjoy their usual Sunday brunch then went for a drive. Anne cooked dinner – an excellent T-bone steak divided into two servings, salad and microwave baked potatoes. As she handed him an apple and a fruit knife, he asked dramatically, "Will Harry ever see an apple pie again?"

"Probably Harry will be plied with increasingly delectable apple pies from Mary and Robbie forever, if…."

"Don't worry, it will be all right. I'll phone as soon as Sid gets his papers. In fact, I'll phone every day."

They said good-bye reluctantly, reminding each other that they would soon be together again and absence makes the heart grow fonder and the time would go quickly then Harry went back to his stuffy, noisy suite, smiling happily.

He didn't stop in the coffee room the next morning as his meeting was at nine o'clock, but he ran up to Anne's door, rang the bell and kissed her early morning face, chuckled and ran down again.

She wasn't sorry to see him go. It wouldn't be long and she was going to be busy. She was happy among her own belongings as she read all the waiting mail, discarded the flyers and wrote a couple of cheques. She watered her plants and did her laundry in surroundings that felt familiar and comfortable although excessively sterile and clean. Arden began to settle back into the mists of a beautiful dream. It was just a shame that the stove was so very automatic. It wasn't as interesting somehow. By Wednesday it was as if they had never been away as the demands of the approaching bazaar increased. There was so much to do about her wedding that she tried to make a list, but could only postpone each item for now. Everything depended upon something else. She would talk to Harry when he phoned about all the things they should have discussed last week. He would probably say there's lots of time. Back to the demands of the bazaar.

It was approaching quickly and Mary spent every day baking pies, cookies and bread. She didn't like to freeze her baking, but she thought it would be all right for such a short time if she defrosted carefully, for the sake of freshness. The muffins would have to be baked the day before so they would still have the lovely just-out-of- the-oven crispness.

Lottie looked after the handwork. She straightened crooked crocheted doilies and pressed cushion covers.

Robbie was designing an astonishing purple turban and costume. She was going to be the surprise fortune teller under a diaphanous tent, also purple, in the corner of the room. Fortunately the Tenants' Committee was in charge of refreshments and decorations.

Anne was drifting around vaguely pondering what she would wear for her wedding but that depended on where they had the ceremony, which depended on when…should she stay at The Complex until she got married or spend the intervening time at Arden in her holiday house. She would like to be in that house. If they decided to stay in Harry's two storey house after they were married, there was a huge amount of work to be done. Of course they could do that together later. She didn't want to take on a lot of housework either. Harry….

"Anne." She looked around and saw everyone looking at her, half amused and half exasperated. Someone suggested that they put her to work on posters with Lottie, where she could do the least harm. The ads for the bazaar were going up everywhere so it was decided that anxious friends would carefully proofread after Anne finished them for correct dates and times.

The bazaar came and went. It was more successful than usual, partly because young couples in the neighbourhood learned that they were welcome and also that there was home baking. All of the baking was sold. All of the baby clothes went. In fact, the only handiwork left consisted of doilies.

Robbie has a wonderful time with her terrible unidentifiable accent, but since she only foretold fulfilled dreams, unexpected money, love and long life, she made three times as much as she anticipated. Some of the elderly tenants didn't recognize her and one woman complained that strange old street people shouldn't be allowed to make money at their bazaar.

During tea time at the bazaar, the manager of The Complex announced that he was retiring at the end of October, after many years of service. He was efficient but also available to listen to the litany of complaints, the last vestige of control of their own lives. No wonder he was retiring and no wonder everyone was in turmoil.

As a group the elderly tenants saw change of any kind as a threat to their tentative hold on security and this loss was especially felt. Someone was always talking about leaving but now moving vans began to appear several times a week and this increased the complaints and general uneasiness. For Anne, the stability of her home was gone and for the first time she was wholeheartedly pleased to be leaving.

The bridge club had never mentioned moving at coffee time. In fact, they didn't talk about their holiday, what with the bazaar and the news of the manager's departure. Rosalie and Millie joined them one day.

"How was your trip?" Rosalie asked longingly. "It was quiet here because almost everyone was away."

"We had a wonderful time, outdoors from morning to night, doing nothing."

"Do you have to take a ferry to Arden?" Millie asked.

"No, you have to go to The Port and charter a boat from there," said Lottie very blasé.

"There is no ferry. It's almost an hour to get there but it's sheltered water mostly."

They met for bridge on Tuesday but there was so much to discuss that their card playing was more sporadic than ever. In fact they didn't play at all. They discussed Annette, and thankfully decided she was Harry's problem. They talked about Arden constantly in an atmosphere of unreality,

"Remember Brigadoon?"

"That was a lovely movie."

"The town that disappeared and only appeared for one night every hundred years or so."

"I see what you mean. Arden."

"Well, I hope that Arden doesn't disappear."

"Not while Sid and Harry are there anyway."

"It really is an unbelievable place, isn't it? All those empty houses waiting for someone to return and bring them back to life. Everything lying there in the sunlight, waiting."

"In the spring we may be there remembering The Complex."

The cards were still in a deck in the middle of the table.

"Robbie, did you send the wine instructions to Monica?"

"Yes, the next day while Anne and Harry were out. I'm collecting all the bottles from the re-cycling box and washing them for Harry to take back with him next time. There aren't many bottles. Not many seniors have a store room full of them."

"Well…not many." They all chortled. There was one senior not far from there who was well-known for his alcoholic intake and his inability to dispose of the evidence.

"Maybe you should go directly to Melvin and save all this running up and down to the re-cycling box."

Finally, a few days later, the long anticipated call came from Harry. "Hi, my love. I phoned especially to tell you that Sid got the papers for Arden in the mail today. They were sent Registered Mail."

"Is everything all right?"

"Very much so. The delay was caused by the owners having taken time to locate all of the old permits, building permits, licences, and recommendations from the regional government. This means Sid won't have to start at the beginning as far as rules and regulations go…he has his permits. It seems that they were in perpetuity, so he just has to renew whenever necessary. Now we can get going."

"Is the weather still holding?"

"Yes. Do you want to come up again for a while?"

"I don't know. Are you coming here soon?"

"I thought if the weather is good I may be there late in November."

"Don't take any chances with the weather. I'd rather think of you safe in Arden than lose you trying to get here."

"I'm no hero, but I miss you. I'll be so glad when we're finally together. What would you think of a Christmas wedding?"

"Well, I'm leaning toward Easter. What do you think?"

"Suits me. You are coming for Christmas, aren't you?"

"Yes. Harry, what's going on with Marjorie and John?"

"There's always so much else to talk about. They are full of congratulations and will come for the wedding. They are hoping to come to Arden for a holiday next year. Marjorie will be phoning you or writing. She says it's hard to say everything on the phone. She had no phone call from Annette. Take care of yourself, my love, and let's plan on Christmas."

Anne called everyone over to tell them the wonderful news. Sid had Title to Arden which meant they could go ahead with ideas that had been on hold. They discussed the change of management in The Complex and all of their friends who seemed to be leaving. Robbie said even Anne was leaving.

"That's a definite change. Anne, do you think I would be crazy to move to Arden?"

"I don't know, Robbie. It's hard to know what's best for someone else, even you. I feel as if I'm stepping into the unknown even though Harry's waiting for me. I can only say I'd be glad to have your company but I don't want to influence you. You'll have to decide for yourself."

Mary and Lottie were listening and considering leaving The Complex. To all of them, Arden was a lovely alternative to various seniors' housing units in The City.

"We won't have any medical help less than an hour away."

"Well, we're all in good health except for the usual decrepitude inherent in reaching, in my case, eighty," said Mary. "Lottie is eighty-four and Robbie seventy-four. We have regular medical appointments that wouldn't be a problem if we have the charter boat. It's the emergencies in bad weather that could be serious."

"We have to talk to Sid and Harry. After all, Sid could refuse to let us come."

Anne said, "We're invited up for Christmas. We can talk to him then."

"We'll do our most beautiful cooking so he can't resist."

"There are other factors. Our children…."

They're not around much, except for Mary's Ellen. What will she think, Mary?"

"She always goes for what I want. I just don't want her to be lonely when I'm gone."

"And can we still do our own housework? I have a homemaker here. Well, I could go for a bachelor house with rustic décor where the dust doesn't show."

"Are we talking about year round?"

"Otherwise we'll have to find someplace in The Port for winter."

"Or keep our places here."

"They won't let us do that when there are so many on the waiting list."

It was complicated, but always in the back of the deliberation was the peace and freedom of that lovely place, so tantalizingly near if they could only get Sid to agree. They began Christmas plans with this in view. Should they have a traditional dinner or go for something different?

After a long discussion they decided to make a traditional dinner. They were all so familiar with the routine that they would be less likely to forget some essential detail and they would have leftovers galore, for later meals. They began puddings and cakes at once to give them time to season. They also decided to buy the traditional ham for New Year's Day, that would leave the men a few meals.

Christmas plans on the west coast are always made in a mood of supplication. This promised to be one of the impossible years. As they made their plans, the men in Arden experienced the dreaded isolation as one storm after another battered the coast.

Even in the sheltered cove, winds whipped the sea into huge waves and pummeled the new rooves and windows, testing their strength. Harry moved into his kitchen for a few days. It wasn't worth trying to heat any more rooms. The wood piles dwindled alarmingly. Sid was snug in his bachelor house as far as heat was concerned but he was thankful that Harry was there for company. There was always work to do and their preparations for Christmas went ahead although it may become wasted effort.

"We'll still have a Christmas even if they don't make it," Sid said dolefully.

"Let's just hope they make it," said Harry. "My cooking doesn't go much beyond beans and eggs and I'm getting tired of that."

They hopefully rigged lights on the jetty, stapling and securing every wire. It gave a cheerful look to the dock in the darkness, so they left them on every evening until the power plant shut down at eleven o'clock. The unending woodcutting went on and they scattered ashes on footpaths so that they wouldn't be slippery in frosty weather. They lit fires in the holiday house every day to drive out the damp.

The women in The City experienced the same huge storms, with furious east winds bringing excessive cold and pounding rain, but they were snug and simply stayed indoors. Finally, on the twenty-first of December, blizzard conditions brought driving winds and hurtling snow. Anne, knowing Harry's determination, worried that he would try to come to The City in such terrible weather. On the twenty-fourth the sun came up in a blue sky, there was flat calm at sea and, amazingly, warm temperatures.

At noon, Harry arrived in the station wagon. They hurriedly packed their boxes and bags in the car and fled to Arden while the going was good.

After an uneventful trip with no stops for food or anything else, they got the charter boat and were delivered to the decorated jetty and all was well. They moved into the same house, put on the coffee pot and began stocking the cupboards. The only ones missing were Monica and Randy, who stayed in The Port for the holiday with their friends.

Harry came in, looking concerned. "Lottie, I hope you remembered to bring salt."

"Salt! But I brought lots last time."

"We used it to do the walks."

"Salt! Don't tell me we're out of salt! How can we make turkey dressing without salt?"

Sid and Harry guffawed. "Lottie, we have enough salt to last until the turn of the next century."

"Harry, don't tell me you were kidding. I hate being out of salt. I panic."

"We noticed," said Sid. "You could always cook with sea water."

The holiday was even better because of the suspense. They may have had to spend the holidays in The Complex, in one case, and eating beans in the other, but the weather was kind. On Christmas Eve they ate a tourtiere (a big veal pie) accompanied by all the leftovers they brought from home.

The Christmas dinner had been well planned. The rusty stove in the holiday house was cleaned up, sandpapered and blacked before the women arrived, and it did a fine job of roasting the fresh turkey. Every dish was good, and as the men appreciatively ate their way through to dessert, the bridge club crossed their fingers.

When everyone was replete on Boxing Day turkey sandwiches Robbie told the men about the manager of The Complex retiring and the present tenants leaving one by one. She went on to say that she would like to join them in Arden if they would have her.

Sid and Harry looked surprised and doubtful then Mary and Lottie added their blandishments to the general consternation of the men. Harry diplomatically looked at Sid, who said he would have to think it over; it was all very sudden.

"But Sid," Robbie was intent, "Would you refuse to rent us a house, even a teeny little bachelor house each? It would give you income since we plan to pay you a very fair rent."

Poor Sid was forced to make some kind of a comment. He thought, then said carefully, "It's a big decision. Give me time to think and we'll talk it over before you leave, but I can say this. I wouldn't refuse to rent you a house if we can iron out a few problems like heat and light and emergency plans. I need these as much as you do, but Harry and I were just going to take our chances. We can't let you women do that." He suddenly has a thought. "This is summer I'm talking about. You couldn't possibly stay here in the winter…we'd have to spend our entire time cutting wood."

The bridge club looked at each other and decided to bide their time. They had said enough for now but they were still thinking. After all, the previous residents stayed all year round. Didn't they? Admittedly they worked in logging and each house had a young husband to take charge of things. They could see that Harry and Sid could never cut that much wood, but why should they? There must be other ways and this is what they had been discussing in the previous weeks. Lottie spoke up.

"If we did, we could hire some of the young men that Randy knows to do our wood piles. They seem to need work and I'd pay for mine…probably we all would."

"Lottie ! Aren't you clever," said Mary. Discussion moved to the possibility of moving in the spring even if it meant living in The Port for the winter, leaving their furniture in their houses in Arden. They would give up their suites in The Complex, if Sid agreed to them coming here.

Sid finally said that if it could be done, he thought he would like having them here. It would be less isolated.

They went to bed exhausted after all that concentrated effort.

The last serious discussions were about the forthcoming wedding. Harry and Anne thought they would be married at Easter in The City and would spend their honeymoon in The Port, just a few days. They didn't want to be away from Arden for long. Harry spoke of other problems.

"One thing I figured out. I can contract to have a helicopter service if we need to have a quicker response than the charter boat. He's going to bring the boat on a regular schedule if we request it."

"Having a millionaire among your friends is certainly helpful," breathed Lottie. She worried although not enough to let the others go without her.

They went back to The City in a very different mood. They were quite proprietorial about the weather for one thing.

"There will be quite big waves when we go back," Lottie said, "but I can't see any whitecaps. The wind goes down at noon." That wasn't quite right but she was satisfied.

"It's funny," mused Robbie. "I don't feel as if I'm going home to The Complex. I feel that I'm leaving home to bring back my things."

Chapter Eight

The returning travellers needed a few days to adjust. The intimacy of good friends in an atmosphere of sea washed air, wood fires and rain was exchanged for the indoor stuffiness and the constant stream of grey-faced, unsmiling people who were also recovering from their Christmas holidays. Coffee time conversation was of grandchildren and great grandchildren, bus tours, and…it's good to be home.

Until they actually gave notice to vacate their apartments they didn't want to mention moving. As the days passed they began to dread it. Now that they were back in The Complex, Arden receded and with a slackening of their first enthusiasm, the thought of saying good-bye to so many longstanding friends was daunting. Never had their large well-fitted bathrooms seemed so opulent or their electrical appliances so desirable. On the first day of February the four women gave notice for March first and Anne would be married, not on Easter weekend but on June twelfth. Easter didn't fit in with the new plans.

The wisdom of their move was confirmed when The Complex management announced at the middle of February that they were taking the unprecedented step of closing the facility at the end of the year. This would give the tenants almost a year to find new accommodation and re-locate at their leisure. They hoped this would lessen the stress of this drastic step for everyone. Management would be pleased to assist in the process as much as possible.

In anticipation of their move, the bridge club started discarding and buying to accommodate their new houses. There would be no dishwashers but Lottie had her little spin-dry washing machine. She wouldn't part with it when she moved in although there was a laundry at The Complex and now her decision was justified. It was powered by electricity but used little power or water. It was very easily repaired. They packed all their kitchen appliances, reasoning that there was no shortage of storage space in Arden, and there could be electricity soon. They would be expensive to replace.

Harry and Sid began to make serious plans at their end, preparing the houses and arranging trucks, a barge and men to help. Harry's eagerness to have Anne closer was probably the reason that the packers would arrive in the third week of February to pack containers, whatever that meant.

Suddenly, the bridge club realized that they were running out of time. They bought copious amounts of food. Harry told them that there would be plenty of room in the containers and on the barge. Without freezers in the near future, dried and canned food took precedence. Coffee and tea. Rice. All kinds of pasta. Flour.

They haunted Garage sales and came home with a heap of various essentials. Big plastic five-gallon pails and three fifteen gallon ones for storage of dry supplies. They all bought garbage cans with the locking capability of a bear trap. Any camping equipment they saw was snapped up. Kerosene lamps and gas lamps and a camp stove and coolers (if we can get ice.)

"We could have campfire evenings out there under the stars with the rush of the sea in the background."

"And loons calling."

"And a whiff of wood smoke."

"Buy those barbecue tools, Anne. I'll buy that huge black pot. Don't you people want to cook out any more?" she asked the owner.

"Sure we do, but we're going to Africa for two years to work for CUSO and we're selling everything."

"We're moving into a remote little coastal town up Island and there isn't always power. Just an old Lister light plant."

"I have a dinghy and a little sailboat for sale. You can have both of them for one hundred dollars."

"Done," said Anne, "but I want to make it one hundred and fifty to help you with your African tour. I don't know how we're going to get this home though. When are you going to Africa?"

"We leave in June."

"Could we leave the stuff here until the truck comes on the weekend?"

"Sure. Where is this little place?"

"It's a little ghost town called Arden that we seem to be restoring. It didn't start out that way but there things often seem to happen."

"Only if you're flexible, and if I might say so, you're the most flexible people I've met in a long time. My wife is working in a motel that is now under new ownership and they are doing a complete renovation. You can get a hundred woollen blankets for a dollar each."

"Wonderful. Just what we need. Can you…."

"Yes, I'll phone right now, and we'll put them with the rest of your purchases." He laughed.

They were so pleased with each other that they subsequently exchanged names and future addresses.

When she excitedly told Harry about their purchases on the phone that night, he roared. "Two boats and one hundred woollen blankets. That truck had better get there soon or he'll have to bring a pup."

"A what?" Anne laughed at his terminology.

"That's what it's called. It's a little addition hitched on behind for an extra load."

"I want a real pup. I thought that's what you meant. When you come on the weekend, Harry would we have time to go to the S.P.C.A. and get a dog?"

"Or two, and a couple of barn cats, but Anne, don't go without me, please. The way you people are buying in bulk, you're apt to fall for their entire stock. In the meantime, can you content yourselves with buying pet food?"

"I promise we won't go without you, Harry. I don't really trust our resistance, either. We're too excited."

The next time Harry phoned, she was even more excited after hearing his news.

"Have you a pen and paper handy? Sid and I have been discussing the big move. It's going to be hard on the bridge club, so we decided to help. But first, you have to phone around and find a moving company that can deliver some containers on Wednesday night or very early Thursday morning, like five o'clock, and place them close to each of the apartments we are going to vacate. We want to arrange for packers to come on Thursday and Friday to pack everyone's belongings and we'll get some men to pack the containers. We'll chalk the owner's name on each one. Any overflow can go in mine if necessary. I know I won't need all that space. Please tell the movers that the truck must take the containers to the wharf at The Port. I have a barge to take it from there and Randy's friends will take care of this end. Randy has a lot of friends who are out of work and keep themselves in shape by working out all day. We're turning into a local industry, at least for now. This is an ambitious project, isn't it, especially if it's only for the summer. When they go out for the winter they can leave their belongings here. Does that sound all right?" When she agreed, he continued, "Can you arrange for a cleaning company to come in and do the apartments after they're empty? Also, get everyone to pack an overnight bag for moving day. How's that?"

"Harry, if I hadn't already said I love you, I would now. We've been pretty worried. Moving is traumatic at the best of times and moving to Arden has so many new problems. Now, I'm to phone the movers, the cleaners and what else? Oh, yes, tell everyone to pack an overnight bag. Containers for late Wednesday. The truck is to go to the wharf at The Port. Then I'll explain everything to Lottie, Mary and Robbie. They are looking tired already. I think we've all been worrying a lot. When can we get our animal crackers? I really want a dog, Harry."

"So do I. We can go after the furniture truck leaves. If necessary, you and I can come to town later and get them."

"Just think. By then all of the hard work and worry will be over. By the way, did I tell you we bought one hundred wool blankets? We met a couple who knew of a motel shutting down and we took them all, at that price."

"Yes, you told me. That should solve a lot of problems for the next fifty years but I would have done the same thing. You and I won't need more than one...."

"Harry, you...."

"Hurry home, darling. Tell Mary to remember to get salt. We only have seven pounds left." Talking to him on radio telephone wasn't the same as being with him but it was lovely. Soon.

"I love you, my darling, and among all these plans I never forget our own plans for June."

"I love you, too, and I'll always remember your thoughtfulness during this move."

The elaborate plan went forward with Anne on the phone for hours. The bridge club discussed the new plans. They wouldn't need to get boxes or packing materials. They wouldn't even have to pack. They only had to spend time filling out Change of Address forms and cancelling power, telephone and cable services.

"No more bills! Just rent." crowed Robbie.

"I wonder why we pack an overnight bag."

"Yes, what was that for?" They discussed it and decided that if the containers weren't opened right away, they had the basics. "They have been putting a lot of thought into this."

"They will never know how much we have been worrying," said Lottie. "I confess I wondered if I could do it. Stress isn't good for this old lady even though I would never have let you go without me."

"We know this is going to cost someone an awful lot of money, but I don't care, I'm going to let him pay for it. But I'm going to love him forever, and Anne, of course. We're lucky you two fell in love."

"Moving gets a lot worse when you get older."

"Like a lot of other things," Mary chimed in, "but not impossible, and we have more time to do things just when we need more time."

"I think it's just that we get out of the habit of deadlines and it's disturbing when we have to go back."

They had one more bridge night in The Complex. Quite a few extra people wanted to join them so they played in the coffee room. Although the four women didn't think about it much their many plans had transformed them.

"Bright eyed and bushy tailed," said Rosalie. "You make the rest of us feel better about the coming changes. They don't necessarily have to be for the worst, do they?"

Old people see change as threatening because it is so often downhill to their way of thinking. Never ending pills and therapy and eventually to the nursing home then the grave. As their options diminish the smallest change brings apprehension. Unless, as in this case, usefulness is called into play again, plans are made for the future and adventure beckons. There was even a spice of danger to make the change even headier, and to take the focus away from aging and health concerns.

"We really are going to have to improve our bridge. We are impossibly slack."

"Maybe we should go back to playing bridge."

"Next winter we'll have time to get into contract if we want to."

"Now let's not get hysterical. I think we should buy a book of rules though."

"Hurray, one more thing we can buy." Shopping was the best part of the move.

"And a stock of playing cards."

"We got those in November, remember? At a Christmas sale?"

"Let's face it. There's nothing else we need. I'm going to spend the rest of the time on clothes. We won't need much but it will be all different. Warm and sturdy is my new image."

"Wasn't it lucky you found that treadle sewing machine. We should be getting it back from the repairman tomorrow."

"Who's going to keep the sewing machine?"

"Anne. They have the most extra room."

"She could have a sewing room in Harry's two storey house." For apartment dwellers the thought of so much storage space was intoxicating.

Soon, the day came. A rusty van brought Randy, some muscular young men, and, surprisingly, Monica.

"I came to help," she said. "This is a oner of an experience and I don't want to miss it. Besides, it's no fun being in Arden alone when it is happening here. I might miss something. Harry is coming right behind us with the station wagon. We don't know where we'll stay yet but there seems to be a lot of apartments involved and we all brought sleeping bags."

Now windows all over The Complex were open and curtains were twitching. People they knew came over to listen. After all the planning, the move went ahead smoothly. Harry arrived and took the bridge club out for lunch in the country. While they were out there they bought a supply of potatoes and carrots from a vegetable stand. It was too early for this year's bounty. They were able to buy turnips, onions and a box of apples. They found eggs and milk and had a lovely time. Buying was the favourite pastime at present, they needed food, and this was not expensive. In fact it was good economy.

They returned to The Complex for dinner and were astonished that Lottie's, Mary's and Robbie's apartments were already empty of furniture. Cleaning was finished in Lottie's and Mary's.

The guest suite had been reserved for the young workmen, who were grinning at everyone's astonishment. Instead of inviting them for dinner, Harry handed over a few bills and said they would meet in the morning. Randy joined them. Monica told Randy she was tired and she would go to bed early.

"Have fun and remember me." Nice woman.

She joined Harry and Anne and the others for dinner. Later they slept on various hide-a-beds offered by friends. Rosalie took in Robbie and Mary. Monica and Lottie shared with Anne. Harry was in solitary splendour as befitted his present status.

"Harry deserves the best, " they said. "He can have his own apartment."

Whatever fleshpots the men found didn't prevent them from knocking on the doors early the next morning to pack the remaining suites, make sure the cleaners were there, and return to The Port by noon. At one o'clock the truck appeared, the containers were loaded, and it left in a remarkably short time, hopefully stopping en route to load the boats, and blankets they bought at the Garage Sale.

Harry asked, "Does anyone have anything they want to buy? Last chance." They left by mid-afternoon.

In the car, Anne said accusingly, "You couldn't wait to get a dog could you?" I know why you wanted to be here. You wanted to help choose. You're as excited as I am."

They drove up to the pens at the animal shelter and parked. There was a lovely din of barking, some staccato, some deep. There was howling, baying, whining and many feet scratched busily at the locked gates. The visitors scattered like mercury to the various pens. Harry moved close to one of the big pens.

"But these are golden retrievers!" he exclaimed. "Who could possibly have put them in here?"

The attendant came over to join them. "The owner died and his children didn't want them. There is a mother and two male pups. The pups are four months old and she is three years old. They just came in yesterday."

"Anne, what do you think? What about it?" Harry was excited. "We have to talk." The attendant listened as they discussed the remarkable situation.

"Sid will want one of the pups. I know that. Do you like the breed? They are very gentle and good tempered. They will look after you."

He turned to the attendant. "What is the procedure? Do we have to speak for them and then wait? Has someone else requested one? We could take the three and keep them together."

The attendant thought it was time to talk reality to the group of grey haired dreamers. "They are big dogs and will need a lot of room." The listeners glanced sideways at each other and smiled. "We prefer that they go to the country away from traffic. I do hate to see them confined. Even now they are not as relaxed as they were yesterday. Have you got room for even one of them, really? I have a little cockapoo that…,"

Again they described Arden and the dog paradise that awaited these three lucky dogs and a few other pets. The women were looking at the cat section.

"All of the animals that we adopt are spayed or neutered. Possibly we can make special arrangements for these three, though. When are you going to take them?" Again, a young man was charmed by their description of Arden. "Come and see the cats. We always have plenty of little cats in here. You can pick your colour, sex and age."

"What about that one in the corner with the wild eyes?" asked Lottie.

"She's an older cat, maybe six years. She was left in an apartment when the couple split and she wasn't found for a few days. She may be permanently traumatized, we don't know."

"I want her. I like a long haired cat and marmalade is my favourite colour. She will be peaceful in my house and will never be left alone. Anyway, it's a house and she can sit on the windowsill and look out, poor little thing. Is she spayed?"

"Yes, ready to go when you want her."

Harry told him what he planned. "I think it would be best if we left them here until next week. We'll be settled by then and they can go directly from here to their new homes. Can you board them for a week? Are you open on Saturdays?"

"Yes to both questions and I'll come then to help with this fantastic show."

Anne was concerned, too. "Would you take special care of the dogs until then? You said they are suffering from being confined and I'm worried about them waiting for a whole week."

"Yes, I'll be glad to. They're nice dogs."

"It's just that the move would be so disturbing for them on top of them coming to a strange place," explained Harry. They arranged to come back the following Saturday. It was the best they could think of, in the circumstances.

Robbie and Mary chose a little house cat each. "Barn cats indeed," said Robbie.

Harry laughed. "They'll be outside whether you like it or not, Robbie. All of that grass is teeming with little grey mice that will keep them busy for a long time. You'll have to bring them in at night at all costs until we know about the resident wild animals. Wild mink or raccoons are hard on cats, never mind foxes and coyotes."

"Neutered animals are especially vulnerable, I think," added the attendant, getting into the spirit.

"My black and white tommy is called Walter," said Robbie suddenly.

"Walter," they chorused. "Where did you get that name?"

"I don't know, but that's his name." Walter was a classy large short-hair with elegant black and white markings. He moved with macho male arrogance, graceful and confident. He cuddled against Robbie when she picked him up, in affection and easy recognition of where his next meal was coming from.

Mary's cat had the pointed little face of a Siamese even though she was black and obviously cross-bred, perhaps several times. The Siamese would always come through in her knowingness, her long slimness, and her infrequent but astonishing wail. She was five months old and the expression in her eyes a thousand years old.

Anne picked a grey striped kitten that was barely weaned.

"You'll have to have her spayed when she's six months old. We can help with the expense if necessary but she's too young, at present."

All was arranged and they left quite a lot poorer, what with shots, spaying and boarding charges. They bought carriers, flea collars and calendars. Their individual donations to the shelter raised the monthly income considerably. Every one of them was quiet, thinking about the new pets and pure pleasure shone in every face. In The Complex, pets were not allowed and these were people who had always had animals in their lives. It was part of the old way of life. Childhood memories of first responsibilities of feeding and caring for their pets were still there. Childhood lessons are clear and relevant throughout life and they seem to keep their freshness forever, even to advancing age. Memories of ever-present affection and non-judgmental love and faithfulness in retrospect can make an almost mystical experience. These fortunate people were moving back into the world, for good or bad.

"We are going to stay overnight at The Port. We'll have a quiet dinner and loaf. Tomorrow, we'll go over just in time for the celebration. No more work and worry for us. All those men are unpacking the containers and then you're settled," said Harry.

The following day they did absolutely nothing.

It was true. They went over in the charter boat with prepared food for dinner at six and found a transformed Arden. They didn't have bachelor houses. Each of them had a house on the second tier. Anne was in the house they had occupied previously, the holiday house. Robbie was next, Mary then Lottie.

There was a tractor and a flatbed wagon with small wheels that Randy had made, for the furniture.

Sid produced a bottle of wine and they drank to the end of the old life and the beginning. "I thought I was going to have to live here alone, then Harry came for the winter and now you're all here. I am very happy tonight. It all came true. Back to decent food and conversation."

They re-heated the pizza and talked for a couple of hours and found that was sufficient for the day. Peace fell over Arden as beds were made, hot water bottles filled before the light plant stopped. Just the lapping of the calm sea could be heard as the stoves slowly burned down. The cold, damp air was a soporific if anyone needed one.

Chapter Nine

Waking in the new house was bliss. It was bliss to lie in a warm, comfortable bed and look at the piles of boxes to be unpacked and the contents put away in all those cupboards in all those rooms. Well, lots of room anyway. Robbie had had the foresight to put her coffee supplies in a separate box, well marked.

She got up shivering, lit the stove, and started the big pot of coffee. She put mugs, muffins and margarine on the table, opened her door, and yelled, "Coffee." She closed the door and began finding things to sit on. One by one everyone appeared, had breakfast and talked for a while, then went back to their waiting chores. Possessions were unpacked and placed lovingly in new locations, and houses slowly became homes. Living in four adjacent houses meant they were closer together than they had been before so it was easy to consult about arrangements and drink cups of tea on the run when anyone had the urge to make one.

Sid spent time with each of the women to listen to suggestions. They also discussed rents and methods of payment and hopes they all had for the future. He decided to get the roofer back to do some carpentry as each tenant seemed to want a cupboard or shelves in addition to the existing ones.

The group as a whole made plans for Arden. "If we move away I think we should donate our furniture to Arden. If they don't want it they can burn it but we can't afford a barge and weightlifters every time." Heads nodded in agreement. "And I think we should pay the carpenter for special little improvements that we want done."

"Costs are going to be so low that we will all accumulate some money. Imagine! That's why I want to put some back into general improvements."

"We could use picnic tables."

"For morning coffee."

"There will be other things as we go along. What we are trying to say, Sid, is that we want to feel a part of things and we know that you own Arden. It's just that we're grateful to you for arranging the move. We simply couldn't have done it without you and we appreciate someone looking after taxes, garbage disposal and the light plant while we have homes of our own without any hassle. We want to be part of it." Mary handed him another cookie.

By the weekend Anne and Harry were ready to go to the City to bring back the pets. Now that they had everything together at Arden it was a chore rather than a pleasure to leave. Only the waiting pets justified going away again so soon.

In the station wagon on the way to town they discussed their approaching wedding day. Anne tentatively remarked that it wasn't plausible to travel to The City for the wedding when every wedding guest, except for Harry's family, lived in Arden.

"Could we be married in Arden?"

"There's no chapel or anything."

"I remember when home weddings were popular. Your house has a nice, big living room."

"If the weather is nice, we could have it outside."

"We could get a minister to come from The Port."

"Harry, do you think Marjorie and John would like to stand up for us? I don't know about Annette…I don't think she would." They could laugh about it now.

"Marjorie would love it. I know she would. Thank you for thinking of it."

"My pleasure. If they could stay for a weekend or a week even, they could have a house to stay in. We could get one ready."

"There's no beach for the kids. Too bad. They liked the beaches."

"We can keep them busy, Harry. We'll have as many children as possible at the wedding to keep them company. We don't know any but no doubt Randy's friends have families."

"We'll have the ceremony in the morning then have a cookout in the afternoon." It sounded feasible. If the weather was bad they could go inside. "Have a cook in," said Harry.

As they parked at the shelter, Anne wondered if they had to put the dogs in cages.

"It may save some anxious moments but they have been confined for so long I wonder if we can get away with it. We'll just have to make sure we don't open the doors without checking on them." Harry pondered. "I think we'd better confine the cats. I hate to think of one getting lost on the way home."

They went into the animal shelter at the time arranged. Cardboard carriers were placed along the second seat and the three dogs, whining with anxiety to get the heck out of there, were placed in the back with the big door slammed and carefully locked behind them. They said good-bye to the friendly attendant and thanked him for tending the dogs so lovingly, and insisted on paying him for his extra time, then they left slowly, so that the gravel wouldn't hit the car and cause any more comments from the back than they already had.

"On the road again," sang Harry. It was true that he had uncomplainingly spent a big part of his life driving back and forth from The City to The Port.

"Never doubt that I did it for you, my dear. I wanted you up there with me. I thought that the other women would keep you from getting cabin fever. The barge was needed for building materials so we just added your furniture. I even bought this old station wagon for your sake. If faith can move mountains, I think love can too, because I sure moved a mountain of stuff for you. What an exodus it was, eh? It will give us something to talk about on the cold winter nights in front of the stove. Oh-oh." The wail of a siren behind him caused Harry to drive off the road and stop.

"I'm not speeding. Wonder what's up."

They looked around but there was no sign of a police car, a motorcycle or any other vehicle. They looked at each other in puzzlement, then toward the back seat. A tiny pointy faced cat was out of her carrier, crouched in the center of the wide seat, and complaining about her unsatisfactory tan upholstered world. When they stopped laughing, Harry put the baby cat on Anne's lap.

"We'll have a story to tell Mary tonight. So that's what a Siamese sounds like when it wants attention."

"Poor little one is unhappy with her world."

There was some apprehension about the dogs when they were led onto the waiting boat but they were lovely dogs, well behaved and calm. The cats thumped and rustled in their individual carriers and each carrier had one beady eye behind an airhole. It was a relief to release the dogs in Arden. They trotted peacably enough up the wharf, then, realizing they weren't leashed, they left. Just like that. Straight up the road toward the farm and away, with everyone huffing after them for a few yards.

"We may as well let them go because we can't stop them."

"I hope this isn't the end of our noble experiment."

"Which one was mine, Harry?" asked Sid plaintively.

"It's up to you. I thought that Anne would like the mother. We could have a pup each but that's only tentative, maybe futile. I hope you enjoyed your ownership while it lasted."

They looked up the track anxiously while they gave each cat carrier to its owner. All doors and windows were carefully closed. Everyone disappeared to fill water dishes and litter boxes.

"Litter boxes? In the country?" Sid was surprised.

"They have to stay in for a few days so they will know where they live."

After placing the cats, Sid walked to the road, thought the circumstances through in his deliberate manner, then whistled in the manner of "The Whistler And His Dog." Immediately there was a stampede of tan fur and hanging tongues as they came back laughing. "Easy, when you know how," he said.

That evening around nine o'clock, Robbie was heard outside, calling. "Walter. Waaalllter" until doors began to open and Mary joined her, then Lottie. Finally everyone was there to help search for the missing pet. Since it was his first night in the location, his disappearance was worrying. Nobody was sure what kind of wild animals lived in the area. Perhaps he would get lost and never find his way back because he was strange to the area. They called even louder. They got flashlights and searched the beach area. They looked up into the trees in case he had got treed.

After an hour of exhaustive searching, Robbie was forced to admit it was no use. "He's gone if he's outside and we'll just have to wait and see." She said, spouting tough love all over the place, but her voice was weak. "Come in and I'll put the coffee pot on, the stove is still hot."

They trooped in, mugs were produced and the coffee made. While this was going on, the house was searched very carefully. Walter may have been shut into a cupboard, or gone to sleep in a drawer. No Walter. Every cupboard was searched carefully with flashlights. He really was gone without a trace.

When coffee was ready, Sid pulled out a chair from the table and began to laugh. He hugged Robbie happily and said, "Look."

There was Walter, sleeping the sleep of a very tired cat on the seat of Sid's chair.

"Oh, Walter," cried Robbie, picking him up. Walter gave her hand two quick licks and lolled his head back in complete contentment. After that, all they wanted was an early night.

In the mornings, Sid often stood on the jetty and looked, not out to sea but landward, admiring the changes since he had first seen Arden. Thin lines of smoke from chimneys, pots of flowering plants, Anne's huge hanging basket and now, in four of the windows, a cat looking out and proclaiming home to passersby. There were no more sagging porches or leaning chimneys of flapping tar paper sheets on rooves. The jetty was level again and one or two broken planks had been replaced. Sid thought he could get on with the big projects now. His dog leaned against his leg and looked up happily.

"Rover," Sid stated. "It may not be much of a name to the others but the best dog I ever had was called Rover and I like calling out Rover if I have to."

He walked away from the foreshore and up to Randy's house. He wanted to see how Monica was keeping. They had just told him he was going to be a grandfather at last. He wondered if they would choose a traditional name for their pup.

Now that there were dogs, walks up to the old farm became a daily pleasure. The new green growth there was constantly producing something new. The dogs found every burrow in the fields and the people took to propping twigs across them to see if they were occupied. Many sticks remained in place after several days but others seemed to be occupied burrows. City people longed to know more about the occupants.

"Maybe those are back doors and they don't use them often."

"I think we need a nature book."

"Someday we'll go shopping again."

They began to carry a thermos and sandwiches and the expeditions grew longer. Anne and Harry took Beauty and Seeker on an upward trail to the left where the dogs enjoyed a workout on the hillsides. They weren't there long when there was a series of crashes in the bush and Sid's dog joined them while thin voices in the lower fields called in vain. Then Seeker disappeared with Rover and another commotion in the bush told their whereabouts as they rejoined Sid.

"Harry, I think that we're destroying their good training," said Anne lazily. "They were so good when we got them. Now they come when they're called as soon as it's convenient."

"They don't need discipline out here." He defended his precious dogs. "Or not much. They do obey when you mean it. They've just learned to interpret the urgency in our voices. You never have to call Beauty anyway. She's always with you."

"Mm-hmm. I wonder why I never had a dog before. She's a part of my life already….I never knew anything about dogs."

"In the city it's better not to have one," Harry suggested, then "Two more weeks, my love. How are our arrangements going?"

"All right. We're just going to have our group and they're all getting ready. If the weather is co-operative how would you like to have the ceremony on the jetty. We can place everyone so that they face the sea and we will too. That way it will be a real Arden wedding, and imagine the pictures!"

So the modest arrangements were made but Arden had a way of inspiring extravagant gestures.

Chapter Ten

A Proclamation appeared on a post at the shore end of the jetty, the creation of Sid and Harry. "Hear Ye. Hear Ye. This is to proclaim that everyone who reads this is invited to the wedding between Harry McInnis and Anne de Kyp on Saturday, June 12 at 11:00 a.m., Rev. John Butterworth officiating. This will be followed by a Barbecue and Horseshoe Tournament. Children Welcome."

The carpenter, who had a name, Chris, and frequently used it, asked if he was included in the invitation with his wife and son. This was very satisfactory because Harry's grandchildren would be there. They had received a letter from Marjorie and John who were accepting their positions as Matron of Honour and Best Man with alacrity.

Marjorie asked about clothes—what to wear and accommodation—was there room for them to stay in Arden, and food—what could she bring to help out. Anne answered her questions then gave Harry the letter. He added two pages of instructions on how to find them and don't bring anything. We have it all, especially blankets and salt.

Marjorie subsequently forwarded a surprising wedding invitation from Annette who evidently was getting married on June Ninth. The groom was a tennis player from Miami, whose only name seemed to be BG. Harry just shook his head. He thought of the money he had given Annette.

"Maybe I'm cynical. Maybe it is love. After all, we're in love and look at all the money I have. Maybe it's the fate of this family…everyone married at once.

Anne nodded. There wasn't anything more they could say about Annette and her life.

The charter boat arrived unexpectedly one afternoon. Everyone went down to see what was going on. Two women stepped onto the wharf.

"Rosalie!"

"And Millie!"

"How did you find us?"

"We just followed your instructions. You told us we had to get to The Port and charter a boat for Arden, and we did."

Rosalie spoke. "Is it all right? Are we in the way?"

It was a facer. All of the Arden residents looked at each other in confusion. "Coffee. Let's have coffee, then Sid and Harry will be back for lunch and we can talk."

"Are we…you're not mad at us, are you?"

"No, it's all right. Come up to my house," said Mary.

The two newcomers were looking around avidly, noting the number of empty houses they had heard about and admiring the tanned, active residents.

It seemed that the change in Anne's wedding plans had started it. They wanted to be at the wedding. But that wasn't all. The Complex was definitely being closed, at least for seniors, because it was to be a residence for people visiting the hospital patients from out of town.

"And also for those having out-patient treatment."

"It's so close to the hospital. They said we would have to be out by the end of the year as you know but we didn't really believe it. Now we have to put our names in all over The City…."

"So we decided to put our names in here," Millie finished quickly.

"It's all up to Sid, you know. He owns Arden. It's a private holding."

"But Anne, you're here."

Robbie said, "Well, you know Anne is going to marry Harry and he and Sid are friends."

"Well, what about the rest of you?"

"We're leaving in the fall. It's a summer place and Sid doesn't think it would do for us over the winter."

Rosalie and Millie were terribly disappointed that they couldn't put their names on the list for Arden.

Sid and Harry wandered in, followed by the two pups, Rover and Seeker who joined Beauty on the porch. Very pretty. The men were ready for coffee and anything edible that was offered. They were told of the dilemma and Sid laughed.

"Are we going to have the whole Complex wash up on our beach?" he asked, patting Rosalie's arm so she would know he was teasing.

"No, we didn't tell anyone else how to get here. We were sneaky and asked the bridge club but we didn't tell anyone else. If they do turn up, it won't be our doing, Sid."

"The problem is that this is a summer place. You'll have to find a place in The Port or somewhere for the winter and we don't know how long Arden will be cut off in the winter. It was only two weeks last year but you'd have to leave in plenty of time. We don't have any way of getting help in a hurry."

"Well, we could go over to The Port for a couple of days after the wedding and ask around. That is," poor Millie was on shaky ground, "if we're invited to the wedding."

"When you get a chance, go and read the sign on the post by the wharf. You must have missed it when you arrived," said Sid. "The other thing is that we're not going to be able to have another moving day like the last one. We'll never do that again for anything!"

Triumphantly, Millie said, "You don't have to. We sold everything! Every stick of furniture! We decided to buy what we need when we need it."

Everyone laughed. They couldn't help it. They were such an unlikely pair of conspirators to fling themselves into their final (probably) adventure.

"Millie, you'll freeze to death here," said Robbie. "It's cold at night even now and it's always damp. What will you do?"

"I can do it, Robbie. If only Sid says yes."

"Well, there are bed...those ones we bought originally. And there's blankets."

"And salt," added Harry.

"We brought lots of food. It's probably unloaded on the dock by now. We shopped at The Port. There's four cases of, well, bathroom tissue. I went to camp once where we had to use leaves." Individual experience makes everyone look at things differently. Still, it was very funny.

Sensible Sid. "You can stay for a week and then you can see how it works. If you want to stay and it seems possible, we can make a firm arrangement about rent and expenses for the rest of the summer."

"How much for a week?" Rosalie was business-like.

"Wedding guests are free if they help," said Sid.

"There's a house like this right next door to Lottie if that's all right."

"What about those dear little places down below. I would like one of my own and so does Millie. Just for this week....Please?"

"Do you know anything about outhouses?" asked Sid as they strolled down the slope. "What a lot you'll be learning."

Anne said, "He's teasing. You have indoor plumbing to go with your four cases of tissue."

They read the Proclamation about the wedding and were ecstatic that they could attend because they read the Proclamation. (They were not as brave as they sounded and wouldn't have been surprised if they were told they couldn't stay at all.) Not the same at all as a printed invitation. More fun, somehow. They didn't consider that mail delivery at Arden was non-existent. They had been unsure of their ploy and were relieved to see all of the houses, and now, to know they had achieved a week at least.

They settled in happily. Millie only wore one sweater over her track suit the next day. They walked up to Robbie's house where they saw everyone with a cup sitting on the edge of the porch. They joined the walk to the farm and helped plan the wedding, just days away.

"Remember how we used to make a flower arch for a wedding? I've made lots of them. We could have one of those for them to stand in for the ceremony. Rosalie and I will come up here early in the morning and pick the flowers if you can have the arch ready, Sid. If the weather is nice we'll set it up on the jetty. You have to get it to stand up."

Mary was cooking a turkey and Lottie and Robbie volunteered to make and decorate a three tier cake. Finally, they made one last list for the charter boat to bring on Friday. Oddly, when Friday arrived the charter boat didn't. The same skipper, Pete, brought a cabin cruiser so it didn't make any difference. The cruiser did the job.

Saturday morning was clear and the sea was calm. Arrangements went like clockwork. Millie and Rosalie were back with the flowers and decorated the arch on the jetty. A turkey had been started in the middle of the night to be ready by noon. All possible food preparations were completed. The women went to help Anne and Marjorie dress and do their hair, then their friends went home to do themselves up.

The cabin cruiser arrived with the minister. He walked to the flower arch erected on the jetty. It was placed close to the land on the jetty so that the minister faced Arden and the others faced the showy, timelessly beautiful cove. In minutes two sailboats appeared, and anchored close to the jetty. The charter boat, strangely draped with tarps, tied up in its usual place. It had even been painted pure white for the occasion. Small boats continued to arrive, and Arden's young strongmen began to unload women and children and picnic hampers. Soon there were a dozen boats clustered around with still others arriving.

A little portable organ was unloaded from the charter boat and placed strategically on the jetty. A young woman played appropriate music before the service.

As Harry and John walked down the track, with little puffs of dust rising around their shoes, Harry was eyeing all the strange boats. They took their places behind the arch. Both were appropriately pale and nervous.

Anne arrived a short time later with Marjorie. Anne wore a soft, pale yellow flared dress that set off her clear skin beautifully. Marjorie was in a darker yellow and both wore flowered hats. Harry had contrived to obtain gold orchids arranged in glorious trailing bouquets.

There was no sound equipment, so the organ was still as Reverend Butterworth read the traditional service, then resumed playing afterward, sounding thin and inexpressibly poingant in the open air.

Everyone sang "Blessed Be The Tie That Binds" as the sailors took Anne and Harry to the transformed charter boat. The black trim had been whitewashed and the boat had been festooned in white scallops of cloth, in three tiers. On the rail, the cabin and the flying bridge were white scallops fastened with pink rosettes. As Anne and Harry mounted steps to stand on the flying bridge, the stern line was released and the engine slowly turned the boat to face the dock. Everyone began to applaud and cheer as Anne and Harry became the bride and groom on an enormous wedding cake. The people on shore launched rockets and lit fireworks. A Camcorder recorded it all for posterity as Harry was handed a top hat to make the picture complete. He kissed his bride and the crowd jumped up and cheered again.

What a wedding. Harry and Anne disembarked from their wedding cake and changed their clothes while one of the local men set up a barbecue and added his huge salmon to the planned banquet. Monica brought out the blackberry wine they made last fall.

Dogs and children were reasonably good but they certainly added an element of feverish activity to the day. The young parents insisted on learning to play horseshoes (you promised on the Proclamation) and a group on the jetty, including the bridge club, danced to recorded music.

At four o'clock Harry and Anne left on their floating wedding cake. The guests ate another meal and left as the sun was sinking (also recorded on the Camcorder).

Harry and Anne delighted the onlookers at the dock in The Port by resuming their positions on top of the cake when they came into port. Harry donned the top hat, grinning. Anne felt embarrassed among all the strangers but as Harry said, "This is no time for timidity. These guys worked for days on the boat and it's their chance to show off their creation. But wasn't that a wedding? I think we're well and truly hitched."

He raised his top hat and kissed the bride. Anne realized that she had married a ham.

The only detail that Harry had arranged was the bridal suite in the biggest hotel in The City for their wedding night. The huge rooms, the fruit basket and champagne were all present. The round bed smothered in cream and peach satin was a fitting end to a fantastic day.

They planned to be away from home for a week. They visited The Complex at coffee time once more to see where they had met, but it was changed. Already there was an impermanent atmosphere. A few acquaintances were there but all the talk was of moving, and the relative merits of their anticipated homes. They compared costs, with baleful looks at Anne, who had cut them out with Harry and who now no longer had to worry about such things. If they had only known, they seemed to infer, Anne wouldn't have got Harry and come out so satisfactorily.

It was a dispiriting visit and they put it out of their minds as soon as possible. After all, all the good people had come with them. They had a predictable dinner at another expensive restaurant.

"When do you want to go home, Wife?"

"I want to go home right now and move into our house that doesn't that doesn't have a circular bed, but does have a view, and does have Beauty and Seeker. I want to spend time with Marjorie and the family."

There was nothing wrong with their honeymoon at all. They just wanted to spend it in Arden.

Chapter Eleven

Sid was on the wharf when they arrived.

"There's been an interesting development, Harry. Welcome home, you two. From your honeymoon. Not anything you might expect. It's just that Chris went for a walk that day and saw the farm."

"It seems that he's a farmer and their rented farm is being sold for a housing development and he's looking for a new location. He didn't know there was a farm until the day of the wedding. He really wants to rent the place."

"By the way, Randy and Monica came for the wedding and they're still here. I think I can pay him enough to keep him going and there may be another Fisheries contract coming up later. In the meantime he can live rent-free and expenses are low. Anyway…Randy knows Chris. He says Chris is good at farming. He grew up on a farm and that's all he's ever done. He does carpentry for extra cash. I think he can do that from here if he needs to. Randy says Chris has had more than his share of trouble lately and could use a break."

"Is he married? Does he have children?"

"Yes, he's married. That's part of the trouble. He married a really lovely girl (according to Randy) who is a deaf mute, and they have a three year old son. His wife had a bad experience a month ago and is afraid of being left alone although nothing actually happened because a neighbour arrived and caught the guy. On top of everything else she was terrified by the balaclava and black clothes. The neighbour was one of our friends, a weightlifter, and he sorted everything out. Chris wants this particular farm for many reasons but also because she would feel safe here and she would be safe, too. Chris told me about it as well as Randy, so it's not just gossip. All of their friends just want what's good for Maggie. He's bringing her over today which is why I'm waiting here. I'm glad Anne's back. You can go back to your honeymoon after they leave."

It was nice to be back to enjoy Sid's humour again.

Soon a small boat appeared and Chris lifted out a little boy and the girl that must be his wife. She was beautiful, dark haired, dark eyed, with a trembling smile that revealed her nervousness. Chris proudly introduced Maggie and Sammy and they all strolled up the easy slope on the road to the farm. The little boy skipped after the three inseparable retrievers. He was happy, seemingly unaffected by the dark changes in his family life.

Again they were aware of the gentle, waiting atmosphere in the house. Maggie shook her head at the state of the old, old gingham curtains. She ran to peek up the fireplace chimney and before they could stop her, she ran quickly up the stairs. Harry warned Chris of the possible danger and Chris followed her up, sticking closely to the wall. The rest of the party went out to wait in the back yard. There were no crashes or even loud creaks and they came out later, hand in hand. Their luck wasn't entirely bad; the aging staircase had supported them.

They came outside and inspected the chicken house, barn and drooping fences. Chris sat on the steps facing the old bench Sid had found. They all followed suit on stairs and bench.

"Mr. Donovan, I would sure like to rent this place, if you are willing."

"There's a lot to be done before it's habitable. When would you be wanting to move in?"

"As soon as possible. Maggie loves it. She's worried she won't be able to have it."

"I'll tell you, Chris, what I'm hoping to get from the farm. Because Arden is a bit remote, I would want to buy eggs from the farm, and milk. Hopefully you can get some vegetables and fruit going. We would pay you a decent market price for everything we buy. You would be a source of groceries for Arden. On the other hand we'll help you to ship what you grow. We have a pretty good boat service now that you would be welcome to use. Later you can share expenses on that, but not yet. The boy could go to school on it maybe. Does that fit in with what you're thinking?"

Chris turned to his wife whose eyes were tense and questioning. As he signed to her she nodded, again and again. Her eyes shone.

"Tell her that the only access is through Arden and tell her about us, the people who live there." Again, as Chris signed, she nodded, and then began to cry. Anne walked over and sat beside the distraught woman.

"She's up and down like a yo-yo. She says to tell you that we have chickens that we will bring and dairy cows, three of them. We have three ponies but we can sell two."

Harry spoke up. "If you need the money, fine, but otherwise don't sell anything for convenience. My two grandchildren will be here from time to time and ponies are a real asset for Grandpa. There's a lot to be done before you can move in. The house isn't great."

"I can get the guys to help with the fences and the out-buildings. The barn isn't bad. I think…." He turned to consult his wife. "Yes. We have a tent that we can live in for now. Would you like to sleep in a tent, Sammy?"

"Yessir, Dadnunc. I like the tent."

"We've done some camping so he's used to it."

Harry said. "Sid, I don't want to interfere but can I say something?"

"Sure, Harry. I'm glad you're along."

"Putting the place back in shape is actually improving the property, Chris, and as such, I think Sid should pay the initial costs, and he could put you on payroll until it's back in working order. The first thing you must do is get that well safe, before Sammy plays outside. That's the first thing. There seems to be half a dozen strong men looking for work, friends of yours. We hate to waste time once we get an idea. You don't have to give notice that you're moving because they're shutting down anyway."

Sid thought for a while. "We'd better think about a lease for both our sakes. I'll get the paperwork ready if you're agreeable."

"You haven't said how much we'll have to pay, Mr. Donovan. We haven't got a lot but I can pick up some carpentry work to begin with."

"Your carpentry work will be right here for now. We'll have to figure it out but I assure you, Chris, you'll be able to afford it. I need the food and you need the place. We need each other. I just want to know that you'll stay…say for five years at least." It seemed that Maggie could follow the conversation to a fair degree because at that point she clapped her hands.

On the way back down the slope to Arden they discussed the barge they could hire and the plan began to move. "In the meantime I can bring milk, eggs and vegetables over right away. We also have some ham and bacon left, things like that."

"Talk to the women. They'll want to order their own supplies."

All of her friends rushed to welcome Anne and Harry home, and were introduced to the newcomers who would come to mean so much in their lives. Sammy suddenly had a lot of grandmas and grandpas. Marjorie and John joined the group and Catherine, Chad and Sammy ran off, the three retrievers in attendance.

Monica had coffee ready for Randy's friends and everyone joined them at the new picnic tables for a break.

"Isn't it funny," Rosalie pondered. "In The City I never drank coffee. It gave me heartburn. It doesn't here…I guess it's the water."

Robbie asked, "Do you think that Maggie would like to live in Arden? The farmhouse needs such a lot of work."

"Sure," said Randy to Chris, "you could commute."

Chris asked Maggie and she was decided. The farmhouse for her.

"We'll be up to help if she'll have us. She must take time to visit us, too. Sammy as well."

"Will we still be able to walk the dogs in the fields?" Lottie asked Sid. She turned to Chris. "Every morning, we walk the dogs across the fields at your place."

"It's Chris' place now, Lottie. You'll have to ask him. What do you think, Chris?"

"We'll make sure they can. Those dogs won't bother the stock and our animals are harmless, but if the ladies are nervous we can put in fencing and gates."

"Of course we're not nervous. We live in the country." Lottie said.

"You know," said Mary, "We hardly have time to do everything in a day, what with coffee breaks, walking the dogs, and bridge on Tuesdays. Now Kevin is going to give us sailing lessons. There just isn't enough time in the day."

"Will Chris and Maggie be staying here year round?" asked Millie innocently.

"Are you still here, Millie?" asked Sid. "I thought you were only staying a week." Her face fell. "We'll have to see about a decent house for you until you leave in the fall. We haven't had time to winterize Arden, Millie. We'll make sure you're told of any progress."

Monica piped up. "I've been thinking."

"Oh-oh."

She continued. "Wouldn't it be nice if we opened up one of the big houses for a store. We could buy stock in The Port as well as food from the farm, and we could have a consignment part so we could sell things back and forth among ourselves."

"Wouldn't that be nice!"

"Good idea." Comments were all favourable, so Sid asked her if she would have time to run it a percentage basis.

"Yes. Since we are on our own little planet we could sell home made wine along with our baking."

"We could sell a few blankets."

"I don't think we have to keep all the playing cards we brought with us. It would give us more space at home."

"Sid, we like it. When she applies to you, say yes if you please."

"I know you're going to laugh at me," said Mary, "but I have some salt we could pack in smaller amounts." They did laugh. "It's always better when you don't have to go all the way into town for little things."

Sid reminded Monica that she may be taking on more than she could handle when the baby arrived.

"I think it's all right. I would only have to stay open for a little while each day when we get organized. And the baby can come to work with me if I get busy."

Maggie's eyes moved constantly from face to face during the animated conversation, sometimes turning to Chris questioningly when she missed a point or wanted to make a suggestion.

"Maggie says she has honey and some jams and jellies she made. She says she'll bring the bees over if you like."

Everyone looked at Maggie and nodded vigorously, making her laugh. Monica and Sid walked to the top row of houses and they decided on the one on the opposite side of the dividing road from Harry's house. They went back to tell the others.

"Say, while we are about it," he added, "Can't we think of names for the trails so we know where we are. Something like North Road or Farmhouse Road and First, Second, Third? Something?"

Harry liked it just that way. "Let's call it North Road, (it goes North) and beginning at the jetty, First (the lowest), Second and Third."

Sid looked crushed. "That was only an example. You can come up with something better."

"No, Sid, I mean it. I like the simplicity. What does everyone else think?"

"If North Road goes North, and facing north the left is west. So, right of North Road is east and I live at Number Two East Second Avenue. Mary is Number Three, Robbie, number Four and Anne is…moved to great heights." They were all back together in their old cameraderie and somehow Chris drawing a map for Maggie made them feel more of a cohesive group than ever.

"Anne is Number One West Third Avenue," said Millie. Mary looked at her with more attention.

"When did you start wearing T-shirts, Millie?" she asked.

"I'm not cold any more," she said with dignity, "and by the way, let's take our morning coffee down to The Point tomorrow for a change. That's the rock beside the jetty on the beach. I do it every morning."

"She does, too," added Rosalie. "I'd freeze to death."

Chapter Twelve

The next morning before breakfast, Millie, Robbie and Lottie took a thermos down to The Point so they could enjoy the sea view. They were rewarded for their ambition by being the first ones to see a tall, graceful sail heading for the jetty. The sail dropped and the ship touched the bumpers softly as a man jumped out and tied up quickly. He turned to the open-mouthed spectators, his curling silver hair blowing slightly in the morning breeze. Sid came from his house, still chewing, and extended his hand to the newcomer.

"Sid Donovan. What can we do for you?"

"Well, I'm just here to satisfy my curiosity. I went by a week ago and was curious about all the activity in this old deserted town that I've known for years."

"This is Arden and we are the inhabitants. All these old grey heads have come home to roost."

"Here's another grey head to visit you. I'm a retired doctor, sailing these waters trying to get my stress levels back to normal." A sudden stillness settled on the onlookers as the magic word was considered.

"A doctor…he's a doctor…retired, but a doctor."

"Come and have breakfast with us."

"Mary's. Let's go to Mary's. She was making muffins…she probably has them out of the oven by now."

They sat, strung along the edge of Mary's porch, feet dangling, watching the water and eating succulent orange muffins, fresh from the oven.

The doctor's name was Roger. He had practiced in Toronto until a couple of strokes put him out of business, as he told the story. He would be all right but could no longer take the stress of a practice. Two years ago he had even completed his B.C. certification but decided against starting a practice. He was a widower of many years.

"Nice boat you have there."

"It is, isn't it? I rented it a couple of weeks ago. I love sailing but it's expensive to own one. You can't even afford to tie one up."

As they idly watched seagulls and Roger's anchored sailboat, a boat towing a barge drew slowly around the point. It was loaded to the gunwales with furniture, boxes and bales. From the center came moos, bleats, cackles and Sammy's high excited voice.

"Looks like Chris has arrived," said Sid. "Lock, stock and barrel."

Harry turned to Anne. "Sid and I are going to help a bit. I'm really worried about that well and we're going to put it in shape before Sammy falls in. There's probably a cesspit around and we'll check to see if there are any other dangers." He glanced at the doctor. "His mother is deaf and wouldn't hear him if he yelled." He and Sid started up North Road. Suddenly there was a blare of noise.

"WHAT IN HELL IS ALL THE GODDAM RACKET!"

A woman appeared, nude except for the towel wrapped around her head, on Roger's sailboat. She proceeded to tell the people on the barge what she thought of being disturbed. The onlookers hadn't heard such language since they left their television sets in the City. Roger stood up reluctantly and said,

"That's Liz. I think I'll cruise around these islands today."

"Sid," he called, "Can I talk to you?" He joined the men on the North Road. "Do you have any of those small houses available? I would appreciate it if I could rent one for tonight. I have to get Liz ashore for a while."

Sid was in a quandary. Here was the answer to his biggest worry, a doctor, and with him, what sounded like an even bigger worry, Liz. Roger seemed all right. Could he handle the lady in his state of health? How do people get into such messes.

"We live pretty quietly, Roger. I don't think your friend would care for us. I can't see that one night would be much of a problem though, if it's any help." It was agreed. They helped him fill his water containers and the others filled a box with food, including fresh muffins, for his day of cruising.

"Thanks." Roger was delighted. "There's plenty of food on board but Liz refuses to eat any more sardines or canned beans. I don't know where she gets her funny ideas. I'm hoping she'll go back to Toronto soon. At least she'll eat today."

Anne invited them to dinner when they returned. "I'm not a very good cook. My food won't tempt her to stay long."

"I'd appreciate that." He was embarrassed. "I don't know if you usually serve drinks, but I'd prefer not to have any tonight."

He walked toward the jetty through a mob of muscle shirts and shorts, tame animals and sacks of chickens (sacks?) toward howling abuse from the sailboat.

"And he's trying to reduce stress."

"He has an alcoholic there," offered Mary. "I know the signs." They looked at her in sympathy. They all knew the life she had led with her husband's alcoholism that only ended when he drank himself to death.

"He's a doctor, Sid, licenced and everything."

"I know. He would be perfect for us. He could handle a dozen adults and Sammy." He always had plans for the future. "I would like to have him here for Monica's sake. They plan to get to The Port for the baby's arrival but I personally would rest easier if Roger were here."

"But Liz. She's violent."

"Never mind the strip tease."

"Harry and Anne can check them out at dinner. We'll put our heads together about Liz if Roger seems all right. We need that doctor!" exclaimed Robbie.

"Incidentally, Anne," said Mary, "I'd better make a casserole for you and maybe a pie. You can do the salad. Oh, what it is to be in love."

"Let's go up to the farm. We can mind Sammy, at least. If the kitchen can be cleaned up she can use it even if they sleep out in the tent."

They gathered pails, rags, cleaners and rubber gloves and walked up the slope with the dogs to help. The ponies, cows and sheep were before them on the road. There were the peculiar moving sacks that seemed to contain chickens if the cackling was to be believed. They came on a scene out of bedlam.

Poor Sammy was put outside by his mother, then told by Harry to sit on the porch so he stayed forlornly on the bottom step. Harry was wading around in the tall grass with a long stick. Sid was tearing the old wood from the well.

When Sammy saw the newcomers, he cried, "Granunc, Granunc," in his own unique style and ran to hug them.

Millie volunteered to take him and the dogs for a walk, and away they went after he told his mother by tugging at her jeans and pointing at Millie. Maggie nodded in distraction.

Chris sent one of the men to erect the tent and the women set to work on the old stove and sink, floor and finally walls and ceiling. With the windows shining, it wasn't such a bad old place. Maggie was delighted. At least she could cook inside. The rest of the house would be checked for rot and repaired where necessary, beginning with the floors and stairs.

"Sid," Mary called out to the yard. "Can someone check the chimneys and see if it's safe to light the stove?"

"Later, later," said Sid brusquely, and Harry guffawed.

"Sid just found the old cesspit. He walked into it."

Monica arrived at noon carrying sandwiches, beer, tea and cowboy cake. They found apples in the seemingly moribund orchard. The species was unfamiliar but they were juicy and delicious.

"We've got to prune the apple trees."

One of the men groaned. Another said, "not today. Please."

Monica invited Chris and his family for dinner since it was their first day in their new home. Everyone would join them later for a Welcome to Arden party.

"Remember, no liquor for Liz." Explanations followed and new plans were made.

"Maybe she wouldn't come anyway." Anne and Harry promised to join them in any case. Mary left to make a casserole and Harry asked Anne to go for a walk.

"Newly weds," someone said fondly.

"And we're the nearly deads, I suppose," added Lottie.

"And now two young families, to add life to the place."

"And Sammy."

They didn't stay long after that, thinking that Maggie would want to enjoy her own kitchen and new home and the security she felt she had lost. It was Tuesday and they had missed bridge, and nobody noticed.

Harry and Anne strolled across the fields and opened a new gate to go into the forest beyond. "The reason I wanted to talk to you, Anne, is this. I've been thinking about Maggie and Sammy. Don't you think it would be a good idea if I gave Seeker to them? We have Beauty and the kitten and each other. What do you think?"

"I think you're wonderful but never mind that. It's a fine idea. Sammy will be ecstatic, but mainly Maggie will feel very safe. Seeker will be fine with the farm animals. He's a good dog but around Beauty he just acts like a pup. Perhaps he needs some responsibility. It's so good of you, Dear." They were still on their honeymoon.

"One of the blessings of getting married after you retire is that you can be together as much as you like, just getting to know each other." Beauty pressed against them when she thought she wanted to be the center of attention again. Harry went back to his well cover and Anne went home to get Seeker's belongings.

Maggie was unbelieving when they handed her Seeker on the leash but she was obviously excited. They decided it would be wise to shut him in the house with her as much as possible until he came to know his new home and family. It wasn't much of a change for he had been spending more and more time outside on the farm and he took to Sammy at once.

Later in the evening, the residents watched an approaching boat with sinking hearts. From their individual houses they watched Roger anchor and come ashore in the dinghy. No Liz.

"Liz is sleeping and I'll fetch her for dinner at six or so." Roger was told that Harry and Sid were up at the farm and he was last seen walking briskly up North Road.

"Stress again. Look at him rushing up there. We'll have to slow him down for all our sakes."

"We'll make the care and keeping of the doctor our secret project." The five women (Anne wasn't there) chortled and made plans.

Liz was heard to bellow once but when Roger didn't appear she went below and wasn't seen again until he went out in the dinghy to bring her ashore.

Dinner wasn't a great success. Mary had made a salmon casserole and Liz didn't care for it. She ate some salad and was obviously looking for some kind of decanter. She lit a cigarette and smoked while the others ate the smoked salmon and cream cheese concoction.

"Pure heaven, Anne. Where did you learn to cook like this?"

"I didn't actually, Roger. I just had the good sense to pick a friend who cooks like this. Did you like the salad? I made that. Mary made the pie that's coming, too. We always eat well here. It's one of our pleasures."

"You'd better watch it. You'll soon be as fat as pigs. I'm a nurse and I know about nutrition. Old people should cut their intake and drop fat, sugar, meat and eggs. You shouldn't even buy that stuff. Baked goods are bad for you, too." She helped herself to a second piece of blackberry pie.

"I'm a lot younger than Roger so I can still eat what I like. He's sixty-two and has a bad heart. I'm just thirty-eight, twenty-four years younger than him," she said, looking at Roger maliciously. "He doesn't like me to smoke or drink."

She shifted in her chair restlessly. "Everyone is so old around here. It's like an old folks' home. Except for you," she said to Harry. "How would you like to show me around Arden while these two clean up?"

Harry laughed. "There's nothing around here to see, and I just got married on June 12. I haven't got time for sightseeing with anyone but my darling."

Since the trouble with Annette, Harry had learned not to equivocate with aggressive females. Roger said nothing, but Anne noticed that his hands were shaking. Harry stood up.

"Come on, Roger, let's go look at the little sailboat that the bridge club brought over."

Liz yawned widely.

"Why do you call them the bridge club? They play bridge?" asked Roger, who enjoyed the game. Anne and Harry smiled at him. "They used to play it."

"We played terrible bridge, once a week."

"It's just that the bridge club is easier to say than Mary, Robbie, Lottie and Anne."

"Oh, Gawd," added Liz.

The men left and Anne cleared the table. Liz lit a cigarette and went into the living room. If Liz didn't leave soon, she would have cigarette butts in every room of the house.

The men returned, and Liz said, "Come on Roger, let's get to our little cabin in the woods. I'm beat." She walked out. Harry and Anne walked after Roger to make sure that the cabin was ready for the night, in case they got home after the light plant stopped at eleven o'clock.

Later, in their own house, they checked the stove and picked up flashlights and put them by the front door, then walked to Randy's house. It was wonderful to rejoin their friends.

"How is she?" asked Sid anxiously.

"I don't want to discourage you all but she's impossible. She smokes like a chimney, she's ill mannered and has a mouth like a sewer. She insults Roger constantly and if he doesn't get rid of her, she's going to be the death of him. He's really on the edge and she's pushing as hard as she can."

"Maybe she will go back to Toronto."

"I don't share Roger's optimism. She's onto a good thing and won't let go easily, but her leaving is our only hope. She won't stay here. She thinks this is like an old folks' home."

"To be fair, Harry, I think her bad temper came out when she realized there was nothing to drink. She probably expected it. That's why she didn't eat," said Anne.

"Didn't she like the casserole?" asked Mary in surprise.

"Mary, she said if we eat like that, we're all going to be as fat as pigs." Since they were all thinner than they had ever been, and healthier, no-one worried much.

"Aren't they going to join us?"

Harry shrugged.

Suddenly a series of shrieks shattered the quiet. They scrambled outside in time to see a pale body pelting up North Road. Roger was in faint pursuit. The loud, foul language seemed to be insisting that she was getting away from that herd of teddy bears at any cost and he could keep the giraffes, too. Randy and Chris ran to intercept her before she got past Third Avenue. Randy said later that all he could think of was how he was going to get an effective grip on her if he had to, but he didn't have to. She ran screaming toward them then wheeled and headed for the waterfront.

"No! No!" everyone was shouting, but she was too far gone to hear. She ran straight off the granite shelf and landed on the rocks below. After she disappeared from view scream after scream erupted from her torn throat. Roger and the others ran to the beach, Roger holding his chest as he looked down. Randy and Chris jumped off the shelf, and assisted the doctor down to the pebble shore.

"I saw him bring his bag ashore," puffed Robbie. She went into his cabin and retrieved it then sent it down to him. He filled a syringe and after a few minutes the terrible screams finally subsided. Roger said,

"There's a radio on the boat, Randy. Could you radio for the air ambulance? Her legs are both broken and she has head injuries."

Harry was already on his way to the radio telephone. Monica herded the others back to her warm house and made tea. They were pitiable. At that point, they looked ten years older than they had an hour ago. She immediately wrapped Millie in a blanket and filled the stove with wood. She eyed the clock and found the light plant was good for another hour. Anne sat beside Robbie with her arm around her. They looked like the aftermath of a train wreck. Beauty licked Mary's hand and leaned against Anne comfortingly.

"I don't know what we're going on about." Rosalie said staunchly. "Nothing happened to us. We just saw some of the real world."

Lottie spoke. "It just brings the bad old times back but you're right. Monica is the one to worry about. Are you upset, dear?" she asked hopefully.

Monica didn't need ministering to, so they refilled their mugs and went out on the porch to watch the helicopter team take charge of the situation. Liz was strapped to a stretcher carefully, placed in the helicopter and taken away. If anyone needed care it was Roger. He should have gone, too, but he said,

"I've had enough of hospitals for a while. I just need rest and quiet." Strong young arms helped him into his house and put him to bed. After hot, sweet tea and a sleeping pill he seemed all right. They took turns watching him for the night and by morning he was frail but calm.

"I can't apologize enough for what happened last night. I couldn't handle her on the boat and I was afraid she would drown. I couldn't find her stock of bottles on the boat and I thought that if we were off the boat she wouldn't have any more to drink. When she went into withdrawal I had drugs to help her but she got away from me. She was my office nurse at one time. She won't go for treatment. I don't know what will happen now."

"Let's hope she never tries to come back here. There's nothing we can do for her. You're different. You can stay as long as you like," Sid said, and smiled to himself. The women were halfway to their goal; Roger without Liz.

"No, really, it's too much of an imposition."

"You're settled here now, Roger, and you don't want to make a move. We can give you a hand when you need it. It's no problem—unless you decide to peg out." Sid said.

"I think I can promise I won't do that."

Roger was only in bed for a couple of days but once the women took control he rested much more than he had ever done. He couldn't always talk them into giving him his sleeping pills but he found that the lapping waves and the night wind were pleasantly soporific.

Sid met him by the jetty one morning as they were going to Robbie's house for morning coffee. "The thing is, Roger, I'm trying to establish some kind of medical emergency care in Arden. I've always told the women that they can't spend the winter; it's just too risky. I think they are half planning to move into a motel in The Port when necessary but they want to stay. Their belongings are in their homes, and I guess it's hard to think of going but what if there was an accident or somebody had a heart attack. We're all getting on. Now that Monica and Randy are here it's better but even that's a problem with a youngster on the way. If a bad storm hit at the wrong time she couldn't go to The Port readily. Until you came along I just couldn't see how we could ever have a doctor just for Arden. Could you stay for a while?"

"It's a thought. I haven't any definite plans for the next while."

"Do you deliver babies?"

"That's what I do, Sid, or did. I was a G.P. and that's how I burned out. There's nothing like a family practice to keep a man out at all hours. There's no let-up."

"Well, none of us is young but there are no specific health problems among us. I wondered if twenty-five or so patients would suit a retired doctor. You wouldn't be tied down much, you could go where you please, when you please but in bad weather we'd appreciate having you here. The rest of the time we could manage, I think. What do you think? And what about pay? How do we do that?"

"One thing, Sid, money's no problem. Around here, there doesn't seem to be many ways to spend it. I could buy a boat and take it out in anchorage fees. I could arrange billing but I don't care much. I could take it on for this coming winter and see how it goes."

"I thought you could take one of the two-storey houses on Third Avenue, and set up a clinic, and live there as well. Could you just make a list of equipment and supplies you will need and I'll take care of it. When Liz was hurt I realized that we should have a stretcher, and maybe splints but all we have now is a First Aid kit from the drugstore. We'll buy everything you want. I should tell you we have all the money we need, especially for improvements to the town. Harry has our finances all set up."

After coffee, they wandered up to Third Street and studied the last house on the right, Number Two East Third Street. Roger became quite enthusiastic about the project. The whole town population kept watch on the men and waited anxiously for an announcement. It all depended on Roger. Teasingly, the men separated and Roger returned to his little house on the waterfront, where he would stay until his furniture and equipment arrived.

Robbie made cinnamon buns and invited everyone for afternoon coffee, so that the women could grill Sid. Laughing, he said,

"I don't know if it's important, but Roger is going to rent that two storey house we were looking at this morning. He thinks it would make a good clinic."

Unlikely as it was, the little formerly abandoned town of Arden had a resident doctor. For now, at least.

Chapter Thirteen

"Hello, Grandma," said Sammy, suddenly appearing in Anne's kitchen doorway.

"Hi, Sammy. Hey, you've learned to say Grandma."

"Millie taught me."

"Isn't Millie a Grandma?"

"No, she's Millie. Millie teaches me a lot of things. My dog used to be called Seeker but I called him Keefer. Now he wants to be called Keefer so I can't change it back. Is that all right?"

"Whatever Keefer wants, goes. Have you got any room for a piece of cake?"

"Did you make it?"

"No, Mary did."

"Yes, please."

"You know, Sammy my cooking isn't all that bad. Harry eats my cake. I did a lot of cooking for a long time and I'm pretty good, Harry says."

"I know, Grandma, but Mary's really good." Sammy stood in the doorway and ate his cake while Anne continued to do the lunch dishes. She worked for a while then said,

"Did you want something special, Sammy, or did you just come for a visit?"

"Grandpa said to come up to my house." Sammy's calling everyone Grandma or Grandpa sometimes posed problems. Grandpa could be Sid, Harry or Roger. She translated this as Harry. My house must be Sammy's house because she was in Harry's house and he wasn't.

"Come, Beauty, let's go for a walk." Sammy and Keefer fell in beside her as they walked up to the farm. Soon Rover joined them. When they got to the top of North Road Harry was waiting for her.

"Come and look at this, Anne." He led her to a track leading away from the farmhouse in a way they hadn't walked before. There were faint wheel tracks disappearing to the northwest, partly hidden by saplings that had sprouted up here and there. They walked into a big clearing where Sid and Chris were standing, grinning.

"But…Harry! Where did all that lumber come from?"

"It's cedar."

"I've never seen such long boards."

"Someone must have been cutting up in here with a portable sawmill. These cedar planks are priceless nowadays; they're tremendous. They're like this because cedar doesn't rot. I thought you'd like to see such a historical sight. We're trying to think of uses for them. Can you think of anything?"

"Well, if I could have some of the comparatively short pieces I would build a couple of planters—two feet wide and two feet deep—across the frontage by the sea. After that awful accident that Liz had I've thought we should do something but a fence would spoil the view. Is that the kind of thing you mean?"

"Yep, that's what we mean." He looked at the others. "I'm confused because they're precious and I don't want to find a use for them. What do you think, Sid? You own them."

"I don't want to sell them because I don't want anyone else to have them. Isn't that awful?"

"Chris, what do you think?"

"Well, I hate to cut them up for smaller projects and I wouldn't know what kind of building would warrant these huge boards. Maybe a barn for unicorns or something."

"Do you think you could rig up some kind of shelter somewhere so that we could lift them off the ground on racks of some kind?"

"I'd like to sort them anyway. They would be more accessible if we stored them closer to the farmhouse. I'll start bringing some in with the tractor and wagon a few at a time. When we get some smaller ones or damaged pieces, I could stack them beside the road and we could sure build some wonderful planters. Plants are your thing, aren't they, Anne?"

"Yes, that's what I do…or used to do." She stood in the quiet woods enjoying the perfect air. "Have you ever stopped to think that all of us at Arden are doing exactly what we want to do? Everyone is doing what he loves best. No wonder it's such a happy place."

She turned to walk back down the track. "Even Sammy and the dogs seem to be right in their element. If you come across any less esoteric wood, we are looking for shelves in the store."

She called Beauty, made sure that Sammy stayed with Chris and walked to the farmhouse to see how Maggie was making out. She hadn't seen her for days.

Maggie drew her into the house and showed her the kitchen. New red and white gingham curtains, ruffled even more fully than the old ones, blew in the gentle breeze. Chris had installed their own cookstove, definitely an improvement over the old one. A big pot simmered enticingly. The floors had evidently been fixed because there was new red brick patterned vinyl with red rag rugs in strategic places. Maggie was going for rustic and it suited the house.

In the living room, the fireplace was fitted with brass tools, wood box and fireguard. Red rag rugs were scattered in the living room also, with a large oval braided rug in the center showing red throughout.

Anne pointed to the rugs, then Maggie, mimed sewing with her eyebrows raised in inquiry. Maggie laughed and nodded then beckoned Anne to the back room.

The large low-ceilinged room had a loom on one wall and a rug frame on another. Maggie had a serger set up ready for use on a handmade sewing table. It was easy to see Maggie's interests by the equipment she had. No wonder they didn't see her very often.

Anne was smiling as she walked down to Arden. Chris and Maggie had only moved onto the farm a couple of months ago and already it was hard to imagine it without them. Sid seemed to have an instinct for congenial people.

Since she was out of the house anyway, she went to see how Monica was doing. Her young neighbour was nearing the end of her long wait.

"How are your plans for the store coming, Monica?"

"I'm all ready to go."

"Are you going to wait until after the baby comes?"

"No, that's another month yet. I want to get going."

"Right. I'll tell the others and we'll come up and help clean the house. When?"

"Whenever you like. Now that the chimneys have been cleaned we can go ahead anytime."

"Tomorrow we'll get together up there and decide what's to be done."

So it was that the seven women met at the house (Number Two West Third Avenue) to begin the mercantile project. The big living room with fireplace would be the main store for groceries and general merchandise. The dining room, directly behind it would be consignment goods. If they wanted one, the kitchen could become a tea room in future, and the front room, crafts. The rooms upstairs were to be held in abeyance. For now the grocery and consignment rooms could go ahead.

"I want to paint first," said Monica.

"Monica, you know we have never passed on any Old Wives Tales but I don't want you to do any painting. It's very bad for you right now." Lottie said. The others agreed so Monica stated indulgently that someone else could do it and she'd be back when the smell was gone. That brought about a novel event.

Roger met the women going down to bring back mops, pails, brooms and cleaners. He was working on the dinghy and the small sailboat that they had brought from The City. He was looking for boat paint. When they talked about the need for a painter, Roger jumped at the chance to be industrious. He would be there as soon as Sid gave him the paint. The women spent the day cleaning and, after dinner, Roger produced paint, ladders and brushes. Soon the store was painted in an almond shade with French grey trim.

Chris produced an old set of kitchen cabinets, painted the same pale grey and they became the front counter. Shelves were constructed and painted before they were brought in, at Mary's suggestion.

Monica produced lists of stock she wanted to buy in The Port and people began to carry in saleable items from home. A trestle table in the consignment room was soon covered with socks, slippers and knitted dishcloths. Maggie brought in woven place mats and wall hangings.

Monica had Randy carry up jams, jellies, pickles and blackberry wine for the grocery store. Maggie brought in honey, as well as jams and jellies. Later, when the store was in operation, she would deliver milk, butter and eggs daily, garden produce as it grew, and chickens, then meat on request after Chris did some butchering.

One day Monica said she was going over on the charter boat the next time it came, to do some shopping. The Magic Word. All of the women decided to go. Everyone downed tools and talked about shopping. Harry said he would like to take Anne shopping in The Port. Randy said Monica wasn't going without him, and Sid said he had to buy more building material. Chris was told of the trip and he decided that he and Maggie could use a day off, too. Only Roger would stay home, "to mind the dogs," he said. This time they would not go as a group but split up into singles and doubles.

Two days later the charter boat arrived and they were off.

Harry and Anne wandered down Main Street. Harry bought Anne lunch around noon, then stocked up on wine and liquors. They bought groceries that the store would probably not provide. Anne bought a sweater for Harry and he bought her a pale green jogging suit. They bought exotic treats for Beauty and a new flea collar for the kitten since had outgrown his old one. Harry thought they might call him, not Seeker but Fleaker, sometime soon. Right now he was the kitten.

They both had time to get, in Harry's case, a haircut, and in Anne's, a cut and set. When Harry had admired her hair soft and uncurled, she stopped having permanents. Finally, they took a taxi around their morning's circuit to pick up their purchases and take them down to the wharf. This wharf was much more imposing than the one at Arden.

The others obviously had an equally busy day. When they all congregated on the jetty there was a huge pile of freight.

Pete, the captain, handed Harry a brown envelope with a big smile. "Look at this when you get home. You'll be amazed."

The days were drawing in and they went back under cloudy skies with the setting sun sending brilliant rays through the clouds and dusk.

The following morning Arden was busy, with people nipping back and forth between houses displaying their purchases. Sid went from door to door distributing starting whistles that he had bought in a sporting goods store.

"Emergency equipment, Arden style." He put a nail beside each front door and hung up the whistles on strings. Harry bought pulleys and clotheslines for the houses.

Everyone bought Roger a gift because he stayed home. He got a dozen huck towels for his surgery, all kinds of cleaning materials and curtains for his kitchen windows. He had asked them to bring back a case of sardines and a bag of oatmeal.

Monica opened the store and new articles kept appearing. She had bought coffee, tea, plenty of canned goods and baking ingredients. Everyone that came in brought something.

"I thought you could use this for the store," was followed by, "What's that awful smell?" until Sid came in with a whistle for her and said,

"Oilskins. That's a good idea."

"Sid, can I hang them in one of the empty houses until they lose that first great glorious stink?"

"I'll carry them out to the back porch for you now, then get them over to another house. They will be good to have in the winter."

"I got rubber boots, too, in various sizes." Heads turned when this conversation was reported because it was looking good for the temporary residents. First a doctor, then a whistle, then oilskins and rubber boots.

The store looked lovely. Mary brought six loaves of whole wheat bread. Shelves were filling up with canned tomatoes, mushrooms, soup, beans, spaghetti, corned beef, sardines and fruit. There were packages of pastas, noodles, rice, flour, sugar, coffee and tea. Other shelves held home-made jams, jellies, pickles, and wine.

There was a display of salt in plastic bags.

There were flea collars and flea powder and flea soap (ah, the joy of living on the Coast), dog food, cat food, biscuits and treats. The consignment room so far had woollen blankets, double sheets (from Robbie) and single sheets (from Anne), along with the previously arranged hand-made articles.

Harry produced a tin cashbox to put in the drawer of the new counter, then bought a bottle of pickles and a jar of honey. One by one, customers depleted the stock bit by bit as they showed their appreciation of the new venture. Maggie appeared with a huge bouquet of wildflowers from the farm, arranged carefully in a two-quart preserving jar.

A few days later a shabby little boat tied up at the jetty and a meagre little man came ashore. Sid was standing on the jetty by the time he docked and helped to tie up the boat.

"I hear you have a store here and I'm low in supplies."

"Well, we don't have much of a store. It's just for the town. What were you needing?"

"Anything, but beans and sardines would be good. Anything fresh?"

"Let's go and look." Sid led him to the house on the slope.

The newcomer walked into the store and looked carefully over every shelf. "Do you give credit?"

"No," said quick-thinking Monica.

"Is there a discount for cash?"

"No, this is for Arden people really and they all pay cash."

"Senior's discount?"

"No, they're all Seniors. The discount is already off. We have no reason for that sort of thing anyway. Do you want to buy something?" Part of Monica's hurry may have been caused by a compelling smell that was beginning to pervade the store.

"I'll have four cans of sardines and four cans of beans, a dozen of eggs, two bread and some carrots."

With Sid hovering, the groceries were packed in a small box and paid for. Sid walked back to the jetty with him.

"Are there any empty houses for rent?" the stranger asked.

"No, not at the moment."

"I want somewhere to live, just for the winter. I could pay you rent for one of these cabins plus fees for tying up at the wharf. I can pay you in advance. I don't drink, don't smoke. I could run you back and forth to The Port."

Sid was careful not to look disparagingly at the dirty, rusted little craft, listing slightly at the jetty. The clinker built hull was streaked with rust from the uncleaned metal fittings.

"We have all that organized."

"I'll be back later in the fall. Think it over and we can talk again."

Sid went back to the store where they all discussed the visitor. "I just don't like it. There's something odd about him. I hope he never comes back. If he does, come and get me wherever I am. Whistle and I'll come," he joked.

"Sid, I forgot to buy grocery bags," said Monica. "I realized what was missing when I packed his groceries."

"Never mind," said Millie, who happened to be in the store. "We'll donate all the grocery bags we have and then we'll bring a basket for our own shopping."

"I'm just using a bathroom scale too. I know it's not legal but I'm hoping nobody here will mind until I find a secondhand commercial scale."

Nobody objected so Monica continued with her temporary solution. Roger's hospital equipment arrived soon after. He had lived in a small house on First Avenue all this time, but Sid decided that he should be in a two-storey house (Number Two East Third Avenue) and everyone got busy putting the house in order for him.

Roger thought the big room to the right of the front door would be the best location for the surgery. Out came their mops and pails as they began work on another of the four houses on the top row. When everything was scrubbed, they herded Monica out while the room was painted in almond enamel. The fireplace was cleaned thoroughly. Randy used the wagon and tractor to bring up furniture and supplies for the little "Hospital".

"Isn't this thrilling," said Rosalie. "This is the most important event of all. A doctor. We have a doctor. I hope we never have to put him to work, but imagine, our own doctor!"

Roger moved his belongings up to the new house and his little house was made clean and ready for the next tenant.

Sid stood on the jetty and, with his back to the water, looked at the town. "It's filling up." Soon the cleaning crew joined him and they admired their work.

At one time an approaching vessel was an event but soon it would be commonplace. Here was a cabin cruiser tying up, a modest one that looked as if it had been used a lot over the summer. The group was speechless when Liz hobbled onto the jetty.

"I'm looking for Roger. Is he still here?"

Myopic Rosalie assumed a most sincere expression. "No, he left a long time ago…just after you did."

"No, he didn't. The sailboat was seen around the islands."

"Well, there you are. He left here."

Liz turned and stumped over to Roger's cabin. It was very clean and obviously unoccupied. Liz blustered.

"If I find out you've been lying, you old fool, you'll be sorry." She turned to the boat operator and he helped her into the boat, accentuating her lingering lameness. They left.

"Whew! I hate lying."

"Maybe so, Rosalie, but you're very good at it. I was struck dumb. I couldn't think of a word to say," said Millie.

Lottie, standing by, was in one of her growing-out black hair times and was at the magpie stage, adding a bizarre touch. They looked up at Roger's new location and say Harry and Anne sitting on the porch. Harry waved vigorously.

As the story was told later, Roger watched the boat tie up. When he saw Liz he told Anne and Harry that he'd better go and straighten it out but Harry told him to wait.

When Rosalie spoke up, standing close to Liz so that she could see her, and at her full five foot ten inches of bravery the body language was unmistakeable. Little round Millie stood behind her, but she didn't leave. Behind them was Lottie, black and white hair flying, but with her feet very firmly set. Roger knew he was free.

For weeks, various young men told of questions being asked and nobody knowing a thing until Liz flew back to Toronto. People all over the area could see the benefit of having a doctor at Arden.

Chapter Fourteen

One day, while he and Anne were having lunch, Harry finally opened the brown envelope that Pete had given him. It contained eight by ten photographs of their wedding boat, with Harry waving his top hat and Harry and Anne kissing on top of the cake (that was a converted trawler.) Behind these pictures were newspaper clippings that grew longer as the dates progressed. Now it seemed to be a national story, "DO SENIORS HAVE MORE FUN?", "LIFE BEGINS AT…", then "WHERE ARE THEY?", "HEY HOW ABOUT AN INTERVIEW?", "IS THIS A FAKE?"

And "WHO ARE THEY?"

As often happens with West Coast events, Arden was thought to be in Washington or Oregon, and this fortunate presumption saved them from invasion. The identification numbers on the boat were obscured by the white festoons (illegally) and they were saved.

"Your secret is safe with us," wrote Pete.

Harry laughed. "Let's make coffee for the gang this afternoon so we can show them our publicity."

"You like this stuff, you show-off, but I'm glad they couldn't find us. I can imagine the questions they would be asking."

Harry leered. "We could make a fortune in the tabloids."

Soon everyone congregated at their house for coffee. It was still warm enough to sit on the porch. Morning dew was heavy now but it was warm in the daytime when the sun shone. Sid looked as though he had something important to say so they waited for him to marshall his thoughts. Sure enough, he told them that it looked as if they could stay over the winter this year, if they wanted to.

"I suspected that when you gave me my whistle," boasted Millie.

With Roger in residence, and Harry and Anne, Chris and Maggie, Randy and Monica all staying, it didn't seem fair to expect Robbie, Mary, Lottie, Millie and Rosalie to remove to The Port.

"It's taking a chance, though, at our advanced ages, but this whole Arden business is taking a chance. There is the problem of winter fuel that I haven't figured out yet."

"I have a suggestion, Sid," said Robbie. "I'd like to hire one of the young men to cut a good supply of wood for me and stack it beside the house. I don't think it's your responsibility; it's up to the tenant to buy her own wood. We won't have to bring in logs yet, will we?" Sid shook his head. "Well then, I'm going to pay for the labour."

This seemed to be a good idea so the others went along. Monica was asked if she could get Randy to contact someone to come over and talk about chopping wood.

Harry showed them the pictures and clippings.

"Pete saved us again."

"Imagine if they came to Arden! It would be the end of our peace and quiet."

"But why?" asked Lottie. "It was a wonderful day but a wedding is hardly international news."

"I think it was the boat," said Harry. "Novelty weddings are in, and us on top of that floating wedding cake was interesting. Also, we're not teenagers."

"Let's not be modest," teased Millie. "It was a very handsome couple."

Anne poured more coffee. "I can only say that I'm glad they didn't find us."

They gazed down over their houses with the new clotheslines already in use at each occupied house. Over the water there was a faint golden haze of fall in the air. Not a ripple showed in the cove. A slight coolness in the sweet evergreen scented air heralded the approaching need for sweaters. Their thoughts were obviously in accord. Sid broke the silence.

"If anyone has any broken putty or missing weatherstrip or bad draughts, let us know so we can fix it before it gets cold. Rosalie and Millie had better get moving soon. Have you two thought about it?"

"Could we share?"

"Whatever you like, but there's no need. There are still six vacant houses on Second Avenue. You could have Anne's old house at the end, Number Three, and Number One East, or you could have Number One East and Number One West and live across the street from each other as well as next door. Or you could go on the West side together, or share a house. How's that for a choice."

"Well worth waiting for, Sid." Rosalie and Millie put their heads together while the rest resumed looking over the water and the islands to the south of the cove. The sea was grey in harmony with the faded sky. It could mean a change in the weather. Rain. It didn't matter, they weren't going anywhere.

"Sid, we think we would like one on each side of North Road. Sammy could find us easily. They can drop him off when they want a sitter. Anyway, it's a nice idea. We both have corner lots."

The cleanup crew enthusiastically continued to go from one house to the next as required. None of the houses on Second Avenue had been re-decorated. They were cleaned in the rush to get settled and they were not bad but next year…they all had plans. At present, they cleaned the two houses for Millie and Rosalie and re-arranged furniture temporarily. This would mean a shopping trip for them soon but in the meantime they had beds and dressers and Anne lent her couch. They borrowed pots and dishes from the cabins they had been staying in, and began making lists. When they took their chances and came to Arden, they had intended to buy everything new for their homes and now they could do so.

"Now we'll have to introduce the cats to their new homes."

"Start all over again, just when they knew their addresses."

Millie laughed and Rosalie corrected herself, "Just when they knew where they lived."

When the charter boat came, Millie and Rosalie were ready, lists and chequebooks in hand. Roger also decided to go to The Port to talk to his medical associates again. Sid was talking to Pete before the boat departed.

Mary, in her house, was preparing to make bread. "Yeast! I'm low on yeast!" She ran out onto the porch and waved frantically at those on the jetty. When nobody seemed to notice, she fled down the steps waving and calling. Somehow her foot came down awkwardly and she tumbled down the four steps and lay in a shocked heap on the ground. She just had time to give a startled squawk before she fell. Robbie, next door, heard the strange sound. She looked out of her door, started to run to Mary then went back into her house for her whistle.

She gave a loud, long blast as she went to her friend. Roger and Sid ran up the slope followed by everyone else on the jetty. Roger asked someone to get his bag from the house as he knelt beside Mary's oddly positioned leg.

"We'd better get her on the boat," said Roger. He gave her an injection. "She'll have to go to The Port. Lucky the boat is right here."

Pete, Harry and Sid carried a makeshift stretcher down to the boat.

"It's all right," said Mary drowsily to her friends, "I'll buy my own yeast while I'm over there."

The dreaded accident had finally happened. Her friends were tearful, pitying Mary who was suffering so much. Gradually they began to think of her future in Arden and became grave and silent. They could only hope that the accident was minor but the odd angle of her leg and Roger's careful handling indicated more that bruises.

The boat left, travelling faster than usual. The people who stayed went back to their work, worrying about Mary. It was the first bad day in Arden. There had been the usual disappointments and worries but these were only the small setbacks that were to be expected. This was a catastrophe.

When the boat brought Roger back they were all waiting to hear about Mary. A stranger, a man, disembarked first.

"I'm looking for Harry McIsaac."

"That's me," said Harry, friendly as ever.

The stranger handed him a piece of paper. Harry looked up in surprise, read the front and opened it. He read for a minute, went red and then white. He took Anne's hand.

"Excuse us for a while. See you later. Sid, you'd better come up to the house, too." They walked to the house. Anne could feel Harry's hand shaking in hers. He never had shaky hands. She poured a small drink of brandy for him and put on the kettle. He was more upset than she had ever seen him.

"It's a Subpeona. I have to appear at a hearing because Annette is challenging Ivy's Will citing undue influence when Ivy was in a state of incompetency."

"That's not going to go anywhere, Harry," said Sid.

"No, it can't. However, they want the company books from the time they say Ivy invested in it. I think we can expect that all of my assets will be frozen until this is settled."

"How could she? How could Annette do such a thing to her own father, when she knows it's false?"

"The problem is going to be Arden," said Harry, recovering a little. "There is no longer any available money. Everything has to stop for now."

"How long is this going to last, Dear?"

"I think it depends on a court date but it could take years to settle."

Sid looked sick. Anne was weeping.

Harry went on, "We're going to have to tell everyone else as soon as possible."

Anne said loudly. "No. Don't tell Monica and Randy. Not when the baby is due anytime. Let's not say anything to them yet."

"She's right," said Sid. "Or Chris and Maggie. They just moved in. We've led them into a terrible position. Let's not panic until we've had time to think."

"Anne, could you just talk to the bridge club…."

"Poor Mary," she mourned, "There are only two others left."

"And Roger and the other women and get them to come up here tonight? Sid, could you go to Monica's and tell her we're having a meeting but it's only about tenants. She can stay home and rest. Randy needn't come either if he happens to come home. Say, about seven."

Anne went visiting while Harry and Sid sat gloomily at the kitchen table, thinking. Harry placed a call on the radio telephone to his lawyer, making an appointment for the earliest possible date. He couldn't say much in view of the nature of radio telephone. Anne returned to say they would all be here at seven.

After Sid left, Anne talked Harry into resting for an hour in his recliner. It had been a physical blow, as well.

The vital foundation of Arden's revival was the unlimited funds, thanks to Ivy's, then Harry's generosity. Without this backing the future of the town was bleak. Unfinished projects seemed to mock the men with the futility of their plans. When the group assembled that evening, Harry started right in.

"Today I was served with a Subpoena, as you all know."

"I thought this was about Mary."

"Shhh."

He resumed. "It's only a spite action on my daughter's part but it has caught us at an awkward time. I am most truly sorry to say that there is no more money."

Millie started to cry. "Is this forever, Harry?"

"No, Annette has no basis for her claims and she won't get anywhere but it could take months or even years to get it through the courts. We don't have years."

Everyone was quiet as Harry gave them time to think. This group of people had experienced the Depression and two wars, as well as all of the disasters people are prone to. A long silence followed the news as they thought and considered. Lottie was the first to speak.

"Harry, I don't know much about business, but what is the situation for Arden?"

"Houses half renovated. The sewage system must be brought up to standard. We are dependent on an aging light plant for power. We must pay for the services of the charter boat to keep in touch with The Port – with the world. On the other hand living costs are low. We have fuel, the occupied houses are weatherproof."

"Isn't there a word…I don't know how to ask this. Do we owe a lot of money? Are we in debt? And can we get along on the money we pay in rent? You know."

Harry was touched. "It's called the break-even point, Millie. We don't owe anything. The money you've been paying has gone back into renovations. Nine of us are paying rent at present. We will talk about Mary in a minute. That rent will cover costs like fuel for the light plant and the boat and the radio telephone. We don't have many current expenses. We're certainly breaking even. We can pay taxes and so on. But there are problems. Randy and Chris have been led to believe they can make a living here. We haven't told them otherwise yet."

"We can't let them down," insisted Robbie. "I don't think they should be told anything until after the baby comes. And Chris and Maggie have put everything into the farm. We'll have to think of something."

"We're not leaving," said Rosalie. "We just got a doctor! I think we can all afford to pay more rent. I wouldn't mind investing my whole pension if necessary. It's only money."

"We won't take your whole pension. You have to eat."

"Harry, could you please do a plan to pay Randy and Chris and see how much we will each have to pay," said Millie.

"You say this is not forever. I have savings and I would be glad to lend it for the time being until this is settled. We need to know how much."

Sid thanked his friends. If Randy and Monica were secure he could accomplish anything.

"The other ghastly thing that happened today is that Mary went to the hospital. Roger can tell you what he told me."

"Mary has a fractured hip. She is going to be in the hospital for quite a while. Because her hip joint is deteriorated she will probably have to have the joint replaced. She is in for a long spell of immobility."

Sid took over. "I can't see any way that Mary can come back here. The boat trip, the slope, the stairs at her house all make it too difficult for her. She would have to have more care than we can provide. I thought you should know the facts," he finished weakly.

Almost everyone was crying and those who weren't, wanted to. This was the first of the group to go. This was a black day for Arden, indeed. The first really bad day, but they were determined to keep going and keep the young families going. One more crisis to meet. Two more. They all grieved for Mary.

Lottie turned to Roger. "Can Mary have visitors? When the charter boat comes I would like to go and visit her."

"I can set that up for you…one at a time for now. I wouldn't mention anything about her circumstances to her just at first."

True to her promise, Lottie was ready to go to The Port on the next charter boat trip. Everyone was. Roger went to see Mary and finish his business trip. Harry went to talk to his lawyer and Anne went to support Harry.

In the lawyer's office, Harry learned more of the impending Court hearing. Charles Wall, his lawyer, talked to Annette's lawyer in The City. She and her husband intended to take it right through to the end. Annette had dual citizenship now because of her marriage and lawyers in Miami thought they could make a case. Charles had talked to Mike, Harry's previous business partner and longstanding friend. The financial records of Mikhar were being submitted to the Court. Harry was correct in assuming that his assets would be frozen.

Charles was surprised to receive the Release that Annette had signed on receipt of her gift of money from Harry.

"I don't see that there is a case at all," said Charles. "The Court date is six months from now and if you think of anything else that may help just come in anytime."

Anne and Harry spent the rest of the day idling around The Port.

"This is a sobering experience, Anne. Let's eat at MacDonald's to celebrate our new status." Anne was relieved to see that Harry was recovering his usual insouciance. They did eat at MacDonalds's and it was fine. Harry bought Anne a plastic toy which was ninety-nine cents with a meal.

They went to the hospital to visit Mary, who was subdued and obviously suffering. She wanted to hear the news from Arden and they told her the latest developments around home. Harry, taking a calculated risk that his troubles would take her mind off her own, told her of his Subpoena and the effect it was having on Arden. Mary was indignant.

"We can't let Arden die now, Harry. My money is yours for as long as you want it. Poor old Ralph didn't leave much but it's there as soon as you know what is needed to keep Randy and Chris working. Maybe Arden will have to wait for the next generation before it goes ahead but we'll die trying, won't we."

Lottie arrived. "How are you?" They heard that Mary was all right, feeling pain but it was tolerable. She missed her house and her little Siamese cross that she had named Ming Toy, Toy for short. The others came in one at a time and left one at a time and finally Sid dropped in. Mary looked at him anxiously but he was calm.

"Here's a cheque for next month's rent, Sid. I've told Robbie to order my firewood. Harry will let me know what my share of the extra expense is going to be when he figures it out." She kept her eyes on his face. "Please don't give up on me yet, Sid. The facts are not all in."

On the trip back to Arden the throbbing of the engine and the rushing of the sea were the only sounds. It was not a time for chatter but it was reassuring to have everyone (except Mary) together. The engine worked steadily and the gulls cried as they flew in circles overhead and the waves lapped. When they got to Arden they were met by Monica and Maggie and Sammy, all waiting on the jetty to welcome them home.

"Did you bring Mary back?" Sammy yelled shrilly, jumping from one leg to the other. "I need Mary. She didn't make the chocolate nut cookies yet."

Everyone hurried to explain that Mary couldn't come back yet, but she was thinking of him and she was making up some new cookie recipes. This was a time for all of them to grin and bear it. Even poor Sammy had his troubles.

Chapter Fifteen

Anne and Harry went home and worked through the familiar routine of lighting fires, setting the table and filling kettles. Harry had the ability to meet a problem, decide what had to be done, do it then forget it. Anne admired this tremendously and did her best to emulate him. As he re-heated the pizza they had bought in The Port, Anne made a salad and tried to concentrate on other recent happenings. She joined Harry at the table.

"Harry, there's been so much going on lately that I never did ask you about that lumber you found. Why would the company cut that cedar way back in the woods?"

"I don't think they did. This was a logging operation, and I think that there was some illegal activity going on years ago…someone was poaching old growth cedar trees and then something happened. I would love to know what it was. Maybe someone died or something."

"I wondered. That's it, of course. They wouldn't be likely to come back now, would they?"

"Oh, no, there are too many people around. Anyway, that wood has been lying there for years. And it has all been moved to shelter at Chris' place. It's Arden's wood all right." He pondered as he ate. "I suppose we could realize quite a lot of money on it if we had to."

"No, we couldn't…not if Chris doesn't know why and we aren't going to tell him, are we? He wouldn't part with that lumber for any small reason. I don't think we should, either."

"Well, I suppose Chris is one more reason. I'm not selling it for any knockdown price," said Harry.

They ate in companionable silence, both thinking of their day in the Port and planning the tasks waiting for them here at home. Harry sipped his coffee.

"I've been wondering if we should ask Sid for the house next door across North Road for a meeting place."

"Do you think we need it when we all have houses we can meet in?"

"It occurred to me the other night when we had that horrible meeting. The time might come when the group doesn't want to meet here. It could be embarrassing if I get into their bad books."

"True, but you won't. A meeting place is a good idea, though. We could leave it set up if we decide to have a group party. A bazaar or something. It would be useful."

"You could take your sewing machine over and crafts stuff."

"Monica thought we would use the store for that."

"Right. It was just a thought. I'd like an early night tonight. There has been too much going on lately."

"Are you feeling tired, Dear?"

"I think I was in shock. Nobody can get to you like your own."

"I'm afraid that I don't ever want to see her again. I'm sorry, Harry, but that's the way it is. She's doing a terrible thing."

"I have a feeling that her husband instigated it and Annette, bless her greedy little heart, went along. I don't think I'll get over this, either."

"If he did suggest it, she could have said no. We'll have to let Marjorie and John know about it, too. Harry! Their money isn't affected, is it?"

"I don't think so. If it is, so are Arden's holdings. Let's not even think about it until it goes to Court. We'll have a better idea after that."

"Poor Harry, never a minute's peace."

"I'm not feeling that I want peace at the moment." Anne looked at him questioningly. "As I said, let's have an early night."

Anne laughed, and wondered how he could do it; how he could just put all the worry and problems out of his mind. She was learning about Harry, the man who went from building birdhouses to running a multi-million dollar company. He had done all he could, now forget about it. He wasn't a worrier.

The next time there was a meeting, Sid told everyone what he and Harry had decided. He was very reluctant to take anyone's savings. That was a bad idea at their ages. He thought that he may have to raise the rents and there would be very little renovation for now. Their big plans for sewage treatment and power would be on hold. They could just barely continue to pay Randy and Chris at their present rates. They had promised Chris they would pay for transport for his harvest and they would. After Harry's case went to Court they would have a better idea of the long term.

Roger said he wanted shelves and cupboards in his house but he would pay for that himself. Almost everyone had some work they wanted done. Anne said it was time to get planters started. All this would give Randy and Chris extra work and income. It was decided to go along as usual with materials that were stockpiled then see what came next.

All of this was carefully kept away from the younger people. There was nothing they could do and it would only unsettle them. Nobody wanted Randy and Monica worried.

Monica still worked in the store, but she was making arrangements for the time that she would be in The Port. Anne would look after the cash register and Maggie would continue to bring fresh produce. It was getting late in the year but there would be squash and potatoes for the winter. Maggie dreamed of a greenhouse so that she could produce tomatoes, melons, cucumbers and lettuce. For the present, kale would grow throughout the winter. She could get an early start on seedlings and flower stock and outside plants if a greenhouse were built.

"I'm ordering plants for the flower boxes and hanging baskets from her if she gets the greenhouse," said Anne.

"It's no problem," said Sid. "There's a roll of plastic in our stockpile if that would satisfy her until we can manage windows. In fact, Harry and I are looking for a project."

All this conversation took place in the store one morning. Robbie joined in.

"Anne, would you teach a class in hanging baskets? We could all make them at the same time."

"I'd love to. We can gather most of what we need from the woods and I'll order the plants from Maggie so she can plan ahead."

They were back to being creative and inventive but on a smaller scale.

Roger made a permanent place for himself in their hearts when he returned from a trip to The Port the following week. After much panting and commotion on the jetty, followed by loud laughter, he drove up to the hospital in a golf cart. Sid and Harry went over to join him.

"I was worried when I realized how difficult it was to get Mary to the boat so I had this modified so we can put a stretcher on it. Now we have an ambulance."

His house was at the end of the street so they built a shelter for the ambulance beside it, right angled to his frontage. They reasoned that the driver could go straight in. It looked very effective and efficient and small, just big enough to accommodate the machine and operator.

They were all waiting for Monica to go into labour, quietly making preparations. The weather became important. The days were drawing in, there was heavy dew in the mornings and heavy cloud cover make the nights very dark. They switched to Standard Time on October 25 although they had no idea of the official date. They had been preparing for winter ever since last February and now the plans would be tested. It was quite exciting.

Of course, being the West Coast, a violent storm drove rain and spray from the wild sea at Arden just as Monica went into labour. Roger stood by as they considered calling the Air Ambulance. Monica was decided.

"If you think I'm going up in that thing in a storm when we have a perfectly good hospital and doctor in Arden, you're crazy."

In retrospect it was a good decision because she just went to the hospital in the golf cart when labour began in earnest. She could have walked but she didn't want to disappoint the group. Quite a few grandparents and an anxious father paced Roger's living room. They prepared themselves for a long night vigil with wood ready for the stoves. They went around to the other houses and fed the cats while Rover and Beauty waited on the porch. Robbie brought over the BIG coffee pot. Randy rather helplessly brought Monica's suitcase that she had packed for The Port. They were congratulating themselves on the good preparations, especially on snagging Roger when there was a piping cry from the other side of the hall. Soon Roger strolled in carrying a little white bundle.

"Congratulations, Randy, it's a boy. A fine, healthy boy. You can see Monica as soon as I get a few things done. She's fine. That was a very fast first birth. She's designed for motherhood. I could use some help here."

Millie and Lottie bustled off to help and were seen later, important in smocks and masks, tending to the patient, the doctor and the hospital.

Randy was over the moon. "Isn't that great. Isn't he wonderful! The baby. You know what we're calling him? Arden. His name is Arden Cedric Donovan. How's that! The first child born in Arden, at least recently. We don't know about before," he babbled. "Arden Cedric Donovan. Sorry, Dad," he said unexpectedly. "I'm sorry."

"Never you mind, Randy, he's a wonderful boy, my grandson, and I don't care if everyone knows my name but you'd better give him one name he can use."

The onlookers burst into delighted laughter when they realized the truth, and were such good friends that they never called Sid Cedric although they finally knew his name.

The benefits of Arden being born in his own town were many. Monica was home the next day in her own place. Six grandmothers, by inclination if not by blood, made sure she had everything she wanted. They heroically left the baby to his mother unless Monica asked them to hold him. Rover wouldn't leave except for a fast dash outside occasionally. Roger was near at hand if he were needed.

Sammy appeared. "A baby. Dad says there's a baby in here." He was allowed to inspect him and he approved. From then on he visited at least once a day.

The weather was cold and stormy for two days then continued to be sullen and overcast, with gusts of rain throughout the day and night. The wind was picking up to bring in another storm when Sid, in Monica's living room, said,

"Oh, no." A dirty little boat was heading for the jetty, still listing. Sid walked down to meet him.

The newcomer spoke first. "I still want to anchor here for the winter. What do you think?"

"No, I'm sorry. Maybe next winter."

"Why not? I have money. Just tell me what you want for one of these little houses here. I'll pay my own way."

"It doesn't work that way, Sir, it's just not possible."

"My name is Humphrey Day. Can I buy some stores from you while I'm here?"

Sid couldn't refuse that so he and Humphrey Day walked to the store where Anne was doing duty in Monica's place. Humphrey again asked for two dozen of eggs and spread himself to four cans of beans, four cans of sardines, coffee, tea, canned milk and honey. Anne packed it all in a box and Humphrey Day (my name is Humphrey Day, Mrs.) paid for it is fresh, crisp cash.

Robbie came in. "Have you got any wooden matches, Anne?"

"No, I haven't. Millie bought the last box. I should have ordered more of them. We're almost out of yeast again, too, just like the day that Mary fell."

"Well, I can borrow some from Millie until the charter boat comes, I guess."

Anne gave Humphrey Day his box of food and his change. Sid was suspicious but his unwanted guest meekly went to his boat, untied it, and putted away from the jetty. Obviously everything was all right. Sammy appeared at Sid's side, wearing his life jacket as was the strict rule on the jetty.

"Grandpa."

"Yes, Son, how are you?"

"Grandpa. There's a new baby, you know."

"Yes, I'm his Grandpa."

"Mine, too." Sid thought about it and gave up.

"Yes, yours too."

"Well. And Mary's not back yet."

"Mary will be away for a while. She fell and hurt her leg and now she has to get it fixed."

"That's what I wanted to know. Nobody told me why Mary left without saying good-bye. She was hurted."

"That's right, she was hurt."

"Hurt. I think I'll go see the baby. We're the only kids around here, you know."

Amid all his worries, Sid found consolation in watching the activity in Arden. Rover leaned against him. He saw Lottie go to the store, then go home again. Millie went to Monica's house. Monica came out on the porch and sat for a while with the baby. Diapers appeared on the line from the back door. Roger opened his front door and propped it with what looked like a rock from the beach.

Harry and Anne appeared from the fields at the top of North Road with Beauty gliding along beside them. Rover whined.

"Go ahead, Boy, go see your mother." Rover fled up the road, barking joyfully. What is money, after all. It would work. They would make it work and this was a long way from The Complex in less than two years. He went to work on an empty cabin.

The day went along quietly. Everyone was, as usual, occupied with his or her own concerns. In the cloudy evening, a dirty, rusted little boat appeared, chugging toward the jetty. Sid went down to take the line, exasperation showing in every line of his face. Humphrey Day thanked him and produced a brown paper bag.

"I brought matches and yeast for the store," he said, "Is it all right if I take it up?"

"I'll go with you and make sure you get paid."

Humphrey Day went back to his boat and reached in. A hand met his. "Also, I have a lady with me that wants to see the doctor."

As Sid told it later, if his hair hadn't been white already he would have gone white instantaneously. The woman who stepped onto the jetty was not Liz, however, to his profound relief. She was a stranger although Sid thought she had a faintly familiar look.

"Hello, I'm Ellen, Mary Burke's daughter. Mother insisted that I come over here and see the doctor." She was an attractive brown-eyed woman, like her mother but with dark hair that matched her eyes. Mary had become a strawberry blond years ago. Ellen was probably in her forties and she wore blue jeans and a plaid shirt.

"I'm just going to take this man up to the store and then I'll find Roger for you."

"Can I just stay here on the wharf and admire the view until you get back?"

Ellen settled herself on the end of the jetty and Sid and Humphrey proceeded to Anne's house to collect money for the matches and yeast from the store's cashbox. Anne was delighted.

"Thank you so much for going to all that trouble, Mr. Day. We were desperately trying to think how we could hold out. We always need bread."

"Good bread, too. I bought some."

Somehow from there, Sid lost control of the situation. The women were all grateful and impressed that Humphrey had gone all the way to The Port and back for yeast so that they could make bread. He had been available to bring Mary's daughter over…who was, at this moment waiting on the jetty.

"Come on, Humphrey, let's get down to the jetty. Ellen's waiting. Anne, I've got company for you. Mary's daughter Ellen just arrived. She wants to see Roger and I'll bring her here after that."

They walked down North Road with Sid trying to think of a way to resume control. Humphrey humbly gave it to him by saying,

"I sure wish you'd let me rent one of those little houses, Sid. I can pay, I have money."

"You can stay for tonight, Humphrey, and we'll talk in the morning. You use the house (Number One West First) on the other side of the road from me, Millie's previous house. Humphrey, as soon as I finish with Ellen, I'll take you in and you have to take a bath and put on some other clothes before you spend any time in that clean house. Can you wait on the wharf for me?"

How had he got so busy all of a sudden? "Come on, Ellen, we'll go up to Roger's. How's Mary?"

"She's coming along well. She sends her love to you all. I've got a little book that she sent for Sammy. She's going to have more surgery, though."

They knocked on Roger's door and were admitted and introductions were made. Roger couldn't seem to take his eyes off Ellen, Sid noted, surprised at the usually suave doctor.

"Please stay, Sid," she said. "You'll see what I mean. Mother wanted me to talk to the doctor about the possibility of her coming back to Arden."

Roger outlined the problems, the rough terrain, the steps up to the house and the longstanding care she would need.

Sid added, "I worry about the boat. It's our only access and I don't see how she could manage it."

"You do want her to come back, then."

"Oh, sure, I hate to lose one of the group and Mary is special to everyone."

Ellen asked, "Will she ever get better, Doctor? That's the main point."

"Yes, I think she will. It will take time in the hospital then therapy then home rest for a long time but she should become mobile again."

"I'm asking because Mother asked me if I would come to Arden to look after her and I have to know the facts. Would she be better in The City without her friends but with medical facilities at hand? Could I look after her? Is it possible?"

"I can't predict definitely, you know that. I can only say that it isn't an unusual injury at her age and she's happy here. You would have to plan on staying for a long while, you know," he said cheerfully. "She would be sent home sooner if you're here to look after her."

"When can you come over, Ellen?" Sid asked.

"Anytime. Now. I only have to pack my clothes."

"She should be able to leave the hospital next week, seven days after her surgery. She should go into therapy, and hopefully, you can spend time with her there to learn what you need to know to look after her. She can come home by air ambulance."

So it was planned that Mary would come back. The exciting news couldn't be contained for long. The three went to Anne and Harry's house and Anne went to fetch the others. Sid remembered his bane, Humphrey.

"I'll be back later."

Humphrey had gone into the house and spent his time well. He was definitely cleaner and his sparse hair was combed across his bumpy dome. His clothes were rough dried, not ironed but clean. Sid started the stove and showed him the house. It was frigid until the fire took hold to make the place warm and dry. How could he have bathed in that icy house?

"It wasn't bad. The water wasn't bad. I guess sitting in the tank didn't let it get icy. Then dry clothes soon warm you up."

Sid explained about the light plant and promised to bring him some blankets. Although Humphrey said he had bedding on the boat, Sid told him to leave it there for now, and just bring his food. Sid left him to it and walked back to Harry's house to enjoy the jubilation. Mary would be coming back. They visited for an hour and planned Mary's homecoming. There was a knock on the door. It was Humphrey, shoulders drooping, looking at Sid imploringly.

"Everything's done," he said.

Anne invited him in and introduced him to everyone, then they resumed talking.

"Do you want to stay in Mary's house or here, Ellen?"

"Mother's house, I think, and I can begin to get it ready for her."

So it was decided although Anne suggested she should stay here for the night where it was warm and dry. Sid and Humphrey walked down to their separate houses with Humphrey carrying blankets that Sid gave him, from the store. Sid was still worried and determined that he would keep a good eye on his neighbour.

"If I let him stay it will be another house rented for the winter. I wish he wasn't such an old wharf rat. I can't see what the women see in him. We sure can use the money." He dozed off to sleep.

Chapter Sixteen

Sid was always up early in the morning but when he looked out at the misty, dark morning of the following day, he saw Humphrey, dressed and combed, standing on the jetty watching the water. When he walked up to Robbie's house for coffee, Humphrey was already sitting on the edge of her porch with a cup of coffee and a doughnut. He was the first one there but the others soon followed.

This morning break at Arden had been fine tuned over time. Someone usually made coffee and something to eat and the rest of the group turned up. There was no set plan. Humphrey was a fast learner and always was the first one to arrive every morning no matter where it was served.

At last the residents of Arden were able to rest in a comfortable routine except that they had time to observe the changing landscape as the year moved relentlessly on. The sun was later in rising and there was a prevailing wind heralding fall. Animal coats were thick and blooming. They moved indoors for their coffee on the days that were too brisk.

"Well, it's fall and we're still here," Robbie said one morning, with satisfaction. "When Mary comes home it will be the whole group plus Humphrey and Ellen."

"What about me?" asked Roger.

"You were part of the group before you even got here. We knew we needed you."

"I'm looking forward to winter," added Lottie. "It was always hanging over our heads and now we'll find out what we were worrying about and planning for."

"It wasn't a bad winter last year," said Sid. "I just don't know if that was usual."

"The wind swings around to the east and it gets cold, real cold," Humphrey said. "And a lot of the time there's a north wind and then we get snow around here." Somehow Humphrey's tone make them all think of the small man in his damp little boat working ceaselessly to keep out the relentless cold. Millie shivered.

"I'm glad you're here, Humphrey. This winter should be better for you."

Sid narrowed his eyes as he looked around at his sympathetic friends. It looked as if Humphrey had made a place for himself at Arden. This made Sid recollect something else he had hoped for and with Humphrey living right beside the jetty he could get started. When the group was breaking up, Sid said,

"Humphrey, have you got time to go up to the farm and help Maggie bring the fresh produce? Maybe you could even use the wheelbarrow. We want to make sure that Maggie keeps coming to see us but it's getting to be a heavy job now, with the potatoes and squash." Away went Humphrey and Sid and Robbie were alone.

"Robbie, if you moved out of this house what one would you like to live in?"

"I don't want to move, Sid. I like this house so much and with being able to make the changes I have it suits me down to the ground. I hate moving anyway. Is there something wrong?"

"Nope. Say you got married. Would you want a bigger house?"

"Married? Me? Sid, who would I marry?" She sat down across the table from him, never taking her eyes from his face. "You're full of surprises, aren't you?"

"Are you surprised? Haven't you ever thought of me as a prospect?"

"You know, Sid, we've just slid into being together all the time, haven't we."

"Do you care for me at all, Robbie?"

"Oh, yes. Yes, I do. I always have."

It was true. She admired the wide, burly shoulders and strong chest of a man who has used his strength. He wasn't tall. His receding hair was quite tightly curled and attractively grizzled black and white. He seemed powerful and co-ordinated, a man to depend on and respect. She cared for him, certainly.

"I had my eye on you when we lived in The Complex," he said, "but what was the use? I didn't have a bean. I still don't but here it doesn't seem to matter."

"It never did, old buddy, it never did. I'm all right with nothing. You should have said this before and we could have had the lottery money."

"Anyway, after I got you here it wasn't so urgent. We could see each other anytime and I had so much to do and plan and worry about. Now that Humphrey is here I don't have to live at the end of the jetty and we can have a house together. What do you say, Robbie?"

"We've got a lot to thank Humphrey for, I'd say. Let's go for it, Sid. I think we'll get along well. We've known each other long enough."

They had never kissed before, not seriously. They had a long moment of contentment safe in a lovers' arms then parted reluctantly because Humphrey would soon return. He never left Sid's side for long. Usually you saw Sid, with Rover pacing beside him and Humphrey shambling along a couple of yards behind, wavering as he studied the sea, sky and the ground under his feet.

Sid leaned against the table holding her two hands. "Think about a house, Robbie. You can have a two storey house, a two bedroom house or a one bedroom house. You can have any house you want just as long as I'm in it."

"If it's all right with you, Sid, I'd like to stay right here. There's room for both of us and we're neither of us what you would call collectors. I'm not set on it but this house would be nice."

They strolled over to see Randy and Monica and tell them of their plans. They wanted the ceremony in Arden, probably quite soon; as soon as Reverend Butterworth was available. They could have the service in one of the two storey houses in front of their friends, nothing fancy. Randy and Monica approved of everything. Their family was increasing much to the pleasure of Sid and Randy who had been on their own for so long. First Monica, then Arden Cedric, then Robbie.

"Do you have children, Robbie?"

"Yes, a son Gardiner in Ontario and a daughter Shirley in Calgary. We probably won't see them although I'll tell them about the wedding. They're too grand for us but if they saw Arden they might come down to earth. There are no grandchildren in my family." She cooed at Arden. "That's one more good reason to marry Sid." She smiled at him.

They told their friends that evening. Sid couldn't wait to tell everyone, partly because he was so happy and partly because happy news was scarce lately. Congratulations and wedding plans took over.

The only difference to Humphrey was that he was often seen sweeping Robbie's porch and carrying wood for her.

"Robbie's getting two for the price of one," Lottie laughed.

Humphrey had steadily made a place for himself and was close to being indispensable. He was up so early in the morning that he had a couple of hours to wait before coffee time came, his breakfast time. He always went to the store to light the stoves and fireplace for Monica so that it was warm for her and the boy. He went to Mary's house and the first thing Ellen heard in the morning was her back door opening. It was quite startling the first time. He lit the kitchen stove and the space heaters then went back to the store to fill the stove with wood then back to Mary's to replenish the fires then to Robbie's. Nobody asked him to do it but he spent the early hours lighting fires for everyone. He omitted Randy and Monica and he knew Roger liked to light his own. He also knew that Anne and Harry were creampuffs who put off the inevitable getting up in a cold house as long as possible so he lit their fires too. After he had his coffee (breakfast) he filled wood boxes, dug a little ditch here and there to cope with the rainfall and then followed Sid and Harry to the farm. All three of them spent the morning working at odd jobs around the farm that Chris had postponed until he found time. Humphrey helped Maggie with her vegetables, filled her wood box, did any heavy lifting for her, helped feed the chickens and gather eggs.

Maggie and Humphrey were soon good friends. Sammy adored him. It was a constant puzzle to Sid that Humphrey was so popular with the women. To Sid he was an abject old wharf rat but nevertheless, all of the women liked him.

The other newcomer, Ellen, fitted in immediately. The bridge club had known her for years. She was a good baker like her mother. Mary said judiciously that Ellen's scones were even lighter than hers but Mary had a lighter hand at pastry. Roger kept Ellen busy helping him to set up his office system. He came back from The Port with a bale of paper from the government when he decided to practice. He said it was as bad as if he had opened an office in the city as far as the paper work went. Ellen spent the first few days in Arden working with him, and from then on they usually appeared together. Roger saw to that.

Finally Mary came home. Roger arranged for the air ambulance and suddenly, just after lunch, she was there. Roger had the golf cart ambulance ready but the ambulance crew and Randy simply pushed her wheelchair up to her house while she waved in fine style. They lifted her, chair and all, up the stairs into the house and she was established.

Toy came home from his hiding place in the bush, yelling loudly. He leaped onto Mary's lap, stood and put his front paws at each side of her neck and kissed her chin. He was purring like an outboard as he kneaded her lap. Mary put her arms around him and told him all about her accident and how she was sorry she had left him for so long.

All of her friends came in to welcome her but they didn't stay. Ellen and Roger soon had her resting on her bed, warmly covered in yet another wool blanket from their stock. No-one really believed it could be true until Mary was actually back in her house. You can never be sure. As she was dozing off in contentment, a little dark head peeked around the door.

"Mary, I'm not allowed to come in yet but I'm glad you're back. We have a new baby and I'll bring him over as soon as you feel better." The door closed carefully.

Winter arrived suddenly. There was a mighty storm a few days after Mary came home. Shrieking winds blew for several days. The sky seemed to be held up by the chimneys in the small community. Rain fell in a deluge for two days then settled into a steady day and night downpour. Monica was back in the store in time to sell everyone a slicker and hat. Rubber boots were in with the Arden people. Humphrey Day bought the smallest set next to Sammy's and stoically stumped around all day helping as usual.

He mentioned one day that he might go over to The Port soon. He wanted to see a friend of his. Because of this, no-one was surprised when his boat was gone one morning from the mist enshrouded jetty. Millie was making coffee that morning.

"I see Humphrey went to The Port this morning," observed Sid.

"I didn't hear him go."

"Neither did I, but his boat is gone."

About then the door opened and Humphrey appeared, obviously zeroed in on the fresh muffins.

"Humphrey!" He looked bewildered.

"You're here!" Then he looked guilty.

"Where should I be?"

Sid took him to the door, opened it and pointed. "Where's your boat?"

"My boat," he yelled. "Somebody stole my boat!"

He fled down the slope in his clumsy boots with his slicker billowing behind him like a sail. The men put on slickers more slowly and followed him. The women stayed in and waited for the news, looking out of the windows and hoping they wouldn't have to go out in the rain.

They could see the men on the jetty peering down into the water where the Tadpole had been tied up. Someone pulled on one of the taut lines and they turned from Humphrey with hands over their mouths. It was better than a movie. Obviously, Humphrey's boat sank. It had probably turned turtle finally overcome by the list.

"Oh, dear," said Anne and they followed the men's example and laughed.

"Poor Humphrey." Still they laughed.

"It was all he had," Lottie pleaded. They roared.

"Why is it so funny?" asked Robbie.

"Harry will think of something," Anne said.

Chapter Seventeen

Winter was here. The grey sea continued day after day to reflect the grey sky. Rain fell heavily and steadily, day in and day out. It wasn't icy cold at that period, just cold with a rawness that never left. Throughout the day, people returned to their homes to replenish the stoves. Wood heat felt grand, kept the houses warmer than any other fuel would have, they said. Clothes were dried in the house, because laundry could hang on the covered porch all day and be as damp or damper than it was in the morning.

More often than not, high gale force winds blew, slamming against the houses and flinging rain against the windows. Houses were cosy. It was lovely to have a friend appear at the door, banging loudly for admittance, laughing with being buffeted along the road.

Harry raised the question of using the other two storey house for a meeting place and general fun center. It began to look attractive, especially with a wedding in the offing. They could use a place where everyone could get together and do things. When the crafts room was mentioned to Monica she said,

"Oh, good. I want to open a little restaurant in the store, and the proposed crafts room would be the best location."

The bridge club suggested a games night and everyone struggled through the bad weather to get there. Harry and Sid wanted a cribbage tournament as soon as they got the crib boards made. After that, a bridge tournament was to take place. The wedding could take place there.

Soon Mary would be able to get there with the help of two strong men to take the place of a walker. At first, the friends met at Mary's house bringing baking and stories to entertain her. Someone always spent the afternoon while Ellen went to help Roger. At the beginning Mary was completely housebound but everyone made an effort to make it as painless as possible. She couldn't go for a walk but she could go out on the porch every day and sniff the drenched air and look through the mist to the heaving sea. She couldn't bake but she could be with Ellen while Ellen baked. She had been so afraid of never seeing Arden again that being there was all her spirits needed. There was always something going on.

The first necessity was raising Humphrey's boat. The charter boat arrived with one other odd looking craft and the strong young men of summertime. There seemed to be a lot of pumping, slurp-chunk, and pulling on lines and running around and more pumping. The women thought they heard a noise like a huge turnip being pulled from a muddy field and there was the Tadpole with it's fittings still dripping rust but cleaner after they picked off the weeds. They helped Humphrey to carry the contents onto the dock. No wonder it sank. He had an awful lot of spare parts aboard. It was all very confusing to the watchers. After all, he had taken his belongings to his house. This looked like machinery or something. They were relieved to find later that it was all legitimate junk, replacement parts enough for ten Tadpoles. The boat no longer listed.

The men came in out of the incessant rain to Mary's house for a meal and a hot drink fortified with rum. It was nice to see them all again and reminisce about the wedding.

"We have another wedding coming up," said Mary proudly.

"Sid and Robbie are getting married."

"When?"

"Soon. It will be easy to arrange because they're getting married in Arden and we're all here. You're invited."

Sid looked at the streaming windows and added, "This will be an indoor wedding. We'll make sure you know the date."

The young men seemed to think of this day in Arden as an outing rather than a working day. They went to see Randy's new son and came out smoking large cigars. They spotted the ambulance cum golf cart and went to look at the hospital.

"This could be very useful for us one day when there's a fishing or boating emergency. Imagine having a real doctor…and Roger wasn't easy to keep." They teased. "There was a very determined lady looking for him, but we thought we needed him more than she did."

Roger blushed and looked around for Ellen who fortunately had stayed with Mary. There was less of a feeling of isolation after the happy-go-lucky men had spent the day.

Still it rained. Once the sky instead of being dark grey became a yellowish grey for a while but there was no sun left in the universe.

Soon the wind shifted to the north and a storm blew straight down from the Aleutians bringing icy gales and snow. This gave Arden a new look, like the proverbial Christmas card, with the little houses sweetly distributed in the billowing snow. It only lasted long enough to take pictures then it turned into a slippery slop that was dangerous to walk in and nerve wracking to negotiate.

Humphrey still got up early and found plenty to do. With the ground streaming with water and woodpiles melting he was busy. After he got the fires going, first going to help Maggie at the farm, then, after lunch helping Monica in the store. The single women, Mary and Ellen, Lottie, Millie, Rosalie came to depend on him, not only for work, but for company.

In this forbidding weather everyone was inclined to shop every day, sometimes several times a day to enjoy the company. Walking the dogs while in slickers was finished for now and everyone wore heavy coats and pants and winter boots. The snow lasted longer up in the fields away from the salt water and surrounded by trees. Boots were important because nobody wanted to fall and break something. No more accidents.

The dogs naturally adored the snow and Rover usually rooted Sid out of bed in the morning to get a head start on his exciting walk. Beauty was more sedate but she was also eager because she knew Rover would be yelping past as soon as possible. Thus in the snowy weather, most of them just had a hot drink and went for a walk. Breakfast was later than usual. Country snow is better than city snow somehow, prettier and less slippery. It was not too cold. The dogs leaped and curvetted with joy. When they passed the farmhouse, Harry went to the chicken house and filled his pockets with wheat. Maggie waved from the kitchen window and opened the door to let Keefer out so he could go along. Sammy could be heard chirping in the background in the house.

They walked across the fields and when Harry found a bare patch under a bush or a tree he would scatter a little wheat for the wild birds and small animals. They never saw wildlife because of the dogs but the wheat was always gone so he and Anne supposed there were birds and small animals. Later Sid brought a two foot square piece of plywood through the gates to the woods beyond and put it in a tree fork. From then on they brought crusts and crumbs as well as wheat for the wildlife.

Humphrey brought a plastic ice cream pail of water and added it to the bird feeding station. "It will freeze and it will thaw. Birds need water."

"I thought they ate snow."

"I tried that once," he said sadly, "but I got tired and I was still thirsty."

Usually it was so late when they got home that they began to follow Humphrey's example and have a muffin for breakfast then wait for lunch. It was a perfect life.

Sid and Robbie decided to get Rev. Butterworth to come from The Port to marry them in the Fun House. They could cram the guests into the downstairs floor of the house—living room, dining room, kitchen and crafts room. Randy and Monica would stand up for them showing family support. It would likely be in two weeks or so, after they went to The Port and secured a licence and the minister.

The charter boat came over on a calm day and Sid and Robbie went back with it. Roger also went and Ellen had some errands to do for Mary. Rosalie and Millie went for the ride, to do some early Christmas shopping and have lunch in town. They were home again in mid-afternoon wary of the weather turning stormy.

They brought piles of mail. It was taken to the store and they all gave Monica time to sort it. Arden was quiet from then on as they caught up on their ties with the outside world. There were a few bills and a lot of refund cheques for deposits on utilities and insurance and other prepaid accounts. Most of them had family news.

Harry surreptitiously flicked through the envelopes but there was nothing from Annette. Marjorie made up for it with several letters and a small parcel. Harry's lawyer reported that he had gone to Court but the hearing was postponed for six months because of the tremendous amount of paperwork involved. He tried to get some operating funds released to Harry, but that would take time. He reported nothing new from Annette's lawyer. Harry told Anne it was just routine procedure but it was also frustrating.

Marjorie sent pictures taken during their holiday in the City. There was one of Chad and Catherine on the beach in bathing suits, running past a sand castle. Marjorie had it framed. Anne remembered the day and was touched by Marjorie's thoughtfulness. They were all well. John was standing pat for now and the money they had received was at Harry's disposal if he needed it. In the meantime John was studying markets and taking courses at community college.

Later, Harry and Sid discussed the mail situation and thought they should do something about it. They had been relishing their isolation but times were changing. Arden was no longer a band aid solution, it was a living town again. If Monica applied for a Post Office she would have to pay more money than was warranted. They could get someone to pick it up for them surely. Maybe they could put Pete's name with theirs on the mailbox and he could pick it up.

"Why not just give him the keys?" They could manage a little extra on his pay.

Sid also said that Rev. Butterworth would be available on November tenth so that was the day they would be married.

This was a situation that made all of the available houses a blessing. Mary wanted to do the wedding cake. She was doing well on her new hip and she had Ellen to help. The turkey would be cooked in Anne's oven, right across North Road from the Fun House. They could assemble the food at Anne's house then carry it across the road when they wanted to serve it after the ceremony.

Another Proclamation was posted. "Take Notice that the marriage of Cedric Donovan and Roberta Fairley will take place on Saturday, November 10, 11:00 a.m. Sit down lunch to follow. Games in the Games Room. Please park cars at The Port. If you read this you are invited."

The weather was reasonable on the day. Several young men and their wives came over for the wedding, chartering Pete's boat. The winter atmosphere was different because they left their children at home. They decided that if it rained there would be nothing for them to do, and if the weather was bad, the boat trip would be hard on them, so Sammy and Arden represented the young contingent. Humphrey worked on the paths, making sure they were smooth with the muddy places filled with pebbles. Mary's wheelchair would navigate like a limousine if Humphrey had anything to do with it.

Boots were lined up on the porch as guests exchanged them for indoor footwear. In the living room, the arch had been retrieved and covered with cedar boughs and coloured fall leaves by Rosalie and Millie. The mantel was gleaming with candles, holly and cedar.

The traditional service was charming, characterized by close ties of friendship among the group. Robbie wore a teal blue silk suit and Monica wore jade green. Sid had never before been seen in anything but plaid or green workshirts so it was impressive to see him in a navy blazer and grey trousers. Randy was resplendent in the same grey and navy.

After the wedding, guests moved across the hall to the new crafts room for a hearty lunch of turkey with every conceivable addition. The cake was cut. After the toasts and tributes, Rev. Butterworth stood up, smiling.

"I have the very pleasant task of informing the assembly that in a half hour or so, after lunch, guests are asked to return for another wedding."

Heads turned and obviously everyone was surprised and puzzled.

"Roger has informed me that the only way he could prevent Ellen's return to The City now that her mother is so improved is to marry her, so he will. This afternoon."

Guests from The Port laughed. "We should have expected something wild at Arden."

"You'll have to take I.O.U.s for wedding presents, Doc."

The second wedding was performed as planned. It was noticeable now that Ellen had worn a white crepe afternoon dress with purpose. Roger in his elegant dark blue suit stood handsome and fit beside her. Anne and Harry were recruited as matron of honour and best man.

Mary announced that cake and coffee would be served in the living room. She had made two wedding cakes so her daughter Ellen also had a three tier formal wedding cake. Ellen hadn't even realized that there was an awful lot of cake being baked. It was probable that she had a lot on her mind, even though Arden people went in for surprises and were becoming increasingly adept at putting one over on the others.

The charter boat left quite late in the afternoon with the two new couples and the minister. Clouds of steam rose from the deck from the damp cold but guests laughingly said it was actually from all the mulled wine and hot rum provided against the cold.

Garbled accounts of recent events at Arden eventually reached The Complex in The City giving rise to the most astonishing of rumours. There had been a Baby Donovan born at Arden and Sid Donovan and Robbie did marry soon after, but how could anyone jump to such a conclusion! It did, however, reinforce the myth-like image of Arden to remarkable proportions. There is no fountain of youth nor is there a cult of rebirth.

Chapter Eighteen

The second Christmas at Arden. The bridge club talked about the differences this year.

"For one thing", said Lottie, "two of the bridge club are married."

"Remember how we planned so carefully what we had to pack. We didn't want to forget anything," said Mary.

"Salt," they chorused.

"And the weather was awful! We weren't even sure we were going to be able to make it until the last day."

"We did manage fresh turkey from the farm."

"And everything else; brussels sprouts, potatoes, sweet potatoes, pumpkins. How did we do it?"

"Well, we know now that we had two very eager men doing everything possible to get us here. They didn't want to be alone here on Christmas, eating beans and listening to the gale."

The weather wasn't a factor any more, except that they were all looking for a good day to go to The Port for shopping. They had ordered turkeys from Chris, who would have them ready at the right time.

Other plans were made. They would meet at the Fun House on Christmas Eve to sing carols and decorate the tree. Nobody was going away this year. They all wanted to be home. They would have a communal Christmas dinner but most wanted to cook dinner in their own houses.

Humphrey was more popular than he had ever been in his life; he was the token single man in Arden. He decided to have

Christmas dinner with Mary so he could help her with any lifting, and Lottie, Rosalie and Millie would join them. Sid and Robbie were having Randy, Monica and Arden in. Anne and Harry invited Roger and Ellen who accepted with alacrity. They wanted to spend the morning sailing, not cooking. The community plan was for everyone to eat early in the afternoon. Later they would carry leftovers to the Fun House where they would open gifts and have dinner together at night. That was the plan for Christmas Day. The men wanted paper plates so that there would be no dishes but that was going too far. However, everyone was to bring their own dishes and carry them home again, to be washed whenever. On Boxing Day they would switch around and have other people than they had on the 25.

Early in December they all took the charter boat to The Port for the last scheduled time before the holidays. Shopping separated them into singles and couples. They had haircuts and bought last minute specialty foods then things to add to the store shelves.

Chris and Maggie took Sammy in to see Santa Claus. Fortunately, the others heard of this so all the grandparents went to admire Sammy and Santa together. Arden sat on Santa's lap and pulled his beard askew and got a candy cane to keep for later when he had teeth, then Monica and Randy took the baby to visit friends in The Port.

Sid and Pete met so that Sid could take him to the Post Office to arrange mail pick-up.

"Sid, I want to ask you something."

"Shoot, Pete. You know me well enough by now that you only have to ask, if it's anything possible." Sid was concerned that Pete wanted more money and he certainly deserved it, but there wasn't any at present. He always seemed to be worried about money lately. "What is it, Pete?"

"They're shutting down my trailer court at the end of the year, making way for an industrial estate. I'm looking for a place to live and I thought of your little one bedroom houses. Would it be possible to rent one?"

"Well...let me think. In time I want to rent them, but we're not ready. We need a new sewer system and a better power supply and other things."

"I thought it would be good if I were based in Arden anyway instead of The Port. For you, I mean. I would be there for extra trips, I mean."

"There's that."

"And the trips would cost less because I would only have to travel in and back, instead of out to Arden and back, then out to Arden and back." He was talking faster out of anxiety. Sid could tell he'd thought over the arguments very carefully.

"The problem is, Pete, that almost everyone out there is retired. We want it quiet, no parties or anything unless we're making the noise. No loud radios or men roaring around at night. It's very peaceful there."

"I know that. After the trailer court I could use some peace and quiet. I don't like noise either. Randy and Chris and their wives spend time in The Port and we meet over there. I guess I can do the same thing. We all hang out together."

"You know, Pete, I always say the same thing. Let's try it for a week and see what happens. And the same thing always happens. They never leave. Pay a month's rent and try it. After that, if one of us isn't happy, we can always make different arrangements."

They decided that Pete would rent Sid's former house on First Avenue for a month. Both of them could see advantages in the arrangement. When Pete tied up his boat at Arden, they went into the house to look it over. It might work out very well, they decided.

"I'll have the water turned on and the stove lit for you to get the damp out." They shivered and went to Sid and Robbie's house, into the warmth and the smell of soup simmering and biscuits baking. Humphrey was waiting with Robbie. He was inclined to worry about Pete's presence until Sid explained the new plan and said that, as far as Humphrey was concerned, nothing was changed. He would go on the same as ever with the job he initiated.

"By the way, Pete, if you bring any animals over I hope they will be spayed or neutered."

"No pets. The trailer court wouldn't permit them. After a month, if I stay, I'd like a dog like Wishbone. You know, the one in the kid's show."

"We'll go with you to the animal shelter," said Robbie.

"Careful, Pete. They go nuts when they go there. Remember what we brought home last time?" They all laughed at the memory but Pete, looking at Walter and Rover, thought it had been a very good deal for the people and the animals.

Robbie added, "Pete, if you're looking for a place to go for Christmas dinner, you're welcome here. I mean it. I'd love to have you but the others may not let me keep you. Remember that now, we have lots of plans." Pete was excited about his prospective home. Mentally, he had already moved in. He arrived in Arden next day with a load of Christmas trees. They unloaded them onto the jetty and sorted them. There were six big trees and seven smaller ones and a 15-foot beauty for the end of the jetty. He got them when he saw a crew clearing the hydro right-of-way to his trailer court.

"That's wonderful, Pete. We hated to cut our trees and were probably never going to do it. Now we can heel these in after the holidays and use them next year."

"The big ones I thought would be for Chris and Maggie, Randy and Monica, the store, Harry and Anne and Roger and Ellen in the hospital. Oh, and one for the Fun House."

Sid could see that Pete really wanted to deliver them so he left him to it, suggesting that Humphrey give him help.

"Harry and I will build some stands, won't we Harry."

As they worked they recollected that Pete had gone all out to decorate his boat for the wedding. He seemed to enjoy the community spirit that motivated Sid and Harry. They were optimistic about him joining the population.

Pete planned the move into Arden with pleasure and relief. He was well over 50, with greying dark hair. He was tall and, for the present, big but lightweight. He was watchful and seemed to see everything going on around him. When men were working, he would lift the end of a board, or hand a mechanic a tool, and the next thing, he would be working along. He was liked in a quiet way. He was a quiet man.

He had seen his living as a fisherman deteriorate until there was nothing left. His comparatively small boat was inadequate in the new system when boats went 200 miles out to sea to bring home a catch. His was too small to make that distance economically viable. He couldn't see borrowing a fortune from the bank for an ailing industry.

He had been an unemployed single male with too much time on his hands and his solitariness had taken him to the bars where there was always company. This life backfired and he found himself too poor to support his drinking. It was only later that he recognized his close brush with alcoholism. He was on the beach, sick and sober.

Pete pulled himself up, stripped his boat of the aging fishing gear and offered himself as a charter boat. He met Sid. Arden had put him back in the working class and saved his self respect. He was left with a monumental boredom with bars and a penchant for people. In Arden he found his place.

After he finished his rounds with the Christmas trees and drank a couple of gallons of coffee he went back to The Port, leaving a feeding frenzy of Christmas decorating. They invaded the store to see what they could buy.

"I know Monica bought rolls of foil...I'm going to make decorations. Maybe we can steal some of the egg cartons for bells."

"Let's plan to spend a day at the Fun House making them."

Monica had in fact brought back strings of lights and all kinds of sparkling, glowing, flashing, shining ornaments. She and

Randy were depressed because they feared that they had overspent on seasonal delights. She happily told the shoppers to come into the back room. Everything…candles, balls, ornaments, chimes, streamers and wrapping paper were on display. Customers fell on them and the young people were ecstatic about their Christmas bonus.

They and Chris and Maggie and the two little boys joined the others at the Fun House to decorate. The tree went up in the living room window so that it could be seen at sea. The homemade stand needed only a few adjustments, then it did its job nobly. Handmade decorations were put up. Huge foil cutouts of angels playing trumpets were pinned to the walls every few feet. Strings of foil wrapped egg carton bells were looped below the ceiling. The room got the full treatment, angel chimes, candles and cedar bough ornaments.

Harry and Anne bought a keyboard with all possible rhythms on their shopping trip. A little portable organ was a gift to the Fun House from Roger and Ellen. The men constructed buffet tables from doors and Lottie covered them with oilcloth Christmas tablecloths. It looked fine.

On Christmas Eve there was a violent storm. "Who cares?" they laughed. Again, they ate tourtiere and drank coffee and red wine. They sang carols accompanied by Roger who had been practicing on the little portable organ. Sammy would probably never forget his first Christmas Eve at Arden…the fire, the wonderful smell of cedar, the voices and organ music while the storm pounded against the rear of the house, excluded and futile.

On Christmas morning Humphrey went to Mary's house to light the stoves and make coffee. He was joined by Lottie, then Rosalie and Millie and Christmas plans were underway. Sid and Robbie slept late. Surprisingly, so did Rover. He was becoming used to more civilized hours now that he lived at Robbie's house. Monica and Arden stayed in bed while Randy got up and lit the stoves. Harry and Anne lay in bed, awake and snug. Harry, as usual, had an idea.

"Let's stay here and maybe the stoves will light by spontaneous combustion." Eventually they had to get up and get going.

Roger and Ellen were able to lay the fire the night before because their fires were out when they got home. Ellen slid out of bed before Roger was awake and started the fires crackling then nudged him awake to put the heavier wood in.

Smoke rose from chimneys, billowing at first, then diminishing to almost nothing as the fires took hold. A skiff of snow whitened the ground. All the Christmas trees were illuminated, including the one on the jetty. It made a brave display on the cold, grey morning.

People began to go out and stroll around their little town and to the end of the jetty to admire the overall effect. Harry and Anne took a pail of shredded suet and grain with blueberries to the bird feeder with Beauty dancing beside them. They waved as the door of the farmhouse opened and Keefer came dashing out to join them.

On Christmas night they ate yet more turkey and opened presents, the culmination of a lot of activity for at least the past month. Lottie's knitted bed socks were a huge success. Everyone got a pair, including Humphrey. He got a lot of things. Tins of cookies, cake, bread, tarts, turkey pie, sweaters (three), long underwear from Sid and Robbie and a mouth organ from Anne and Harry, who had obviously found a music store in The Port.

Everything they gave has a musical theme. They bought a banjo, ukelele, mandolin and trumpet, battered but operational. There was music. Randy and Monica got tapes and Sammy, a drum.

Chris got tickets to a three-day country fair in the spring, all expenses paid. (We'll all look after things for you.) Maggie got a pair of antique brass firedogs (Dachshunds) for her rustic living room.

Sid made a cribbage board for every house. Harry brought the house down with the birdhouses he made for them.

"You're retired all right, Harry," said Sid. "Right back where you started from."

Roger gave Ellen sailing lessons at the yacht club in The Port and Harry gave Anne a trip for two to the Caribbean in the form of an I.O.U. stuck in the door of the birdhouse.

Sammy would have made a killing but they decided beforehand to limit their enthusiasm to keep him loveable. Blocks, cars, puzzles, colouring books and a splendid green Christmas stocking with his name woven in. It was one of a pair. The other one, red, matched except for the name, Arden. Of course they were found hanging on the mantel. Apples, mandarins, home made cookies and candy kisses and licorice for all, made by Maggie.

"She'll have more stockings by next year for the adults," Chris said. "They are fiddly, Maggie says."

They all went home early in a bemused state of love and contentment. The black clouds over Arden would go away, or not.

The New Year's Eve party started out all right. The problem was that nobody stayed up past nine o'clock anymore. They ate, they drank wine, they danced and sang, and by ten o'clock they were finished. Finally, Sid suggested that they move midnight up a couple of hours before they all collapsed.

"It's bound to be midnight somewhere." They drank champagne and toasted absent friends, Randy and Monica, Chris and Maggie, Marjorie and John, Pete, The Complex, then went home.

Harry said to Sid, "I think we should re-set the light plant. We're running it unnecessarily for two hours every night."

New Year's Day was at least half over before anyone got going. At lunchtime Sid noticed that not even Humphrey was in evidence.

"I think I'll go down and see how Humphrey's doing."

"Bring him for breakfast. We're having buttermilk pancakes and maple syrup. Happy New Year, my dear old Sid."

"Not so heavy on the old. I'm a newlywed, remember. Same to you. Be right back."

Robbie wasn't watching him; she was busy at the stove or she would have seen him walk to Humphrey's house, then back to Roger's house. The two men walked back toward the jetty.

Later Sid came home.

"Robbie, it's Humphrey."

"What is it? What's wrong?"

"He's dead, Robbie. He must have died in his sleep."

"Oh, no, Sid. Oh, no." She started to cry and Sid put his arm around her. "Again, thank the Lord for Roger. He's taking care of all the formalities."

"Poor Humphrey."

"When I went in I tried to wake him. The place was freezing. He didn't look any different. I think he had been gone for a long time."

Sid and Robbie went their separate ways to let their friends know the sad news. In the short time he had been in Arden, Humphrey had made a place for himself in their hearts and lives. It was such a pity that he went just when he found peace and security. Later, the general consensus was that they were glad they had known him and pleased that he had this final time surrounded by friends and work and a good home.

When Sid went into Humphrey's strongbox, he found old papers, old photographs and old death notices. He had been alone in the world before he came to Arden, predeceased by his family and most of his friends. There was one crisp new twenty dollar bill.

The Arden people chipped in to give him a funeral at The Port. There was only one stranger there, one elderly man that nobody recognized. It turned out to be the man whose boat was tied next to the Tadpole in The Port. When the service ended they talked to him.

"I haven't seen him for a while because I lost my boat. We only used to meet at the marina."

Sid and Harry looked at each other, both with the same thought…that they knew what to do with the Tadpole.

The old man was tearful when he was given the Tadpole. "I don't suppose I have to do anything about a licence nowadays. I wouldn't want to go fishing anyway."

"Can you meet us at the wharf next weekend? We'll bring it in if the weather holds. No, wait." Weather considerations changed his plans. "Come back with us now and get it while the weather is reasonable."

The plan went ahead with the old man returning on the charter boat and loading the Tadpole with Humphrey's machine parts that he would later sell. Pete took Humphrey's clothes and Christmas gifts over to the Tadpole still at the jetty. The recipient was pleased but dignified.

"Funny. I never expected to be Humphrey's heir but that's how it turned out. Funny how things go. Thanks for everything, tell the people up there. It'll be used."

Pete topped up the gas tanks and waited while he started up, threw him the lines and watched the Tadpole chug back to its old anchorage at The Port.

At Arden, it could have been as if Humphrey had never lived there when his boat and belongings were gone, except when Randy lighted the stoves in the store, once Humphrey's job. As Monica filled shelves or Maggie brought in potatoes and pumpkins Humphrey almost tried to help. As muffins came out of the oven or coffee was brewed, Humphrey's sad eyes brightened with love and good feeling for his friends and their good cooking. He was missed. He had worked hard for Arden and made a place for himself there.

Chapter Nineteen

The new year marked a change in Arden, unnoticeable at first but inexorable. Several circumstances contributed to the new atmosphere. There were three newly married couples establishing their homes and their lives together. The Fun House changed their system of early morning coffee breaks. Now if someone felt like making coffee for the group, he or she would go up and light fires at the Fun House. A new refinement was a large red plastic pail that was put on the porch as a signal. Sometimes fires were lighted but there was no coffee brewing. Coffee for the whole group was different now. In fact, Arden was a living town again.

The new restaurant was a change. In the cold and rainy month of January it was practical to light only one set of stoves. When Monica got going it became quite fashionable to have coffee or lunch in the store's coffee shop. She called it Pete's Retreat in honour of her first customer. Sometimes there were several tables in use. She served wonderful pies and cakes, baked by the good cooks of Arden. She made soup daily and sandwiches for lunch. Sometimes she opened at six o'clock in the evening or on Sunday for a special dinner, one menu for all. Once it was roast beef and once she baked a huge salmon that Sid brought in. She thought they wouldn't have turkey for a while, but Chris raised some big, tasty roasting chickens that were an instant success.

Chris and Maggie brought Sammy fairly often so he could learn about restaurants. At these times a line-up of cats and dogs on the porch proclaimed the same message as the red pail on the Fun House porch. The whole community knew where the In Group was dining so they could all be In if they chose.

Sid set up his Crib Tournament for the last Friday and Saturday in January to give everyone time to sharpen up. It would be a tough fight with enviable prizes. The bridge club began meeting again in each other's homes. Mary, Anne, Robbie and Lottie went back to their unique style of bridge thus providing stability in lives that had experienced so many changes. Sammy often spent a day with Millie while Maggie worked in the crafts room at the Fun House. Anyone who wanted a lesson in weaving or sewing could find her there. Anne's sewing machine found a home.

Anne and Harry still walked the dogs. On many mornings, others joined them but often they went alone together. They walked deep under the dripping trees where the conditions underfoot were better for walking. They talked about the looming Hearing. Harry tried to re-assure Anne but she was growing more apprehensive as the day approached.

"You can never be sure how it will turn out once it goes to Court," she brooded.

"There's no way that it can go against me, my Darling. Try to trust my certainty on this. I know how you were burned in Court but you didn't know all the facts. I wish I had known you then. I wish I had been there for you, but this time…this time there's a sequence of fact that can't be denied."

"Harry, can you say absolutely that nothing can go wrong?"

"There's always an outside chance that Annette's husband is trying to pull something, but as far as Ivy's will and my business go, there's absolute clarity."

"That's what I'm afraid of…the outside chance. Oh, dear, I shouldn't try to pull you down, but I worry so." There under the weeping trees, they held each other for comfort and longed for the day to never come, and for the day to come soon, when it would be resolved.

Roger and Ellen were passionate about sailing, and walked down North Road every morning to the sea. They went sailing almost every day in the small sailboat that Roger had re-furbished after the bridge club bought it on spec a long time ago.

"We have to get a boat, Ellen."

"We have a sailboat right here, Roger. Are you wanting to have one of our own?" She was mischievous, sitting the length of the boat, four feet away from him.

"Next time we go to The Port, we'll start looking around. It's a good time to buy. What I really hate is not having a boat when it's practically free mooring…I used to pay a fortune just to tie up and now when it's free I don't own a boat."

Sid and Robbie also went to sea. They did a lot of fishing using the dinghy, returning at odd hours depending on the tides and weather. They were content together, bobbing up and down on the winter sea while they garnered a surprising variety of seafood for themselves and for the store.

"Here we were worrying about money, Robbie, and we're doing all right. We eat a fortune in seafood. Maybe it will be over soon and we can go back to having financial backup, if we need it."

"Money always seems to be there when we get desperate. It's never enough but we get by. This is such a good time with us being together. Christmas was nice and yet it was all very low cost. I feel sorry for Harry and Anne with all this worry all because of Annette. His own daughter!"

"Just a couple of weeks and we can all breathe easier."

"Pete is going to be good for Arden, isn't he."

"Yes, I like Pete and I think he's going to stay. I hope he does."

Pete's arrival meant that there were two retired fishermen in the community to discuss the vicissitudes of the industry. With that and the rest of the group welcoming him Pete had no intention of leaving. When his first month was up he and Sid happily established his rent and moorage fees. The charter rates were adjusted to the halved distances he had to travel.

He was never alone unless he chose to be. He worked on his boat and got it in good order. He repaired and improved the jetty. He replaced two floats and added more bumpers. He placed a few more buoys for visitors.

He began his day with a visit with the group. If the red pail was on the porch of the Fun House he went there. Otherwise he went to Pete's Retreat or fried some eggs at home.

At lunch time he ate in the restaurant with Monica making a very nice soup and sandwich lunch. There were always pie and cake and not expensive either. There were always people around. He sometimes went to the farm to give Chris a hand if he was needed. Otherwise he cleaned up the beach, gathering up driftwood and anything else that washed in. He was always taking somebody to The Port which gave him a chance to see his friends. Evenings were busy with visits and his new hobby of woodcarving. He even put a few pieces of carved driftwood in the store.

Sid discussed him with Harry and Anne. "He seems to fit in, doesn't he?"

"I like him, Sid. He always was looking for ways to help. Look at that wedding cake he and his friends did for fun."

"He's decided to stay. What do you think, Anne?"

"I like having him down near the jetty. With you moving up to Second Avenue, it's nice to have someone there. And he knows everyone in the area."

Sid, Harry and Pete discussed a better financial arrangement that reflected the changes in circumstances now that Pete was a resident.

He did go to the Animal Shelter for a dog. He brought Sonny back, not like Wishbone, but just as good to a television fan, a male like Brew. Sonny had been around and knew he was in clover. He made it his business to make friends with the other animals at once.

Sid's Crib Tournament took place as planned. Fourteen players took part in the fight-to-the-death battle. Many hidden talents came to light when cribbage was played for the first time in

Arden. It seems that Rosalie's father was a master who taught his only daughter his strategies. Roger was a shark at poker but he was bored by cribbage and kept falling into sneaky traps. Randy and Monica were obvious make weights. Chris and Maggie weren't allowed to play together in competition because they had a method of communication that was reprehensible even if it wasn't mentioned in the Rules.

"Harry, we're going to have to get that signing class going…soon."

Maggie's face was gleeful. They played hard on Friday night stopping only for cups of coffee or tea. The Tournament was to continue on Saturday.

By Saturday afternoon, it was hard to maintain the fight-to-the-finish fiction. Millie and Rosalie were the triumphant winners of the first annual Arden Cribbage Tournament, and as such they won a dinner for two at Pete's Retreat, a round trip charter to The Port, a sack of potatoes, a sailboat trip and a fishing trip. All this of course was to take place if it ever stopped raining.

Another advantage of Pete's living in Arden was the increased frequency of mail pick-up. Often several times a week he returned from The Port and took mail around to the recipients. He soon had every mail key on his keychain, and it was almost as fast as town delivery.

While everyone was gallantly putting in time until the Court appearance Harry and Anne received an exciting letter from John. On the work project he had narrowed his search. He expected to sell Canadian export products to several large construction firms in Japan. For this reason, he and Marjorie were going to Japan in February to investigate further and they would spend as much time as they needed.

"Would Harry and Anne like to go, too? John could use Harry's expertise and Anne and Marjorie could have a wonderful time shopping and sightseeing when the men were in meetings."

"Well, Dearest, what about that? Would you like to go to Japan for a holiday?"

"I've never been there. Have you?"

"Yes, a few times. It's a great place for tourists and celebrations. What do you think?"

"Could we decide after the Court case? It's not long now. Mid-February."

"All right, but would you like to go?"

"Oh, yes! It could be the honeymoon we missed and it would make up for this long, dreary time that you've had to stay in one place."

"Let's tell them we'll go unless we lose the case."

Letters were exchanged and John made reservations for four on his own initiative, taking out cancellation insurance just in case then went on to other problems. They didn't want to take the children on this first meeting-packed trip.

When Anne mentioned this in Arden, Millie said immediately, "Anne, they could come here! We'd love to look after them, wouldn't we?" The others agreed that this would be perfect…a chance for Sammy to have friends and for Chad and Catherine to have a nice holiday, maybe not as exciting as Japan, but nice. The new exchange of letters confirmed that John and Marjorie would come to Arden with the children and go from there after they spent a couple of days getting them settled.

Their Court appearance was to be on a Tuesday and the flight was booked for a Friday, almost two weeks later. In fact, the Hearing was again postponed for one week so that John and Marjorie were in Arden the day before Harry and Anne were to go to the City.

Chad and Catherine were delighted with their new surroundings and were eager for their parents to leave. With final instructions on safety and behaviour, John and Marjorie left with Harry and Anne on the charter boat on Tuesday. The only comfort for Anne in the whole mess was Marjorie's involved and sympathetic presence for the coming ordeal.

They rented a car in The Port for the trip to the City. Court was at one o'clock in the afternoon giving them time for a leisurely lunch before they presented themselves for the Court's decision. Annette was already there sitting alone beside her attorney. She was turned away from the entrance and possibly didn't know that her father and sister were there with their spouses. She made no sign. They sat quietly with Harry holding Anne's icy hand between his two warm palms.

Theirs was the first case after lunch. After the formalities, the judge looked at them all over his glasses and read from his notes.

"We have heard from each attorney in this case. I have studied the documents presented to me at some length. I would like to compliment the principals of Mikhar on the meticulous financial records presented to this Court."

"Just subsequent to World War Two, it is shown by bank records that Ivy Harriet McInnis, wife of Harold Andrew McInnes, transferred her assets in the amount of three thousand dollars to the Defendant. He states that she gave all of her money to him in order to help him in his business. In fact, this sum was transferred to his personal account and was never shown to have been Mikhar records at all. At no time, as Counsel points out, has Mr. McInnes' bank account fallen below a balance of three thousand dollars so there is no indication that these funds were ever included in anything but a holding for Ivy Harriet McInnes.

The second point I wish to make is that although Ivy Harriet McInnes was ill for four years prior to her death, there is no indication that she was ever mentally incompetent or otherwise incapable of attending to her affairs. She did, in fact, at the time of her diagnosis, arrange all of her financial affairs with assistance of her attorney. Her Will left all of her assets to her husband except for a considerable amount of valuable jewellery that was divided in equal shares between the two daughters.

Coincidentally, soon after his wife's death, Mr. McInnis' construction company was sold. He made an outright gift to each of his daughters of half a million dollars voluntarily. Each signed a Release of Claim upon his estate because he planned to invest his assets in a non-profit project.

Subsequent to these events the Plaintiff initiated this proceeding. I would like to say at this time I have never seen such a flagrant abuse of the time of the Law Courts as in this action. There has also been considerable costs accumulated in this case necessitated by the examination of Mikhar's records over a long period of time."

"For these reasons I find for the Defendant with the Plaintiff responsible for Costs."

They left the court room sedately. Anne said later that she was skipping like a lamb but Harry said she wasn't. She was sedate. They were free at last of the burden of oppression they had carried for so long. John drove the car with Marjorie beside him in the front seat and Harry and Anne held hands in the back.

Chapter Twenty

When the decision was handed down, Annette sat for a few minutes, too stunned to move. She was shocked at the realization that she had actually lost the money. BG had told her that she had a right to half of the money from the business when her father died, so she should be able to get more than a measly quarter mil now. BG was no rocket scientist but he was plausible and Annette believed that he knew what he was talking about. She believed every word as he proceeded to urge her on. At first, he expected that Annette's old father would settle out of court. She had said he began acting as if he were senile when her mother died. He was with her for the first Court appearance when he heard that Harry had recently re-married.

Annette took it for granted that he would be with her for this one. She had never felt so isolated as when her father and sister left the courtroom in a happy group of four and she was alone. She needed BG and he hadn't turned up. She finally walked away trying not to think of the huge court costs she was supposed to pay. She wouldn't have more than a quarter of million dollars but considerably less and they had been spending a lot. She walked to the red rental Camaro but it wasn't there. She must have parked it somewhere else. She searched the crowded parking lot superficially and then very carefully before the truth slowly forced itself into her confused thoughts.

In fact, BG had telephoned Annette's lawyer beforehand and had been told that there wasn't a chance of any cash settlement. Harry's lawyer had refused to consider it. BG learned for the first time of the Release that Annette had signed, among other things and he swiftly decided that there would be no more money for him than he already had. He promptly emptied the joint bank account and booked a seat on the noon plane, heading for Miami. He regretfully turned in the leased Camaro at the airport.

From the parking lot, Annette went to the bank to draw some ready cash while she re-grouped and was horrified to find that she didn't have any. The teller was sympathetic but Annette learned for the first time what nothing in the bank means. There could be no transferring of funds, no overdraft, no assistance from the bank at all. She didn't mention her bank card, giving herself time to think.

There was nothing left to do but beg her father for mercy. It couldn't get any worse than it was now, she thought, she was at the absolute bottom, but she was wrong again. She used her last cash to take a bus to The Port. She didn't believe that her father would abandon her when she had the tremendous court costs, and no, absolutely no, money. She arrived at The Port in the evening and walked to the wharf. There was no charter boat there. She asked the man on a small fishing boat and was told that there was no longer a charter boat to Arden from The Port.

She offered the fisherman money to take her over. She wanted to see Harry McInnis, her father. She dropped his name consciously, knowing that he was well known in the area.

"Well, you really are out of luck. Harry isn't in Arden."

"What? Where is he?"

"That I do know. I heard it right here on this wharf when they read the letter from their daughter. He and Anne left for Japan. I'll bet they're going all around the Pacific. Their daughter and son-in-law from Calgary were here and they went too. I'll bet they're gone for six months at least!" The fisherman wasn't often witness to such exciting events and he was making the most of it.

Annette should have borrowed money from Pete's friend, the fisherman because he was the last friendly face she saw that day. She took a pair of running shoes from her big tote and changed her shoes, then walked back toward town, thinking desperately. She ate a large restaurant meal and paid for it with her bank card, thereby suffering horrible embarrassment and finally threats. At least she had food in her stomach, the first time she has eaten that day. She told them it was all a bank mistake, the card was perfectly good, and her father, Harry McInnis, would take care of it. That may have been the reason that the manager didn't call the police.

She walked several blocks along the main street and tried to check into a hotel. She had only her tote for luggage. She explained that there was a mix-up in arrangements, and her father, Harry McInnis, must have expected to meet her in The City and she thought he meant The Port. They would sort it out tomorrow. Since the desk clerk insisted on advance payment she gave him her bank card. After that encounter, she had no room and she could only sit in the lobby for she had nowhere else to go. After an hour the desk clerk called the manager who came and told her she would have to leave because she wasn't registered in the hotel and unregistered women were definitely not welcome.

She left, thinking hard. Were there still Y.W.C.A. facilities? Where did indigent people go? She knew they slept under bridges but there must be somewhere else. It was dark and she had no idea where she was. She was wary of going to the police in this unfamiliar situation. She went into an overnight coffee shop and ordered coffee while she searched feverishly through her wallet. She found an obscure gas credit card she had never used. Possibly she could charge a room on that account. She paid for her coffee grudgingly, out of her remaining change. She went outside and looked around. Two blocks away she saw the flashing vacancy sign of a budget motel and she walked to it and away from the Arden story for a very long time.

She was right in thinking that Harry would have helped her but he had no reason to suspect that she was alone and penniless. A short time ago he had given her a substantial nest egg. Not long ago she married a tennis pro from Miami, so he knew she was all right.

Chapter Twenty-one

When they left the courthouse, soft rain washed away the stuffy heat of the court as they walked to the parking lot.

"It really is like coming out of the dentist's office," observed Anne shakily.

"After finding your teeth are all sound," added Harry.

"And your next appointment is not even booked," said John.

Marjorie walked in silence, smiling hugely.

John drove to the airport. Because of the delay in the court appearance the trip to Japan was only two days away. They decided not to go back to Arden but instead spend the extra time on the mainland, extending their holiday by two days.

It was a short flight to the mainland. They noticed a very curly mane of very yellow hair on a stringy young man beside them. It was so obviously dyed that Harry raised his eyebrows and Anne thought he was silly. They didn't realize that a substantial part of Harry's life work flew out of the country with him when he boarded his plane.

They booked into a hotel and Harry immediately phoned Sid on the radio telephone to tell him of the outcome. The lack of privacy of radio telephone transmission made calls brief and to the point. Harry told Sid that funds were in place and that there would be no more trouble and let it go at that.

"I'll come back as soon as I can, Sid. Don't start anything good without me." Anne laughed at him. He was already back in Arden and they only left home this morning.

The two couples met for dinner and decided to go their separate ways each day then meet for dinner. That was the official beginning of their holiday. Although Harry had been confident, Anne could have never relaxed until she was sure of the outcome of Annette's temper tantrum. This was glorious.

The next day Harry and Anne walked around downtown, carefree. They didn't want to make plans. This was different from Arden and they were in the mood to enjoy everything. They were enjoying the novelty of a busy street when Anne suddenly pulled on his hand.

"Come on, Harry, quickly." She pulled him onto a city bus and they began scrabbling in all of their pockets for change. They had to ask what the fare was. The bus started with a force ten jerk and they grabbed wildly for support, clutching their change. Finally, they paid their fare (the driver disdainfully indicating the fare box) and sat down, subdued as if they were back in school. Anne gazed out, then pushed him out and off the bus.

"There. Look at that."

Across the street from where they stood, an integral part of the elderly neighbourhood, was the Rosellen Flower Shop.

"That was my Dad's florist shop that I inherited with Mom. The whole time I've been here in Vancouver this time, I've been disoriented because everything is changed. All of my landmarks are gone, replaced by tall buildings and sheets of glass. Then I saw the same bus. Now here, just exactly as it was, is Dad's shop. Rosellen was my mother's name. Imagine! It's exactly the same!"

"Come on, let me buy you a flower." After he bought her an orchid corsage and paid for it, he shook hands with the Chinese proprietor and explained about Rosellen. The owner was friendly and pleased to know that Rosellen was the name of an actual person. He gave Harry a rosebud buttonhole.

"We're still newlyweds," he said as the florist pinned on their flowers.

They got another bus on the corner and Anne took him to the house she had lived in for so many years. It was well kept and prosperous looking.

"It's a big house for three people." Harry observed.

"You remember, that's what it was like in the Depression. Many houses were empty and none of them worth much. When I was small, there were unoccupied rooms upstairs where I took visiting children to play, with all the boxes of toys from years ago. There was always a room for visiting relatives when they came to stay. All of our friends lived like that."

"Now you have a two storey house again, smaller, but there are two of us instead of three."

"I didn't know it was possible to be so happy. I love you, Harry, and I love our two storey house."

"How lucky we are, sweetheart. Where shall we go now?"

"There used to be an ice cream parlour down the street." They walked to the end of the block and stood in front of a video store.

"Oh, well, there will always be the Rosellen Florist Shop."

They replenished their change and hopped on and off buses until the rush hour traffic began, when they escaped to the bar in the hotel to wait for John and Marjorie who reported that they had been looking at houses, in case they were forced to move to the Coast. They were in shock, and strong drink was indicated.

"If I could move our house out here, I wouldn't have to work. I could retire on the profits."

They went to the park the next day then admired the new city hall. They decided not to inspect the new court house. The new library was impressive to look at but they didn't need a book. John had already researched Japan and industry extensively. It was a lovely interval, unstructured and undemanding. On Friday they flew to Japan.

Her first trip to Japan was a complete blur of colour and crowds to Anne. They arrived at the end of Japan's winter, almost spring, so their clothes were more than adequate for the temperatures. It seemed to be an early spring and often jackets were adequate when they went out. The time of year brought a nice surprise because their hotel was still on winter rates until the end of February.

The men spent every day in pre-arranged meetings that lasted for hours, sometimes into the evening. Marjorie spoke of this the first time they dined alone in the hotel.

"I like the hotel dining room, don't you? I'm so lucky to have your company, Anne. Imagine if I had been alone while John was attending all these meetings."

"It's nice this way. We have all the freedom we want, with male escorts when we want them, in the evenings. I'm glad we came. It's nice for me to have a break after that horrible court case."

"Annette's always like that. Impulsive, and she never seems to think about consequences. And she's absolutely witless about money. Oh, well."

"Are you saying she doesn't know what she did to us?"

"Probably not. The court case may teach her a lesson, but nothing else has."

They admired their parasol-garnished colourful drinks and forgot about Annette. There were so many other people to observe, with their lovely clothes and customs, who had come here from all over the world. They went back to their separate rooms at ten o'clock and the two men were still not back. Harry arrived in their room an hour later and told her about his day.

"Yesterday was taken up with a meeting with the representatives of a huge international conglomerate. They are looking for a Canadian contact to represent them in Canada. I think John has a chance at the job if he wants it. They showed us all over the city—their various concerns. We had a quick dinner in the boardroom then looked at the communications holdings." He smiled at her, curled up in her kimono. "Did you think we had been to an opulent dinner with geishas and everything? No,

Anne, John is not that important." He kissed her cheek. "It was the boardroom."

"Would this be what he's looking for?"

"It could be. He applied for the position, along with several others. There are a raft of meetings to come. How was your day?"

"We shopped. We left the hotel and tuned left and worked our way down the street. We saw all the big, flashy places, like your conglomerate."

"Take a tour tomorrow. If you want to, I'll arrange it at the front desk."

They discussed it at dinner, and Harry booked a tour. The next day Anne and Marjorie spent hours seeing Mount Fuji and lovely gardens and charming restaurants. One day they toured the harbour and another day went to the Ginza on a shopping tour. That one made their previous shopping day seem amateurish and tentative. Still, they bought little because there was nothing they needed. A few small gifts for the children and a souvenir for the Arden people. They spent the rest of the time looking. The spectacle was more than enough for the first days in Tokyo. They wanted to go on the bullet train but Anne wanted Harry to go with her. That was one thing he had never done and he was fun to go with.

One evening, Harry told her of the meeting of the day.

"This company is a rather traditional family one, by no means outdated. The president is a man of my age with his two sons CEO and Vice President. I kept out of the discussions but it's a huge construction-engineering concern. They buy a lot from Canada and feel that they want someone to represent them solely. It's an interesting offer. John did himself well throughout the day. I'll be interested to know what he decides."

There were still more meetings. For the next two days Anne and Marjorie went together to see the city and Tokyo Bay from the Tokyo Tower Observatory, more gardens and more temples. The Japanese are exquisite gardeners and their tours always included breathtaking gardens. Anne had enough knowledge to appreciate the spectacular effort.

"I don't think I'll ever garden again," she told Marjorie. "All I will ever see are my shortcomings."

When Harry came home one evening, he was thoughtful.

"Do you remember the company I told you about, run by an older man and his two sons?" She nodded. "We met with them again today. John has been leaning toward their company, Tanaka Incorporated. The father is Jiro, sons, Hidemi, CEO, and Shintaro, Vice President. I like them personally. Today we toured their building and a few local projects. I think John has make up his mind to go for Tanaka."

"What do you think?"

"I'm just a spectator but I think he's right. I can ask a few questions when I get back to Canada but it looks good to me. Now, Jiro, the father, has invited us for a very splendid dinner and evening on Wednesday, the day before we leave. You and Marjorie will pull out the stops and look beautiful. John and I, of course, will do our best. We will see some of the nightlife. How about that?"

"Oh, Harry, I'm excited! What an end to our visit. I have to find a hairdresser and a dress shop. Oh, the desk. The girl on the desk is good. I thought evening entertainment was for men, and that they leave their wives at home."

"If that's true, I think Jiro is making a special effort. Anyway he wants to meet Marjorie. He's family oriented. You and I are extras here but I think he likes our family relationship, and wants to know us all. Let's go meet John and Marjorie for dinner and talk about it," said Harry, who under-rated his part in the proceedings.

Marjorie and Anne went in a taxi the next day to a recommended boutique, holding Harry's credit card and written instructions in Japanese. They were smilingly measured and observed. Eventually they emerged with several small parcels. The gowns would be fitted, pressed and delivered on Wednesday. In fact, they would help them dress.

On Wednesday, they went to a hairdresser who spent hours shaping and styling. Marjorie's hair was put smoothly into a stunning upsweep, while Anne's grey hair was voluminized and gathered at her neck with a matching chignon.

"No, this is not quite the way," said the stylist. "Madam, if you will permit, I will come to the hotel tonight and finish this after you are dressed."

That evening, the two women were meticulously dressed, and their hair perfected by the small, capable hairdressers. Anne wore a rose tulip skirted gown with bare shoulders and a tiny rose silk shawl. Marjorie was in a royal blue full-skirted gown. Her dress had large sleeves, fitted below the elbow.

It was a splendid evening. Jiro Tanaka and his two sons, Hidema and Shintaro did everything to make the evening memorable. When five attractive men concentrate on two gowned and jewelled women, it's bound to be a successful evening. Add perfect cuisine and beautiful surroundings and it's memorable.

They did everything to make John feel that he was making the right choice in joining them. Their first contract with him was for one year to explore the relationship with a lifetime commitment to follow if it was acceptable to both parties.

Jiro sat beside Anne. He told her of the Tanaka Inc. building under construction, their new head office in Tokyo. He was obviously proud of the unique design and meticulous planning. He was very attentive when Anne said she was a florist by profession. She was retired, she told him diffidently describing her hanging baskets and planters in Arden.

"Now that I've seen Japanese gardening, I realize how little I know."

"You mustn't lose your confidence." He smiled. He promised to send her a collection of plants for her huge planters that would be compatible with the wind and sea.

It was very late when they parted and went their separate ways, congenial and replete.

On their final day they went on the Shinkansen bullet train and sped over the countryside at 170 k.p.h. "It will go 220 k.p.h. in a minute," said Harry, enchanted.

"I'm glad there are so many people on it, or it would leave the tracks," she replied, clutching his arm happily.

John had signed contracts the previous day and his new profession was launched. He was as excited as Marjorie was. They discussed the business trip and dinner, and decided it was successful.

"A toast to Tanaka Incorporated."

"Success to John."

"To absent friends."

Shintaro, the pleasant Vice President, was in the limousine that took them to the airport. He presented each of them with a small, beautifully wrapped gift, souvenirs of their first visits. When opened later, velvet boxes sheltered beautiful Japanese pearl rings for the ladies and pearl cufflinks for the men.

Fortunately the flight home was uneventful, giving them time to recover. They rented a car again and John, the new Canadian representative of Tanaka Inc. was again the chauffeur.

Pete met them with the charter boat and soon they were in Arden. Chad and Catherine and Sammy, carefully life-jacketed ran down the jetty. Each occupied house had lights onto welcome them home.

Chapter Twenty-two

Every single resident of Arden was waiting to greet them although the cats may not have known what they were waiting for. They may have just been following their owners. Sid helped everyone step off the boat, shaking hands with each one fervently. Considering that Sid was not demonstrative, there was no doubt of his feelings today. He was almost knocked off his feet as Beauty, seeing no-one but Anne, dashed to her, sparing time for a side lick for Harry. Robbie waited with the rest of the bridge club for the first excitement to ebb. Catherine launched herself at John and Chad tugged at his mother's hand.

"I had sailing lessons with Roger. Look at my boat." The faithful sailing dinghy was now called "Chad's Boat." The name was painted right on it.

Plans were made for everyone to congregate in the Fun House for dinner. In the meantime, everyone went home for a rest. John and Marjorie went to the Holiday House with Catherine and Chad.

"We were staying with Millie, but she moved our stuff over here this morning. That's when we knew you were really, really coming home." Catherine hugged her mother.

Harry and Anne lit fires in their house for pleasure for the others had kept everything warm and dry while they were away.

"Harry, look at the kitten; he's a cat."

"He must have been growing while we weren't looking. He couldn't have grown that much in a week. Could we call him Seeker?"

"I don't know. Ask him. It's fine with me. I only know I don't have to cook, so today is another holiday."

Later they walked to the Fun House and into pandemonium. WELCOME HOME was on a long banner on the end wall. Food was arranged on a table in the rear. Harry poured champagne for everyone, with a glass of apple juice (practically the same thing) for the three children.

"I give you John, the new Tanaka Inc. representative in Canada. Here's to success."

Various toasts followed. "Here's to progress" was Sid's and the gleam in his eye told them he had something specific in mind. "Welcome home to the travellers", "Happy days are here again", and so on. No direct reference was make to the Court case in deference to Harry's feelings about Annette, but the joy and excitement were palpable.

In Japan the food had been beautiful and exotic but brownies belonged in Arden. The chicken was delicious and the freshness of the produce from Chris and Maggie was unmistakable. Everything was so very fresh.

"It's a pleasure to breathe in Arden," John stated. They planned to stay for the weekend at least. Now that he was working he needed time with his wife to make plans.

The Tanaka sons had suggested that he and his family return to Japan for six months or a year. In this way, he could work in the home office and understand the company better, while he learned the language and tastes of his Japanese employers. If the whole family went he would not have to maintain two separate homes. That would be economical and they would enjoy the Japanese adventure together. They could live in a Tanaka apartment building to keep costs down. They wondered if they should sell their house in Calgary. What about a permanent location?

"It's a complex world," Sid said. "Chris is in the most ancient profession of all, farming. John is working through the Internet. Randy works by contract and native ingenuity. At one time you just took the job that was available and liked it. I was a fisherman because my father was. Fortunately, I did like it." He turned as Harry came in the front door again. "What's that you've got there, Harry?"

His friend was carrying a parcel wrapped in flimsy brown paper. "I brought you each a present. The men's are dark."

He began taking out silk kimonos in marvellous colours with embroidered dragons, flowers and scenery. The room became a swirl of pastel and jewel colours with elegant dark tones on the men. Chad and Sammy sat on the floor and changed into little karate suits while Catherine tied on a turquoise kimono.

"You must have emptied a store!"

"How did you carry all these? Oh, silk, of course."

Harry smiled widely. Maggie's dark eyes were shining. She loved cloth and understood it. They all donned their kimonos over their clothes and peacocked around. Harry loved to give presents, and as he looked at Anne in her pale blue kimono his eyes filled with tears to think he could indulge his whim again.

Sid put his arm around Robbie. "What a time this has been, and the night's not over yet." He kissed her temple lightly and friends noted this remarkable display by Sid and said nothing. He was always undemonstrative and they didn't want to make him shy.

As they strolled home in the moonlight the scene was like Act One of Madame Butterfly except for the trees. Sid and Robbie walked with their arms around each other. Later, they talked. "You know love making gets better with age."

"Nobody expects anything so whatever happens is great."

He laughed. "This is one time that slowing down is all to the good." The little house settled around them and the town slept.

Next morning, they laughed together and discussed their marriage. Neither had expected much of a sex life. They had accepted the cliché of old people marrying for companionship, as if young people didn't need a companion, and older people needed only their memories.

"They say…."

"They say never knows."

It was spring in Arden. John and Marjorie left on Monday to sort out their lives. Chad and Catherine were sad about leaving Arden and happy about going home to Calgary and excited about going to Japan. Marjorie had her hands full. Millie gave them travel kits with cookies, juice, cards and puzzle books from their friends in Arden.

"Look after my boat," was the last thing they heard from the departing charter boat.

The sea was a beguiling blue to match the benign skies. Anne was occupied with her planters. She found a large rotted tree in the bush beside the town and she and Harry spent hours bringing the nutrition-laden remains back to use with her soil. She prevailed on Sid and Robbie to bring back copious amounts of kelp. They gamely towed in floating beds of it to put in the compost boxes. Chris brought wagonloads of topsoil from remote areas of the farm.

"Dear, are you going into market gardening with Chris?"

"We need good tilth and what's left will never go to waste."

One Saturday she decided it was time to put together hanging baskets. The women headed for the woods and came home with moss and ferns. Tables were set up on the Fun House porch and covered with plastic. Maggie brought down plants from the greenhouse: geraniums, nasturtiams, fuschia, pelargoniums and small yellow biddens. In the morning, the men helped them construct baskets out of wire then went to each house, where there was a location carefully marked in the porches with felt pens. They put in supporting hooks in preparation for the completed baskets.

Pete, Sid, Harry and Randy cooked a large pot of pork and beans, using Pete's recipe and Randy made bannock using the recipe he had learned from the native fisheries inspectors. At noon they carried this substantial fare to the Fun House and they all had lunch. Coffee was served in mid-afternoon and the beans made an excellent dinner, with the addition of a salad and sliced ham from the farm.

That evening, large hanging baskets filled with tender, hopeful little plants, contained in rich earth and wet moss, were suspended on every porch of the occupied houses and some of the unoccupied ones. Each basket was wired firmly to the hook in anticipation of summer winds. When Sid took his evening stroll to the wharf to enjoy the sight of Arden in the evening light, he studied the hanging baskets.

"That's going to be a sight for sore eyes," he said to himself.

Anne moved on to the planters. Chris' topsoil was combined with the compost and rotted wood and loaded into the planters. Anne remembered that Jiro Tanaka had offered to send plants for her but she also planned to augment with plants of her own. In late March, a card appeared in their mailbox to say that Anne could expect a delivery from Japan within the week. Excitement took hold of the gardeners as they tried to imagine what Jiro Tanaka was sending to them. They decided not to touch the big planters until they had the Japanese plants in hand. The bridge club was so fascinated with gardening that they went into the woods, looking for wild strawberry plants. A strawberry jar here and there would be nice. While they were peering unsuccessfully under the ferns, Sammy came running toward them with Keefer leaping around him.

"Grandma, there's a big box coming." He looked at Anne. "There's a very big box on a boat at the wharf. You'd better come and see."

"The plants," the friends chorused as they fled for the beach, then as the jetty came in sight. "It can't be."

Several wooden crates were being unloaded from a barge tied up to the jetty. Pete and three very big young men were struggling with yet another wooden crate. When the women arrived at the scene, Pete said,

"It's all for you, Anne. It's from Tanaka Inc. in Tokyo. There's an envelope in the cabin for you. I'll get it in a minute."

"I think we'd better get Harry," Anne said nervously. The crates made serviceable seats for them while they waited for Harry and Sid to arrive.

Pete handed Anne a manilla envelope. She looked at Harry, questioningly.

"Open it, Pandora, and all will be explained."

"Do you know anything about this?"

"Only what you know. We'll probably both know more when you open the envelope."

She cut it open with Pete's proffered knife and read for two or three suspense-filled minutes.

"It's the plants," she said weakly. "He's very careful to say that he knows I'm a florist but in case I need advice on foreign plants, he's enclosing a plan for planting and care. The Japanese are noted for their beautiful manners. Then he says that he is also sending a teahouse to go with the garden, built by Tanaka Inc."

This was followed by a long silence. Another crate was being unloaded and it looked like the last one, finally.

"He is enclosing plans for the assembly of the teahouse, although he knows that Harry is a builder. He thinks that the foreign elements may give difficulty. Both the plants and the teahouse have been chosen with regard to the waterfront location and the wind and spindrift I have talked about. He says he will think of his new friends sitting in the teahouse surrounded by the plants in Arden. He hopes to join us for a visit one day."

"Come on, girls, get off those crates."

Crowbars were carefully applied and the crates were opened. With the help of the plans they soon had the parts in order. Bags of cement were brought from Sid's stores.

They decided to place it in the area above and east of Pete's house. Inevitably, someone said in front of Number Five East First Avenue.

With so many men working, the work went quickly. In a surprisingly short time, a jewel of a teahouse stood sturdily, close to the waterfront in Arden. It was red and gold with touches of the primary colours gleaming beside the gold.

Moving side panels were of rice paper but the wall facing the sea was of clear plastic, of a type that was new to the builders. It was as clear as glass but thick and light. There were also sliding panels of plastic to replace the rice paper in bad weather. There was a seat across the front wall and thick soft cushions for the seat and for the floor. Folding chairs completed the seating. There was a large low table. A final box held a bonsai tree for the table, quite safe in it's elaborate packing. It was a marvel of a teahouse.

As Pete, Sid and Harry carried the tools back to storage, Pete made several attempts to talk to Sid.

"For a while now, I've been thinking…I guess it's too late now…I had an idea…."

"Pete. Say it. The suspense is killing me."

"Well, I thought I'd ask if it would be possible to put up a small ways in the bush beside Number Five, West First Avenue. If I could clear a bit, I could set it there, and use it to repair my boat and clean it, and I could build a boat or two if you wanted me to."

"How about a sailing dinghy?"

"Sure. I wouldn't need ways for that, but I wouldn't want it too big, just big enough to work on the bottom of my boat when necessary."

This was new to Sid and he walked quietly up the road.

"I guess it wouldn't be good with the pretty little teahouse down there."

"The teahouse is far away from the spot you're thinking of. Don't worry about that. I don't see a problem, if you don't plan on going commercial. What do you think, Harry?"

"Sounds fine to me. What about that granite ledge? Is that going to be in the way? Of the ways?"

Pete chuckled. "No, it may be a help. No kelp. Ha Ha."

Sid thought they would need some heavy timbers. That was the limit of his suggestions. They would let it be Pete's project.

Time went by. Marjorie wrote of their decision to go to Japan for six months. They would take the children, and if possible, they would stop at Arden on the way. John was very involved in his new work. He had already shipped his first lumber to Japan and was deep in negotiations for more. Tanaka Inc. was interested in Canadian products and were all for diversifying. John would be busy. He was following several ideas for some kind of unusual facing for the Tanaka Inc. home office building.

Anne planted and tended her plants, helped by everyone with spare time. This was much more ambitious that she has anticipated. It was planned to be low maintenance when it was established, she was assured by the notes sent to her, but in the meantime she was glad of any help she could impress. Even Sammy began to avoid her if he wasn't inclined to work.

The farm was in full operation and very busy this spring. Several of the young men from The Port were staying at the farm for the duration. Randy was working full-time in Arden, tightening up the occupied houses and working on the rest of the houses when he had time.

Monica was busy with Arden the baby, the store and the restaurant. Pete's Retreat could have been open all the time. Mary and Lottie baked every day and often worked in the restaurant at mealtimes. Robbie and Rosalie worked almost full time on the planting and gardening. Millie spent her time at Monica's house, tending Arden and often, Sammy.

Roger and Ellen worked to get their first home in order. They were bitten by the sailing bug and spent their spare time on the water. Roger was very interested when he heard of Pete's new project. From then on, he was most often found working down on the shore with Pete.

Doors stood open most of the time. The sea air was sweet and sea breezes moving through the houses brought a salt tang with them.

Sid and Harry worked together as they always had, at present on shelves for the hospital. Sid was especially sprightly, Harry noticed. It was as if the poor trapped spirit of the man at The Complex was flying free at last.

"Have you got something on your mind, Sid?" he questioned him.

"Windmills."

"Windmills. I should have known that. What do you mean, windmills?"

"Have you ever heard of the study that was done on the Coast a few years ago? I read that they thought it was feasible to supply all the power for a community by utilizing windmills. There is a constant wind on the Coast which is the main requirement. I'm thinking of how to get a copy of that study and how to apply it to Arden, and how much it would cost." They worked in silence, then Sid said,

"Harry? What are you thinking about?"

"Windmills." Neither said another word until lunch time.

When they got together again after lunch Harry continued Sid's thoughts. "With John being so hot on computers, I think we should get him to research windmill hydro electric power for me. And I wonder if Tanaka makes windmills or maybe someone closer to home. This is a very interesting idea, Sid. Let's get on it before winter. It's hard waking up in a cold house and having to light fires. I had enough of that when I was a kid."

"The only way that last winter was bearable was that Humphrey lit the stoves for us every day and now we don't have Humphrey anymore." He added, "The next thing will be sewage disposal. It's been hanging fire ever since we got here."

"Yeah. One thing at a time, Harry. We have all summer but I think I have a solution to another one of our big problems.

"Now what?"

"You know that big, big lumber we have?"

"Our unusable resource that brings out the worst in us?"

"I think we ought to offer it to John for the Tanaka Inc. building in Tokyo. It would be a feather in John's cap and maybe help him to get ahead in the company."

"I want time to think. Let's think about something trivial until at least Monday."

Harry was obviously excited but true to their agreement, they discussed a trip to The Port for shopping and dinner sometime soon. They thought they could ask the women to begin choosing colours for their houses and also begin planning any changes they might want. If they went to The Port they could look at floor coverings and light fixtures, and decorating books to get an idea of costs.

"I seem to remember the dream of Arden I had was to relax and fish and fix a house once in a while in a leisurely manner just as a hobby. Now it seems that we're running from the time we get up until we hit the sack again."

"It's like the old poster, 'When you're up to your neck in alligators it's hard to remember that your original intention was to drain the swamp'."

They chuckled companionably. "Now we're into international diplomacy…."

"And windmills."

Chapter Twenty-three

Sid was finally able to enjoy a time of relaxation. There was time to take the dogs for a walk or sail or go fishing, time for a few weeks of retirement living. The business of living seemed to take all of the Arden residents' time.

Sid and Harry digested the problem of the monster lumber. The wood was probably unique and they could think of no practical use for it unless it was cut, an unthinkable solution. They couldn't imagine shipping it in it's present form. Someone somewhere would know how to handle it but as far as they were concerned they owned a white elephant. Possibly they were in the position of the original sawyers who had a dream as they worked heroically with cutting the huge trees into boards then were faced with moving them. Or not.

Sid and Harry worried about the dubious origin of those beautiful boards, suggesting death and mayhem, poaching and other illegal activities. For that reason alone, Sid didn't want to try to sell them for his profit would only compound the original crime. He just wanted to admire them or give them away.

They decided to wait until John returned on his way to Japan. They would show him the wood, let him take measurements and pictures and offer them to him. If he wanted to, he could talk to the Tanaka executives about using them.

The windmill solution also awaited John so they were idle.

They thought Roger would like a tall cupboard with shelves in the hospital. They could ask him about a design. They also built more lawn chairs. In time they thought they could put two before every house. They discussed traffic.

Traffic. Chris' farm would soon be in full production so the tractor pulling a big farm wagonload of produce for The Port went down North Road almost daily. He was shipping eggs and milk, chicken, turkey, ducks and geese. Pork and beef were sent over on the charter boat in their seasons. The orchard gave a fair return for the first year but after careful pruning and spraying this year's crop looked better. The blossoms on the old fruit trees had been profuse as well as showy. In the early summer Arden enthusiasts had walked to the farm just to enjoy the blossoms in the sunset then the dusk shading to dark. Now the trees had a different beauty, fecund and calm with tiny fruit forming.

They talked about Pete who was busy with his charter boat and the ways he had originated. Arden residents could go to The Port almost on impulse. Soon the barge would have to take over when Pete could no longer handle all the produce at peak times.

Roger and Pete serviced the golf cart ambulance and kept it running efficiently. It went for an occasional spin to keep the motor in order. Roger and Ellen were sometimes seen heading for the farm in their noisy toy.

"Harry, we're soon going to have a traffic problem. Do you think we should install a light at the intersection of North Road and Third Street?"

"Let's make a Yield sign, for fun. If your windmill works we can install a flashing amber light."

In the evenings, Pete made time to work on his ways with Roger's enthusiastic assistance. Soon he would be able to do the work he originally envisioned—cleaning his boat.

In the lovely summertime, John and Marjorie arrived with the children for a weekend on their way to Tokyo. Sammy immediately joined Chad and Catherine for a pony ride.

It was to be a hurried visit because their flight was on Monday. Harry suggested he and Anne would drive them to the airport in The City. They could turn in their rental car at The Port and go down in the station wagon. After coffee and doughnuts Sid and Harry took John for a walk in the woods. They told him the story of the lumber and showed him where it had been stacked in the clearing then took him to the shelter that Chris built.

They stood back and waited to see his face. He was incredulous. "These must have been first growth cedar! They must have been tremendous, real record breakers! How did they mill them?" he said unbelievingly. They explained that it was a pity that they were cut but they were, quite a while ago, and it would be a shame to throw the wood away in minor projects.

When he was told about Sid's proposal for the Tanaka home office building he sat down on a convenient log (normal size) and began taking notes. He trotted to his house to get a camera while Sid and Harry stood around grinning. They were relieved to leave the problem in his hands. "If they do want them I don't know how in the world they are going to transport them and I don't think I want to. I have enough on my mind."

John appeared, breathless and carrying his camera. "Anyway, there they are for your use, whatever you decide. I just hope you don't end up cutting them up for picnic tables." Harry suggested that John take his time. "When you've been over there long enough to know more about the company, present the suggestion when the time is right."

The weekend flew by with talk of their Japanese adventure, rental of their house in Calgary and the children's excited chatter. On Sunday afternoon, Pete took the six of them to The Port. They picked up the station wagon and drove to The City. They moved into a motel close to the airport, had dinner and went to their rooms until the following day.

Again Anne found herself saying good-bye to the family that had become so precious to her. She could hardly regret their leaving though, when they were so excited and optimistic. She gave them photographs of the teahouse and Japanese garden for

Jiro Tanaka. He would see how it looked against the backgrounds of Arden and the cove.

After the plane left they went into The City for a sightseeing tour of their previous home. It was a beautiful little city with tree-lined streets showing green and brilliant colour in the sun. They drove by The Complex and on impulse, parked the car and went into the gardens, still lovely and well maintained, surviving the upheaval of people leaving and people arriving. They sat on a familiar bench holding hands for a few minutes, then thankfully got into their station wagon and left for home.

When they arrived at The Port, they drove around before storing the car. They ended up attending an auction. It was almost over, few people remained in the littered field and the auctioneer was losing interest. There were a pile of cartons left that contained books from the estate. Nobody bid on the first box so Harry offered five dollars. The auctioneer said "Sold" then asked if he would take the twenty other cartons for five dollars each, so he did. They had to make a few trips in the station wagon to the wharf. When they got back to Arden, it took Pete and Randy an hour to move them to the Fun House. Harry was smiling widely again, pleased with himself although as yet, he hadn't looked at his purchase. "If It's comic books, we're rich," he said.

He didn't have time to look at them in the Fun House either because John had left an envelope with Sid about windmills that were in production and could be ordered. He also included material on solar panels. Correspondence with manufacturers began.

"Sid, I've had it. I'm taking a day off. Anne and I are going for a hike."

The following morning he and Anne went for a day in the woods with Beauty beside them. Time was passing so quickly. They walked past the farm, waving toward the house in case Maggie saw them and strolled through the fields to the gate and into the woods. They climbed the hill to the summit and lay in the sun. A soft breeze blew from the sea, flowers and evergreens perfumed the clean air and the quiet was so complete that the sighing grass was loud. They lay on the grass, occasionally brushing off a visiting ant or grasshopper and lazily discussed life. Eventually Anne poured a drink for Harry from the bottle of water he carried. They crunched on farm fresh carrots and ate cheese and bread and apples.

"What a cook," said Harry happily.

They eventually walked down the hill and further into the deep woods than they had ever been. There was a special atmosphere in the deep woods, self absorbed and watchful. They strolled along the game trails, one behind the other. Beauty padded along behind them. A deer raised her head as they passed then went back to drinking from a tiny brook. Chipmunks chattered and occasional small rustlings in the underbrush suggested other small creatures. Anne noticed a garter snake with a bright iridescent head brightly watching Harry, slowly turning her upraised head as he went past.

They didn't see any bears although they were always hopeful of one day knowing they played host to the impressive beasts. Maybe they would see moose although Beauty's presence kept most wild creatures away. On the way home they optimistically looked for wild strawberries although they thought it was too early. Harry later bought a jar of strawberry jam at the store, thereby cutting out several intermediate steps from picking.

Another day they went to The Port to cruise furniture and appliance stores. Inevitably, they met a young interior designer who was greatly interested in transforming a prosaic 1960's house into a living picture. They sounded him out about coming to Arden, then promised to discuss his work with the other residents and get back to him. He proffered several business cards which seemed to be the custom now. Harry said he thought the guy overstocked on them.

When Harry talked to Sid, they decided to have a meeting, a pleasant one at the Fun House to talk about renovations and redecorating the houses.

The houses in Arden were built to logging camp standards of thirty years ago. They were sturdily built mainly of fir, the most common wood of the time. They had fir floors that were easy to maintain. They had basic power and plumbing. There were three designs varying mainly in size. Each size was built in a row, all of the same design. This produced the Christmas card effect the residents had noted the first time it snowed. The present tenants speculated that couples had the small houses, families the two bedroom ones, and the executives had the two storey houses. They were expected to accommodate important company visitors.

The first row, the smallest houses were on First Avenue. Each was rectangular and divided from side to side into two rooms, kitchen-living room and bedroom. The bathroom is at the right rear, taking part of the bedroom floor space. Each had a small picture window facing the sea and the back door rather awkwardly facing the camp.

The Second Avenue houses were slightly more than twice the floor space of the singles. They had slightly bigger windows. The front door opened directly into the living room, defined by a vertical rail divider. The front bedroom opened off the living room.

Straight back from the door was a small hall with three doorways opening into the kitchen on the left, the bathroom at the rear and the second bedroom on the right. There were wood heaters in the hall and living room. The kitchen had open cupboards and wood stoves. A cooler was cut into the rear wall for food storage. There was one window above the space for a table.

There were four two storey houses on Third Avenue. Each front door opened into a hallway that went the length of the house to the second floor staircase. On the main floor doors on the left opened into the living and dining rooms. On the right the office, then the kitchen and bathroom opening off the kitchen for warmth.

On the second floor the main bedroom was across the front at the end of the hall with bedrooms left and right of the hall. The rear bedroom had a bathroom, and was obviously the guest room. Plumbing lined up with the downstairs kitchen and bathroom.

Sid said the single men were most likely in a float camp. Bunkhouses and cookhouse were on floats in the adjacent sheltered coves because there was no sign of bigger buildings in the townsite.

These were the modest little houses that the present residents would renovate. At the meeting they talked about possibilities. They could buy propane appliances (stoves, fridges and hot water tanks) but the general consensus was to wait for electricity so kitchen renovations would be done later. The living rooms would be first with each resident's ideas.

"I want that through hall changed to make the living and dining rooms more accessible." Anne started the ball rolling. "In fact, I think we can get rid of the hall altogether."

"The design is good for us because of the hospital," said Roger but we'd like to have two of the bedrooms made into one. We're thinking of a Jacuzzi in the back bedroom when we get electricity."

Harry told them about the interior decorator he had met. "He's willing to come over and look around. We could consult with others if he doesn't suit us."

"What if we get him to come over and make a plan so that when the power comes we'll be able to go ahead."

Mary said doubtfully, "A decorator wouldn't have much to work with. They're very small."

"A pied-a terre."

"A bijou residence."

"Boy, that takes me back."

"What would they call them now."

"Too small."

"Not for me. I don't have time for housework."

Sid asked if anyone would like any kind of additions to their houses but they didn't. They chose their houses in the first place.

"I love my house."

"We all do. At my age I like everything being so close."

Anne said, "Harry, couldn't you warn him and let him make his own decision?"

Robbie suggested they get some decorating magazines and "just start planning."

"We could also tempt the man by asking for restaurant renovations and Fun House improvements."

"They're nice the way they are. I love that almond paint." Roger was standing by his original choice.

Nothing was decided at the meeting but Harry and Sid knew the mood of the group and could go on from there and they had other things to think about. They had talked about a church in Arden in the wake of the weddings but it wasn't feasible. Services at The Port were preferred because everyone liked Reverend Butterworth. For several months Lottie and Rosalie had gone to his church happily taking advantage of Pete's move to Arden. Later they were joined by Millie and Mary. Now that Harry and Anne were home for a while they followed suit. It became a custom to go to The Port for church and lunch then an afternoon of individual pastimes, dinner and home.

"I'd like to see a little chapel here anyway. It would complete the town and we could still go to The Port on Sunday." Sid ruminated.

"I wonder where we could come by a design."

They also worked on their basic improvements on a loose daily schedule leaving time for other pastimes. Both men were married now and had separate interests, fishing on Sid's part, pleasure on Harry's. He had been known to knock golf balls around in the fields and he and Anne often went to The Port to play golf on a more conventional golf course. In the field he had Keefer to retrieve balls for him and he often wished he could take him to The Port. Keefer had seen him one day and raced out to join in whatever interesting pastime Harry had going. He learned to fetch golf balls quickly and once he had learned not to chew them up but to treat them like soft little birds Harry was set.

Chapter Twenty-four

Into all this peace and quiet, Pete delivered three people one day. Harry thought he saw John but his eyes weren't always that dependable. When he saw the other two men he called Anne and went to the jetty.

It was John. He introduced two men, both Japanese, who were from Tanaka. One was an engineer and the other was an architect. John told Harry and Anne of the excited meeting when he, after four months of work for the company, told the others of the find at Arden. He showed them pictures of the magnificent cedar lumber and gave them the measurements he had taken. The rest of the meeting was too fast for his level of the language but the end result was this fast trip. The building was nearing completion and the architect wanted to eyeball it, as John said. They brought the engineer to advise and handle the practical problems that the lumber presented.

They were offered ever-present coffee but they wanted only to shower and change before hustling up the hill to the farm. Harry and Sid followed them up; they couldn't wait to see their faces. It was the second best entertainment the lumber produced. The men were stunned, then ecstatic and walked to Pete's Retreat, waving their arms widely.

Two houses on First Avenue were prepared for the visitors. John's house, the Holiday House, was made ready for his short visit. They were invited to dinner at Anne's house because she had more room and everyone prepared food for a potluck. The women debated wearing their kimonos but decided not to. They couldn't carry it off, they thought.

The evening went well. The guests were polite, enjoyed the casseroles and courteously answered all questions they were asked about Japan. They asked about Arden and its strange beginning. They brought messages from Jiro Tanaka and his sons and after dinner walked to the teahouse and gardens. There were many exclamations about the huge planters. Chris explained that these were made of the broken boards from the bottom of the stack and turned good side out.

They laughed at Anne's alarm when she cried, "You're not going to take my planters apart."

"No, Anne," said John, "We didn't even think of it."

"It was a pile of work," she grumbled and they laughed even more.

The engineer took charge of the operation. The next day a boat and barge arrived from The Port and the boards were carefully wrapped in plastic and loaded. There went the last of the cedar adventure, for the three Tanaka employees decided to go back on the boat with the wood. John hugged Harry and Anne and almost hugged Sid in his excitement before he left.

Anne was making breakfast a few days later when Harry said, "I'll be darned." They watched the Tadpole chug to the jetty where Pete was standing by to take the lines. Anne had a lump in her throat as she watched an old man step ashore. Sid soon joined them.

This was no Humphrey Day. A shaved and polished man was questioning Pete then turned when Sid arrived. Pete re-introduced Robert Hall who looked at Sid piercingly and said:

"I could see your ways when I was going past and I wondered if I could put my boat up and work on the bottom. She hasn't been cleaned for a long time. She feels sluggish. I can pay you something."

Sid said it was up to Pete and left them to it. The Tadpole looked as if it belonged there and everyone went down to look at it and meet its owner. It made them miss Humphrey all over again.

A week later the Tadpole was on the ways being cleaned to within an inch of its life. It was true, it was covered with barnacles and seaweed. Pete was on his boat working as usual.

Suddenly, Pete came pelting onto the jetty and then to his house. He grabbed his whistle, and for the first time since Mary's accident, the emergency whistle blast was heard. Everyone flew to the jetty.

"A hurricane!" yelled Pete. "There's a hurricane out of the southwest just passed over The Port and there's bad damage."

"The tea house!"

"The charter boat!"

Rosalie shouted, "The farm! Do you want me to alert the farm, Sid?"

"Yes, …yes…the stock. Thanks Rosalie, will you be all right?"

"Yes, I can really run." Away she fled up North Road, "carrying the news to Ghent." She could run, it was plain to see.

Suddenly large flocks of starlings darted and whirled over the town. They landed in a big fir tree then swooped away again. The women hurried to carry the bonsai and the cushions and table from the teahouse. Harry and Sid ran to take out the rice paper walls and put them in the closest house (Number Five First Avenue East). They debated whether the plastic panels would be useful for protection and decided to leave them in place. The wind was freshening noticeably. Again flocks of starlings darted over the town and settled in the trees to the west.

"My planters." Anne was brokenhearted. Sid and Harry ran for a big roll of plastic and lashed it over the planters with half inch line. They ran to the ways to help lash the Tadpole down, then to the charter boat to help Pete with extra lines and bumpers. The sky grew dark.

Roger ran to his house and drove the ambulance into the shelter between the hospital and the Fun House. He tied it down as securely as he could.

"Could the women do the houses?" yelled Sid. It was hard to outscream the wind now. "Then stay inside. I'll be up in a minute, Dear." He looked at Robbie. "Best not to light a fire for now, don't you think?" She nodded and left. She tried to take Rover to safety but he wouldn't leave Sid's side. She arrived to find Walter, agog, sitting in the front window.

Anne and Beauty ran for cover. She spotted Lottie's marmalade cat under Pete's front porch and picked her up to carry her home. That timid little cat was a rigid, struggling ball of fire, practically impossible to carry but Anne grimly tucked her inside her jacket and kept on going, until she could throw her into Lottie's front door. She tried to take down her big hanging baskets but Harry had wired them so firmly that she had to leave them.

She saw Monica at the store, furiously putting chairs inside and slamming doors and windows. She ran for her house and slammed the back door just as the wind arrived with a loud bang. A loose sheet of plywood flew from the jetty to the beach, fortunately missing the men who were running to their houses at the last possible second.

Later they learned that they had only felt a side swipe from the hurricane as it hit north of them and slammed through the woods and across country. At the time it was violent and frightening. The people stood well behind windows watching the damage being inflicted on the town. The sailboat and dinghy had been beached and tied down but they were picked up and thrown against a house on First Avenue (Number Three). They slammed against the wall one after another, smashing windows. The frail mast of the sailboat tore through the plastic covering of one planter as it went over, leaving the plastic flapping frantically for a dozen feet.

The charter boat rocked and leaped at it's moorings but held it's position. She was built for heavy going. The extra lines tautened then crumpled time after time but they held. The Tadpole on the ways, was in a more sheltered location and rode out the storm quite well with one porthole broken and paint scraped here and there from flying debris.

The storm was noise and wind. Shrieking wind and slamming loose pieces. Under a lead grey sky the sea leaped in huge grey and white waves as the wind swept the wave tops onto the town to mix with the flying rain. The trees to the east and west bent almost to the ground with the wind and could be heard breaking as branches snapped and flew away. Slowly, after an hour the wind began to abate. The sky lightened and the sea slowly won its frenzied battle with the wind, and grew calmer.

People rushed out to talk to each other and survey the aftermath of the storm. They walked in a group to the farm, dreading what they would find there. Sammy ran out to meet them.

"The cows almost blew away. Daddy got them in the barn just in time. He put the sheep in the cow barn! The chicken house blew over and the chickens are up a tree. Keefer got excited and bit one of the men and Daddy's mad!"

They arrived in the farmyard where Maggie was wringing her hands. "Oh, Harry, where's the greenhouse?" cried Anne.

It had blown away and landed in a mess of plastic sheeting and splintered boards in the orchard. The fruit trees were devastated, all the leaves and fruit stripped from them, and broken branches were everywhere.

When they talked to Chris they realized the storm had been much worse on the farm than in Arden. By good fortune he still had six extra men for another project so when Rosalie arrived panting the news, they began putting in livestock and nailing barn and outbuilding doors shut. The pigs were missing and of course, the birds. There were no turkeys to be found and only a few chickens.

Keefer retrieved his reputation when he arrived with a swearing goose in his careful mouth. They followed him into the woods and found most of the birds, bedraggled, limping and bloody, but alive. They found one of the pigs that would have to be butchered, but only one.

When Pete went back to his radio, they realized that they had come out very well compared to the rest of the area. There had been eight people killed along the coast, two of them children, when houses in the path of the storm blew over. Some burned. The flames had spread little for some reason. At that time there were no reports of ships at sea.

The next few days were spent in trying to put things right in Arden. The Japanese teahouse had stood firm and was undamaged. Jiro Tanaka told them it was built to withstand wind and water. It only needed its cushions and table and bonsai replaced and it was back to normal. The flimsy rice paper walls were put in place and its impression of delicacy and fragility was restored.

Anne's planters were not badly damaged. She spent the next few days trimming and clipping the plants and adding soil. The planters themselves were solid. The remarkable survival was that of the hanging baskets. Sid and Harry had secured them well then wired the baskets to sturdy hooks. They had swung around violently and some of them were misshapen from hitting he ceilings of the porches but the hooks held. Their battered plants were tended lovingly in recognition of their brave survival of the storm.

Sid and Harry walked down to the wharf and looked back up at the town. "I'm just as glad the windmills weren't up. We'll have to add additional supports to the specs."

"Judging by the teahouse, I think we should get Tanaka Inc. to build them."

"We'll have to build a new ambulance garage. Roger's not happy that his blew down. Lucky the power plant survived but we have to get going on a better system."

"Windmills," said Harry.

Chapter Twenty-five

Again Sid and Harry had to put aside their restful occupations and do some real work. Chris had survived a real disaster but much that he had accomplished had to be re-done. Actual storm damage meant that fallen trees had to be cut up after they were removed from fences that they had destroyed. Instead of re-building the chicken house Chris decided to build the bigger, more efficient one he planned for the future. The old one was an original building and was slated for replacement. The barn was also original and Chris was reluctant to spend time replacing its roof that had been badly damaged. The sheep had only a shelter that was always inadequate. The small pig house was gone entirely. In the face of Chris' almost total replacement of buildings, Harry and Sid thought their first priority was Maggie's greenhouse. She anticipated quite a lot of her income from it and was now out of the winter vegetable and bedding plant business until further notice.

They had glass in stock now, so they spent the next couple of days building a larger, more secure glassed-in greenhouse. They sent Sammy to bring his mother to see the result. She was pleased and admired the benches they constructed around the inside wall and down the middle of the new structure. They demonstrated the rope and pulley arrangement to open and close glass panels to control temperatures. She was delighted with the new building and began rounding up soil and containers before they were even finished picking up their tools.

They went looking for Chris for the latest report on conditions. It was a relief to see the three ponies grazing in a small paddock and geese stridently running things again. They preferred to observe rather than ask Chris questions and force him to recite more disaster. He said there was surprisingly little real damage except for the disastrous conditions of the orchard. Twenty trees would have to be replaced but they were the oldest ones, lovely old varieties too. About half had survived. He still couldn't find his pigs and they were worth a significant amount of money to him. He figured he would have to write off a few extras as a result.

Harry walked to the barn and got a metal pail half filled with mash and they spent the morning walking in the woods following the line the storm had taken.

"Sooey, sooey," Harry called. "I don't know if they understand my pig talk but it's the only word I know. They'll have to be flexible. Sooey, sooey."

"You don't think they survived, do you?"

"Not really but even one survivor would be nice. Sooey, sooey. Nobody else has the time to search. I should have asked Anne to pack a lunch. She does a very nice carrot stick. Sooey, sooey."

They walked for miles, spending time that the farm workers just didn't have. They discussed their projects.

"When we get time, Sid, how about if we put up some bookshelves upstairs in the Fun House. I thought one of the bedrooms facing the sea would make a nice library and we could put a desk under the window so a person would have a nice place to read."

"I didn't know you were a reader."

"I'm not but I bought a library, remember, and I'd like to unpack them and see what I have. I thought it might be nice on a winter's day. Who knows, we may have a copy of that windmill study."

"Right. As soon as we finish with the storm damage, we'll do it."

"Sooey, sooey," called Harry, rattling the bucket. In the deep silence, they both heard a squeal and they burst through the underbrush following the sound. They found one sow that had farrowed and she was in a nest among the roots of a big tree, surrounded by her piglets. She was starving. When Harry got closer he saw that her back left leg was useless.

"Poor old girl, you've been through a lot. Never mind, it's over now and you have a beautiful family." He tenderly emptied the pail of food beside her and went to look for a spring.

Sid walked back toward the farm for help. In a surprisingly short time he was back, with Roger and a wheelbarrow. Harry watched with delight as Roger took his medical bag from it. "I met Roger driving his ambulance for a test run in the field. We went back to the farm for the wheelbarrow then drove as close as we could and walked the rest of the way."

Roger set the sow's dislocated leg and stitched a long jagged cut. She was loaded into the wheelbarrow after the three men spent a long time running in frantic circles grabbing tiny piglets in each hand and putting them in a sack. They returned in triumph to the farm with the patients in the ambulance and the wheelbarrow bumping along behind. It was all worth it when Chris met them by the barn.

"We marked the place where we found her and we'll keep looking. We may find something else."

Harry told Anne about the bizarre incident at lunch.

"Harry, could a pig be blown through the air, even in that wind?"

"We can never be sure but I think that the wind got under the raised floor of the pig house and took the whole thing away. She must have fallen off and come down through the tree so that it broke her fall. It's anybody's guess."

"How many piglets were there?"

"Thousands, when we were trying to catch them. Maybe six. I'm not sure."

"They couldn't be more than two days old, could they?"

"That's about right. We could have fun naming them, couldn't we?"

After lunch the women decided to join Harry and Sid in the pig search but they didn't find any others, then or later.

Roger was disgusted that his new ambulance garage had been a victim of the storm. He thought some more qualified person should replace it so Pete and Robert Hall, the new owner of the Tadpole, offered their services. They were working full time along with Randy, repairing storm damage. Arden was almost back to normal from it's forlorn storm tossed appearance.

Sid and Harry built bookshelves for the new library and Sid donated his recliner chair that had been in storage since he married Robbie and moved into her house. They found a table that would do for a desk and put it under the window with a kitchen chair beside it. Recognizing their limitations, they asked Randy to carry the boxes of books from Number One, First Street West where they had been stored. The three men Randy, Pete and Robert were working together that day.

"Books," said Robert. "The whole time I've been camping in that house with all those boxes of books I've been longing to know what they contain. What a wonderful thing. Can I help sort them for you?" Robert was very different from Humphrey Day, who was irreplaceable. Robert was immaculate in his person, wearing faded but clean jeans with creases in the legs. His fleece shirts were changed every day and his hair was clipped short for tidiness.

The Tadpole was transformed. Robert said he had sold the spare parts and used the money to buy paint and cleaners. Everything was painted and polished and the small galley and berth were clean and ordered. The last job had been the hull which was Robert's reason for coming to Arden where he had hoped to save some money if Sid charged less for the ways.

While the Tadpole was on the ways, Robert had rented Humphrey's house and shared it with the books for a minimal payment.

"I'm lucky I was ashore when that hurricane hit," he said. "Imagine that in a small boat." Inevitably he asked Sid if he could rent his house and Sid was in favour. He liked Robert. Later they found that Robert's motive was the books that Harry bought, which, as Pete said, proved something or other.

Pete was still busy repairing the two small boats so the Tadpole was useful when Sid and Robbie wanted to go fishing. Now three of them spent hours at a time bobbing around in the waters adjacent to Arden where Sid and Robbie had bobbed around in the dinghy, supplying fish to the store and to themselves.

Pete brought the mail back one day and took it around to everyone. He had begun acting as postman to the community, although Canada Post might have made some kind of objection if the fact was known. Monica was too busy now to do her illegal sorting and delivering. Sid and Robbie sorted their mail in the kitchen and drank coffee while they read their amazing offers for pizza delivery ads.

"Some day I'm going to take them up on their pizza offer," Robbie chuckled. "If they promise to deliver."

"Here's one from Japan. Imagine Jiro Tanaka writing to me. It must be to thank me for the lumber." He opened the letter, read it then handed it to Robbie.

"I guess we'd better have a meeting tonight," she said.

They went around and asked everyone to come to the Fun House at seven. Pump pots and cookie trays were filled for the latest town meeting. Everyone looked at Sid expectantly. He looked at Harry and grinned. For once Harry didn't know what was going on and he was going to surprise him.

"I have a surprise for you. I'm already surprised. Mr. Tanaka wrote to me to thank me for the lumber that was sent from Arden. It's safe in their warehouse and arrived in good, no, splendid condition. Their architect has incorporated it into the façade of their new home office building. We know all that." He glanced at Harry. "Now. They expect that the building will be officially opened at the end of October and he invites us to the opening.

Us. All of us. He quotes John as saying that there are six men, nine women and two children living in Arden and he would like us to come to Tokyo for the ceremony. He wants to pay all of the fares and accommodation. He says please let him know if there are any others we would like to invite and how many would like to attend."

There was a long silence. "This isn't going to be much of a meeting if nobody says anything," said Sid.

"That's going to cost him a fortune," ventured Lottie.

"The lumber was priceless so we didn't sell it to them. They only paid to transport it. Mr. Tanaka is very conscious of this. Now there is so much excitement about it that he wants us to share in it to pay us back a little."

"I know Anne and I are going," said Harry. "It will be a real celebration."

"We're with you," said Chris after signing madly to Maggie. She nodded vigorously. "I'll just have to find someone to look after the place."

"Robert, if you want to join us it will be all right with Mr. Tanaka."

"No, I think I'll stay here and look after the place if you would trust me. I can feed the animals and keep watch."

"Certainly we would trust you but we can hire some of the young men if necessary. We'll talk about it again and if you change your mind before we write back, you'd be welcome."

The group agreed with Sid, and said teasingly,

"We can use another man to help with the luggage."

"Roger and Ellen, you have to give up sailing and come with us, of course."

"I can shop for a boat over there and sail it home."

The bridge club, Millie and Rosalie were all if favour. It was the trip of a lifetime for them. As Sid had expected, there were no refusals, other than Robert's impulsive one. Arrangements were discussed over coffee and cookies in excitement but there was no hurry. They had more than three months in which to anticipate.

Harry and Anne were still talking about the future celebration when they went home. "I'm glad they agree with Sid and me about the unique lumber. Sid found a perfect home for it."

"I'll be able to see Marjorie and the kids again. That's an unexpected bonus. Let's do our Christmas shopping early and take their gifts over. That way we can buy things that don't go very well by mail."

"Right. I think I'll take a lot of pictures for Jiro Tanaka so he'll be able to envision Arden."

"Two years ago we couldn't have imagined that Arden would be like this. Remember when the bridge club came for Christmas?"

"I loved you so much in that sad time and it all turned out so well. Remember the exodus when you people brought the two boats?"

"We must write to them soon, too. They are due to come back from Africa in the spring."

"I want to give them a thousand dollars extra for the boats. They're worth it or they were before the hurricane. Now only Pete knows what's going to happen. But the exodus!"

"And the pets! Oh, Harry, remember when the little Siamese yelled and you pulled off the road. You thought it was a siren."

"And Beauty and Keefer and Rover in an animal shelter…like royalty in an elder hostel."

"They were saved and we have certainly gained by it."

They reminisced about the past couple of years and the people who had come and gone. The people who stayed had changed so much. They still had aches and pains and yet nobody thought it was worth mentioning. At one time Sid limped and Millie was always chilly. Roger's face was brick red with stress and high blood pressure. It is all changed. All the walking of pets and moving up and down North Road, and fishing and sailing and fresh food and activity had been good for them.

"Remember in the hurricane how Rosalie ran up North Road like she was entered in the hundred yard dash? She probably couldn't make that time normally but she was amazing. It seemed normal at the time," Harry marvelled.

They talked in bed until they fell asleep. It seemed that the whole story of Arden was important from the time Sid first mentioned it at The Complex until their projected flight to Tokyo to take part in what Sid called international diplomacy, the opening of the Tanaka Corporation Building. The teahouse would be their permanent reminder.

When Anne wakened the next morning, she was held tightly in Harry's arms, with her head in the hollow of his shoulder. She should have been very uncomfortable but she wasn't.

"What's so funny?" he asked sleepily.

"Well, I remember you telling me one time that you could still make me happy in bed and you were right."

"I told you so," he said smugly.

ISBN 1552129594